MICKEY FINN

21st Century Noir

Michael Bracken, Editor

MICKEY FINN

21st Century Noir

Down & Out Books
3959 Van Dyke Road, Suite 265
Lutz, FL 33558
DownAndOutBooks.com

Cover design by Zach McCain

ISBN: 1-64396-158-6
ISBN-13: 978-1-64396-158-3

TABLE OF CONTENTS

INTRODUCTION

Noir. Put a group of mystery writers together in an on-line forum and they will debate the definition *ad nauseam.* To me, noir is the story of a protagonist who appears to have reached rock bottom before the story begins and for whom things only get worse. Some of the tales that follow fit that definition, but not all.

In selecting the twenty stories in this volume, I tried to keep in mind the many varied definitions of noir that I've encountered, and I've tried to ensure that several are represented. On the other hand, I restricted the stories to the 21st century, challenging contributors to write modern noir stories, stories that don't rely heavily upon the technological restrictions of the past. A character with a cellphone, for example, has many advantages over a character who must find a payphone to call for help, but a character whose cellphone carries a phone location tracker app may be unable to hide from danger.

So, I'll leave it to you, dear reader, to debate which of these stories meet your definition of noir and which only skirt it. But I do hope you'll be intrigued by the way twenty writers have moved noir into the 21st century.

—Michael Bracken
Hewitt, Texas

REFLECTIONS OF THE PAST

Bev Vincent

Back in the old hometown. Back in the old house. Hell, back in his childhood bed if he wanted, but Greg hadn't allowed himself to withdraw that far into the past yet. He planned to sleep on the living-room couch. This move was supposed to be about starting over, but it felt like a retreat.

What had he left behind? A threadbare third-floor apartment with unreliable heating, noisy neighbors and the pervasive odor of mildew. An ex-wife and a lover who'd looked at him when he said he was leaving like she'd known all along he was going to snap. A stack of unpaid bills. A dead-end job as a private investigator. Few friends.

And a reputation he hoped wouldn't follow him, including a six-month stint in county jail. They got the wrong guy, he told anyone crass enough to ask but, in truth, he'd gotten clean away with all the other offenses he'd committed as a P.I., so he should probably consider himself lucky.

Upon his release, his older brother delivered a new verdict— Greg should move into the old family home. His siblings didn't want to sell the house, located at the edge of town, only a block from the beach. It had been sitting empty since they'd moved their mother into a care home, where she now sat for endless

3

hours, mumbling and forgetting bits of her life one day at a time. All Greg had to do was take care of the taxes, utilities, and upkeep. Their parents had long ago paid off the mortgage.

His brother and sister had houses of their own, hundreds of miles away, as well as jobs and families. The implication was that he didn't have any of those things, which was true, but he didn't like having it shoved in his face. Still, it was a chance to start over. Not someplace new, but someplace different from where he'd been spinning his wheels for the past decade.

En route to the house, he'd driven his ramshackle Civic past places that evoked strong memories, few of them pleasant. There was the intersection where he'd nose-dived over the handlebars of his bike when he was sixteen. Twenty-three stitches in his face, busted glasses, two chipped teeth, and a mild concussion. As if he didn't have enough trouble at school without looking like a boxing dummy for two weeks.

Over there, in that unpaved alley, a ruffian named Marcus had pummeled him when he was twelve. The bully had asked, in an amicable tone, "You wanna punch in the mouth?" Greg, his mind racing for the magic answer, had responded, "No, thank you," but his polite refusal hadn't impressed Marcus, who mashed his fist into Greg's lips. That was when he asked his father to teach him to fight.

And in that rusty brick building, perched on the side of a hill, Greg's father had died three years ago after a prolonged illness. His memory of the long bedside vigil, once it became clear the end was near, still haunted him in the dark, quiet hours before sleep. Greg hadn't been back since.

His worldly possessions—those he cared enough about to bring with him—fit into five cardboard boxes and three suitcases. The boxes sat unopened in a corner of the living room. Books, mostly, and DVDs.

Greg wandered the house, swigging from a bottle of whiskey he'd found in a cabinet, trying to decide if he belonged here. Someone—his sister, probably—had draped sheets over the furniture, and he couldn't be bothered to remove most of them. Not yet, anyway. The only thing out of place was a huge wall mirror with an elaborate, gilt frame, leaning against a bare wall next to the couch—his temporary bed. Its reflective backing was scraped in a few places and the frame bore the scars of a rough history. *Not so different from me*, Greg thought.

He had no idea where it came from. Perhaps bequeathed to his mother by a departed friend. There had been enough of those in recent years. She would never have purchased it, given her superstitious beliefs about mirrors. He remembered how she had covered the one in the hallway when his sister brought her newborn daughter to the house. *Babies' souls aren't firmly rooted for the first year of life*, his mother said, *and can be stolen by a mirror.* That wasn't her only strange belief. *You shouldn't stare into a mirror by candlelight*, she said. *Fire is the spirit element and you'll see the devil. Dreaming of your reflection means someone will die soon.* Where she'd gotten all this crap Greg didn't know.

He decided to hang the mirror but, before he could get started, the phone rang. No one knew he was here except his siblings, and he wasn't sure he wanted to talk to either of them. They had a way of checking up on him that seemed both parental and patronizing.

"Greg?" an unfamiliar female voice said when he answered.

"Who's this?"

"Monica. Monica Hicks."

"Mon—I thought you were..." He caught himself. *I thought you were dead* was what he had been about to say. Hadn't she been killed in an accident years ago? Must have been someone else. He had so little interest in his old schoolmates that he rarely paid attention when his mother related local gossip during their infrequent phone calls. Not that she did that anymore.

"...out west," he finished clumsily. He had no idea why she would be calling him. They'd barely spoken in school and he hadn't seen her since graduation night. An unpleasant scene, he remembered. Too much liquor, a habit that had followed him ever since. He took another slug from the bottle.

There'd been a party on the beach. Monica's date had gotten sick and someone had driven him home. Greg's date, a timid girl named...Pamela? Amelia?...had grown paler and more withdrawn the louder and more raucous everyone else became until she had simply vanished, freckles and all.

He and Monica had gravitated toward each other, both of them in that leaden stage of drunkenness when the earth's pull seems irresistible and the air is as dense as water. Few words passed between them. They'd found a spot away from the stragglers and tried to fuck, but he couldn't get it up and she had laughed. A silly, inebriated laugh that went on far too long, even after he'd slapped her.

"You there?" It was like the voice of a ghost.

"Yeah. What's up?"

"I heard you were back in town, so I thought I'd see how you were doing."

"I just arrived. How'd you know where to find me?"

"Guessed. Let's get together. Catch up. Reminisce."

"Okay." Greg kept his voice flat and unemotional. Maybe she'd pick up on his lack of enthusiasm.

"I'll be at Murphy's Pub after six," she said.

That brought back memories. During the summer after graduation, while most of his classmates prepared for college, Greg had worked days in the paper mill and spent his evenings squandering his earnings on pool and beer at the pub.

He stared at the phone. Monica had hung up. He shrugged. She'd been good-looking as a teenager. Some women improved in their twenties and early thirties. Why the hell not? He could use a drink or two.

He decided to hang the mirror first. If he staggered in shit-faced at two in the morning, he didn't want to accidentally kick it on his way to the couch. He imagined shards of reflective glass scattered throughout the living room. Another seven years of misery. He'd done just fine reaping bad luck without benefit of a broken mirror.

Most of his father's tools were still scattered on the basement workbench where he'd left them when he went into the hospital. Greg remembered helping his father on projects when he was young. His brother hadn't showed much interest in carpentry, but Greg had enjoyed the smell of sawdust and the warmth of freshly planed wood. His old man had been a hardass, but they'd gotten along during the brief periods when Greg wasn't raising hell and getting into trouble. They'd worked mostly in silence, but it had been a comfortable silence.

Greg pawed through drawers until he found a stud locator and a couple of fasteners that looked hefty enough to support the mirror. Once hung above the sofa, it added depth to the living room. He stood in the center of the room and scratched the short hairs at the back of his neck. "How about a beer?" he asked. His reflection gave him the thumbs-up.

Greg donned a jacket against the evening chill, locked up and caught the #6 bus. Parking downtown was difficult at the best of times. Besides, he would probably be in no condition to drive later, and he didn't need a DUI.

Murphy's faded sign needed a coat of paint, and Greg identified a thin crack in a window near the corner that he vaguely remembered causing. Warm air rushed out to greet him when he pulled the door open. Cigarette smoke and loud conversation followed. The pub was crammed; it was Friday night, Greg realized. Lately he'd had no reason to pay attention to what day it was. He had no job (*yet*, his conscience nagged) and no schedule.

Most of what happened after Greg entered the pub was washed away by uncounted pints of lager. Only a few vignettes remained. The strange look on a bartender's face when he asked about Monica, who never showed up. Narrowly avoiding a fight with a beefy millworker over a bowl of peanuts. The redhead who repeatedly glanced in his direction only to look away when he tried to return her gaze. Puking on the sidewalk in the alley beside the bar.

Staggering down the street with the redhead inexplicably on his arm, kissing and groping each other at every intersection. Someone in a passing car had hooted at them during one of their passionate clinches, he remembered that.

Nothing more. He woke up on the couch late the next morning, throbbing, spent, naked and alone. He couldn't tell if someone else had spent the night. The doors were bolted from the inside. If the redhead had come home with him, he must have let her out.

Suddenly paranoid, he searched his jeans for his wallet. Not much cash left, but that was no surprise. His lone credit card—a *charge* card, he reminded himself; no one gave him credit these days—was still in its celluloid pocket. He didn't have much worth stealing.

The pounding in his head started at the base of his skull and progressed past his ears to both temples. Acid churned in his stomach and the taste in his mouth almost made him hurl. If he moved too quickly, bright lights flared before his eyes. His back muscles ached, maybe from moving in his boxes of books or hanging the mirror.

The vision staring back at him from the mirror looked like a celebrity mug shot. The rings under his eyes were only slightly lighter than the eye-black athletes wore to cut down glare. Einsteinian hair sprouted in all directions. His mother's voice echoed in his pain-laden head: *You have to remove any mirrors from a sick person's room or they'll suck their soul out while they're weak.* Greg didn't think he had much soul left to worry about. Someday he'd look in a mirror to discover he had no reflection at all.

He collapsed onto the couch.

The pounding that awakened him hours later didn't come from his head. Someone was banging on the door. A groan sprang from his lips when he got to his feet. He pushed the curtain aside.

A uniformed police officer stood on the step. Greg searched his sketchy memory of the night before, wondering what he'd done to bring the cops.

No point avoiding the inevitable. Dressed only in his underwear and a T-shirt, he opened the door and squinted against the sudden onslaught of sunlight.

"Greg Callahan?"

"Uh."

"Mind if I come in?"

Greg stood back to let the officer into the kitchen. He had nothing to hide.

"Can I ask where you were last night, Mr. Callahan?"

"Um, I went down to Murphy's for a while. What's this about?"

The officer scratched a few lines in his notepad. "Did you meet a woman named Emily Perry?"

"Doesn't ring any bells," Greg said. He thought about the redhead, but his gig as a P.I. had taught him to never volunteer information to the police. Answer their questions, truthfully when practical, but nothing more.

"Twenty-nine, five foot six, long red hair. A bartender remembers you leaving with her about eleven fifteen."

Greg molded a wry grin onto his face. "Yeah, well, we weren't formally introduced."

"She came back here with you?"

Trying his mildly befuddled look, Greg said, "To be honest, I don't remember. Rough night."

"You wouldn't happen to know Ms. Perry's current whereabouts, would you?"

"Nope. Sorry. What's the problem?"

The cop craned his neck to take in the adjacent rooms as he spoke. "Her roommate called us to report that Ms. Perry didn't come home last night."

Greg didn't respond to that.

"Then she missed her flight to London this morning. Ordinarily we wouldn't investigate so soon, but missing an important transatlantic flight and all..." The cop tried his looking-around-corners trick again.

Greg sighed. "Take a look around, if you want. Just don't break anything." He went into the living room, put on a bathrobe, dropped onto the couch and massaged his temples.

A few minutes later, the cop reappeared. "Okay, thanks for your cooperation, Mr. Callahan. If you hear from Ms. Perry, give us a call." He handed Greg a business card.

Greg nodded. "Sure thing." He ushered the cop out and relocked the door. The bright outdoor light still bothered his eyes, but he thought his stomach was finally ready to withstand food.

The phone rang while he was stacking his dirty dishes in the sink.

"Yes?"

"What happened to you last night?" a female voice said.

"Who's this?"

"Monica, silly. I thought we had a date."

"I was there all evening...it's you who didn't show up."

"Really? Well that's strange. I could've sworn I was there. What are you doing tonight?"

"Recovering."

"Want to hook up later?"

"I can only handle one night like that a week."

"How about if I come over to your place? Bring a bottle of wine?"

Greg's stomach churned. "Listen, I don't mean to be rude or anything, but why are you so eager to get together? It's not like we were close in school or anything."

"That's not how I remember it, Greg. I remember getting close one time. Really close."

Greg's memory: Monica, naked in the grass beside a stretch of sandy beach. A thread of seaweed entangled in her short dark hair. Beige sand coating the bottoms of her feet. Their kisses angry and bruising. Her breast fit naturally into the curve of his hand and *she* hadn't pushed him away. She had been hot and moist, ready for him. Her legs were spread, inviting him inside, but she was laughing as his body failed him for the first time.

Not for the last.

"Okay, come by if you want. Listen, do you know someone named Emily Perry?"

Monica's snicker reminded him of how she'd laughed that night on the beach. "Of course, silly. She was your prom date."

Emily. Not Pamela or Amelia. Could the flashy redhead who'd been all over him last night have evolved from the pale wallflower who'd blushed deep crimson when he asked her to the graduation dance? Hard to imagine. Had she recognized him? Was her missing-person routine retaliation for ignoring her when she wouldn't put out, wouldn't let him touch her, would barely allow him to kiss her?

"Oh, right," he said.

"I'll be over in a while," she said. "Hang loose."

Hard to hang loose when things stopped making sense, as just about everything had lately. He was still readjusting to life after jail and to being back here. He stared into the mirror for a few seconds. At least his reflection still appeared within its depths. That was some comfort.

He wandered the house, looking for any evidence that Emily Perry had been here last night. Why couldn't he remember? The drinking had been taking a toll on him for years. Had broken up his brief marriage and induced him to make countless unwise decisions, such as the one that sent him to jail. One of these days, he was going to have to find the strength to quit.

Back in the living room, he looked into the mirror again. "But not today," he said.

In case Monica followed through on her threat to visit, he put on jeans and a fresh shirt. He bundled his dirty clothes into a wad that he tossed into his parents' old bedroom. His shoes were by the back door. He brushed light-colored dirt from their soles into the garbage can and shoved his feet into them.

The kitchen he left untouched. Fuck it. She'd invited herself—she could take the place as it was, assuming she didn't stand him up again. While straightening up the couch, he found a red hair clinging to the pillowcase. Greg stretched it between the thumb and forefinger of each hand. One question answered—Emily had definitely been here.

He dropped onto the couch and picked up the remote, intending to watch TV until Monica arrived.

When he awoke later, something round and firm was being pressed into his hand.

"Some party animal you are, pooping out after a few drinks."

He blinked and shook his head. An attractive brunette was standing over him. She held a nearly empty bottle of red wine in one hand and a full glass in the other. Greg wrapped his fingers around the proffered glass instinctively. His mind was Swiss cheese. He glanced at the wall clock. Over two hours had slipped by.

"Am I keeping you up?" the woman said. He looked at her again and revised his assessment. Monica Hicks would be nearly thirty. This girl, in her skin-tight jeans and loosely buttoned shirt, looked like a high school student. Did Monica have a younger sister?

Or was he hallucinating?

Greg stuck his nose in the wine glass and inhaled. Aromatic vapors permeated his nostrils. A sip rewarded his mouth with a deep oak flavor with fruity overtones, sensations more vivid than in any dream.

"How come you're so quiet all of a sudden?" the woman—the girl—asked.

Greg drank deeply before answering. "Sorry. I don't know what's going on. Who are you?"

"Nice one. I've gotten the brush-off before, but never like that."

"I'm not brushing you off. It was an honest question."

"How else am I supposed to take it? You stand me up last night, invite me over this evening, we polish off a bottle of wine, make love, and put a pretty decent dent in bottle number two, and now you're asking me who I am? Is it some sort of philosophical question?"

"Bear with me a second." He took a deep breath, running his free hand through his hair. "Monica? You haven't aged a bit. You look the same as you did graduation night."

She beamed. "Nice recovery." After she finished filling her glass, she dropped onto the couch and leaned against him.

Greg drained the last of his wine and put the glass on the coffee table. Monica slipped under his arm, snuggling closer. He reviewed what she'd told him. Two bottles of wine? Made love? He remembered none of it. He knew he hadn't invited her over, though. She'd invited herself.

His stomach lurched with a sudden bout of nausea. He leapt from the couch, vaulted the coffee table, knocking over the empty wine bottle, and barely made it to the bathroom in time to throw up into the toilet. He retched a second time, but there wasn't much to come up.

Despite the nausea, Greg didn't feel drunk. He could hold his booze, but a bottle of wine would normally have much more effect on him. Other than being disoriented, he felt completely sober, and what he'd vomited into the toilet didn't look like anything more than the meal he'd eaten hours earlier.

The living room was empty when he returned. No wine bottles or glasses.

He stood there, staring at the couch, unable to fathom what was happening. Was he having flashbacks from all the drugs he'd taken as a teenager? Had he poisoned himself with something he ate? Had it all been a dream?

Get a grip, he told his reflection.

He watched sitcom reruns, infomercials and old movies until two in the morning, when he finally felt tired enough to sleep.

His dream: He was standing in front of the antique mirror. Instead of his reflection, he saw two women—eighteen-year-old Monica Hicks and twenty-eight-year-old Emily Perry.

"Why did you hit me?" Monica asked.

"Why didn't you stop hitting me?" Emily asked.

"They never found my body," Monica said.

"They'll find mine," Emily said. "You're the obvious suspect."

"No one saw us together that night," Monica said, forever eighteen. Greg recognized her clothing—the jeans and shirt she'd changed into after the prom. What she'd been wearing earlier, during what must have been a dream. Must have been.

Emily smiled. "But lots of people saw *us*. The police know where to start."

Greg's eyes snapped open, his heart pounding. Emily's voice echoed in his ears.

There'd been a knock at the door, he realized. It repeated. He glanced at the wall clock. Seven-fourteen. Heavy drapes covering the living-room windows were keeping the early dawn light at bay.

"What now?" he grumbled as he pulled on his jeans. He cracked open the curtain to see a man standing in front of the door. He wasn't wearing a uniform, but Greg knew a cop when he saw one.

Bare-chested, he opened the door partway.

"What?"

The man flashed his gold badge. "Detective Irwin. Can I come in?"

"At this hour? On Sunday morning? You must be kidding."

"Got company?"

"What if I do? What do you want? I haven't heard from that redhead, if that's what you're after."

"This would be easier if I could come in," Irwin said.

Greg sighed and stepped back. The detective went through the kitchen into the living room and sat in the recliner where Greg's father used to fall asleep watching the evening news. The only convenient place for Greg to sit was on the couch. He grabbed his shirt and buttoned it before sitting.

"You weren't entirely honest with Officer Klein yesterday,

14

Mr. Callahan."

"I don't know what you're talking about."

"You led him to believe you didn't know Emily Perry." Irwin looked at his notepad. "You hadn't been formally introduced, you said."

"Oh, that. To be honest, I didn't recognize her. Hadn't seen her in ages."

"But you know who she is now?"

"Yeah, I figured it out after he left."

The cop frowned. "I'm having trouble believing you didn't recognize someone you used to date."

"Ten years ago. And we didn't date, really. We only went out once."

"To your prom."

"Yeah, that's right."

The detective flipped through his notepad.

"She changed a lot since," Greg said.

Irwin remained silent. Greg knew what the detective was doing, pretending to review his notes. Let the suspect talk and he'll eventually say too much. Greg decided to wait him out.

"So, if I have this straight," Irwin said, "you didn't recognize your high school sweetheart and you don't remember if she came here with you or not."

"That's what I said."

"What about Monica Hicks?"

"Who?"

"She disappeared the night of your prom. You don't remember that, either?"

"Guess not. Ancient history."

Irwin closed his notepad. "If I were you, Mr. Callahan, I'd lay off the booze. It's affecting your memory."

Greg followed him to the door.

"We'll be seeing each other again, Mr. Callahan. Count on that."

After the detective was gone—Greg watched his car back out

of the driveway to be sure—he tried to figure out what was happening. Six months in county jail had messed with his mind a little and, sure, he was probably drinking too much, but it felt like there was something more going on. Coming back here had been a mistake. The past was haunting him, except he couldn't remember enough about it to understand how.

They never found my body.

What was that about, anyway? He hadn't killed anyone. Sure, he might have slapped Monica that night on the beach, but she had laughed at him. He'd been drinking pretty hard back then—*and ever since*, his conscience nagged—but she shouldn't have laughed.

Emily Perry had been his substitute date to the prom. He and his girlfriend Jane had broken up two weeks before graduation after a screaming fight. A brawl that had taken place in the basement of Jane's house one night when her parents were out. What she'd said to set him off, he couldn't recall. Her reaction to being hit...again...but for the last time, that much he remembered.

Emily had been a plain redhead with freckles that seemed to radiate from her face and upper chest. Someone desperate enough to say yes when asked out only a week before the big event. Someone who looked grateful to be asked at all.

But not grateful enough to put out on the big night, when everyone else was making out all over town. The bitch didn't even want to kiss him other than a peck on the cheek. Had pushed his hand away when he'd cupped her breast. That was when she started to fade from his awareness. He turned his mind away from her and she vanished. He couldn't remember when she left the beach party or how she got home. Didn't care.

He had no future here. Only his past, haunting him. Part of him had known that from the beginning, which is why he slept on the couch and his belongings were still in boxes.

Except now he was trapped. If he threw everything into the trunk of his car—a hundred and fifty thousand miles on the odometer and a terminal rattle in the engine compartment—and left town, the police would think he was fleeing justice.

What had that cop said about Monica Hicks? That she'd disappeared the night of the prom? When she'd called him on Friday, his initial reaction had been that his mother had told him she'd been killed in an accident.

Disappeared on prom night.

After he hit her for laughing at him.

What exactly had happened after that?

He remembered his anger. He ached for her but his body had failed him. Pulling at his pud like a little kid, trying to stroke some life into his flaccid organ. He must have looked ridiculous, which is why she'd laughed—but she shouldn't have. She should have known better. Greg Callahan wasn't the sort of person you laughed at about anything. He'd learned how to fight back.

Later, staggering back to the fire, he'd collapsed onto the sand and immediately reached for another beer. He couldn't remember seeing Monica after that. Nor could he remember how they'd parted. At some point he'd gotten dressed and gone back to the others.

Someone else must have come along and found her there, alone on the beach. Or else she'd run off to let her bruises heal and had just never bothered to come back.

Or...

Another black spot in his memory. How many of those were there in his past? He'd been so drunk the night of his arrest that he'd said things that put him behind bars for six months. He barely remembered roughing up the guy who had cheated his client, but his damaged hands had betrayed him.

Half a year of his life spent in a six-by-eight cell with a guy going through withdrawal, who had screaming fits in the middle of the night when he thought spiders were crawling over him or that green slime was oozing from the cell walls.

Was that where he was headed? Hallucinating and losing his grip on reality?

He picked up a book and threw it at the mirror, splintering it into an infinity of shards, each one a tiny mirror reflecting his image back at him. Seven years' bad luck? He'd never notice the difference. He ignored the fragments scattered on the floor and turned on the television.

Detective Irwin showed up on Monday morning again, this time with a search warrant and a forensics team. Greg sat at the kitchen table drinking coffee while they combed the house for fingerprints and other trace evidence. No skin off his nose. What could they find? Even if they could prove Emily Perry had been here, that didn't mean anything. She was probably over in London laughing her ass off.

Another black spot, though. What had they done that night? He wished he could remember. She might have been a wallflower in high school, but she'd turned into a hot chick. She'd been all over him on the way back to the house. He couldn't wait to do her. She hadn't pushed his hands away when he groped her on the street corner, either. Maybe she wasn't getting back at him—maybe she was making up for lost time. Finally getting what she'd turned down that night on the beach.

Two blackouts, two missing women. He couldn't blame the cops for suspecting him. They scoured the house for hours. Greg went for a walk, got a newspaper and a coffee, came back. He was reading the job ads in the classified section when Irwin announced their departure.

"Have a little trouble with your mirror?"

Greg grunted and didn't look up from the paper.

"Bad luck, but you know all about bad luck, don't you? Familiar with the inside of a jail cell, too, right?"

Greg kept staring at the newspaper page.

"I've dealt with guys like you before. Like to get rough, like you did with that guy. Bet you get rough around women, too."

Greg said nothing.

"We'll let ourselves out. Talk to you again soon."

That night, Greg dreamed he was on the beach again, but this time he wasn't eighteen, he was twenty-eight. Emily Perry was there, but she looked like she had on prom night. Plain, befreckled, scared stiff. When Greg ran his hand up her body to her breast, she squirmed and tried to push him away, but Greg was too strong. He mashed his lips against hers.

She kissed back, but then her lips took on a new shape and he could feel her body shaking in his arms. Was she crying? He leaned away from her, but her eyes were dry. Not crying—laughing. Trying to hold it in but laughing all the same. Anger swept over him. His thoughts clouded. Blackness descended. When his mind cleared, she was gone.

Greg sat up in the darkness, letting the dream dissipate. One thought remained. Sand. He'd seen sand somewhere recently. On Saturday night, when he'd been straightening up the living room while waiting for Monica to arrive. But it couldn't have been Monica. According to the cops, no one had seen her for ten years. He shook that off.

Sand. There had been sand on his shoes when he got dressed that evening. He remembered brushing it off into the garbage can before...

Before he hallucinated an eighteen-year-old version of Monica Hicks spending the evening with him.

The cops showed up shortly before noon the next morning. With an arrest warrant this time. "I told you we'd be seeing each other again soon," Irwin said.

They'd found the sand in his garbage, and a recently used shovel in the basement. This inspired them to investigate the area around the beach. Search dogs found the shallow grave in a copse of trees not far from where they'd partied after graduation. The crime scene investigators noticed another depression in the ground nearby. Two for the price of one, with more than enough forensic evidence to seal the deal.

"You'll be wanting a lawyer," Irwin said.

Greg hung his head as the police led him away from his parents' house, his old home, the place where he'd grown up and the place he'd returned to in hopes of a new beginning.

GETTING VIOLATED
David Hagerty

The deps were holding up feeding, letting breakfast dry and crack in the steamer trollies. I always said there was no way to degrade the sponge cake of eggs and potatoes the jail served up, but the toast would be hard as wood if I didn't get it out soon. In every cell, inmates were mugging me, like it was my fault the assembly line got stalled. When they started banging on the window sliders, the beat became a chant, echoing like approaching footsteps. "Pod time, pod time." If they didn't get let out soon, we'd have a bigger problem than dry toast.

Worse, I was on my own that day. Rolls Royce hadn't made it up for work, a first in the six months we'd been paired as trustees. Probably sleeping off a pruno bender. He'd always been a master brewer of jailhouse wine, cutting it with lemon drops and hot sauce to kill the flavor of rotting fruit.

But when I looked over to his cell, the door was cracked and the dep was standing guard. Maybe he'd drunk a bit too much acid O.J. and was headed to ad seg for a prolonged dry out. No surprise. In anonymous meetings he'd told the teacher what she wanted to hear, but I was never convinced by his "going straight" routine. Everybody here can mimic Oprah and Whoopi with an impassioned speech, but I've seen plenty of them come back on a new beef a week after they're sprung. Catch and release, the deps call it. We say they're doing life six months at a time.

Except when the brass arrived, I knew something was askew. We rarely saw sergeants in the housing units, let alone a lieutenant; once they'd been promoted, deps avoided rubbing up against inmates, like we might stain their dress unis. They'd rather sit at a desk counting us and the overtime they're earning.

This one was typical, with a grey mustache and Brylcreemed hair. Does anybody besides cops still use that stuff? His slack build said he'd have a hard time subduing even the most ragged junkie, but he had the dead eyes of somebody who'd once been a brawler.

I was scheming how to run breakfast solo when Deputy Larsman motioned me over. Lardsman we called him because his love handles overflowed any chair.

"When's the last time you saw Ritchie?" he said.

It took me a minute to connect the name to the guy I knew. Rory Ritchie was always Rolls Royce to us. "Last night."

"*When* last night?"

"Boiling time." Before lockdown, we always passed out hot water so the speed freaks could get a final shot of coffee ahead of lights out.

"Where'd you go after?"

"Where do you think? My cell."

"And you didn't leave it?"

"You the one locked me down!"

"I know how you guys do, jamming paper in the cracks to keep the bolts from engaging."

What could I say? Truth was, as a trustee we did as we liked. In exchange for passing out clothes and food, we got freedom of movement. We could go cell to cell, even wander the halls unsupervised. I wasn't about to cop to that noise, though. From the control booth, the guy had an overlook on everything in the pod but was too lazy to even peek out a window. He thought we couldn't see him through the mirrored glass, dozing, but at night, when the lights were low, the guards were backlit by monitors. It was like a cockpit up there, with windows on all three sides and more buttons and knobs than anybody could memorize. There was a control for everything, even the toilets! If he didn't know what was happening, it's because he didn't want to know.

"I was asleep. Hard as you guys work me, I'm knocked out by lights out."

He gave me his cop's hard look, but I beat him at the staring contest, then watched him waddle toward the cell and flap his jowls at the brass. A minute later, the lieutenant pointed at me and said, "Get a mop."

He kept the door closed, but even so I could smell this was going to be messy. The place had a funk worse than any piss cup or vomit patch I'd cleaned before, so I suited up with gloves and booties. I didn't know what kind of shit RR had gotten himself into overnight, but it must have been potent. For the right price we could get almost any narcotic in our hotel. Since we ran both feeding and linen exchange, we could trade extra food or clothes for whatever we wanted, maybe even help smuggle something in through the kitchen. Still, RR had been on the junk for years, so he should have known how to dose himself.

When I found the mop, hidden behind the linen shelves, it had only half a handle, the top end cracked away, leaving three feet of sharp stick to work with. Then I really didn't want to know what RR had been up to, because a baton like that would put you on equal armaments with the deps. Somebody was going to get added time for that, but I already had my release date calendared six months on, so I thought back. Last time I cleaned was the day before, which left plenty of openings for some break-in artist. Plus we'd just finished linen exchange, when every inmate got a new bundle of clothes, sheets and towels. Anybody could have stashed a handle in that package.

I hadn't much time for rumination before Lardsman came

for me, so I didn't have my lines learned before I had to deliver them. As I started with my alibi, the lieutenant cracked a half smile like he'd just foiled a jailbreak. His pleasure threw me off until I saw through the cracked door to where RR lay on his bunk, blood puddled under him, and a broom handle sticking out of his gut like an arrow. Right off I knew I was fucked.

First thing, they put me in an iso cell and slammed the window slider to keep out any fresh air or light. Even with the sensory deprivation, I was wired, my mind pinballing around memories from the night before, trying to figure how anybody could have escaped a locked cell, stolen a broom, made his way to RR, killed him, then snuck back undetected. Even with Lardsman asleep at the controls, you'd have to be a phantom to pull off that.

Besides, RR wasn't tied into the politics. He didn't associate with the gangs, didn't play cards, didn't even watch TV. He was short to the box by fifteen days and jittery as a J cat about catching any more time. Other than work, he kept himself in solitary. Sure, there was always some friction on the job— somebody who wanted extra privileges without having to pay for them—but we both cut that off quick. Neither of us wanted to be tellers at the favor bank when half our customers were professional stickup men.

Maybe he'd turned down somebody's bid, figuring it would get him a better price the next day, and instead it got him payback. Possible. But RR knew how to say no so nobody took offense.

Or maybe somebody had *keestered* an old vendetta, waiting for a window of opportunity. Not likely in this bunch. Guys were so busy profiling they couldn't overlook even the smallest slight. A bump, a look, a passed word, and they'd be mouthing off for everybody to hear. Really there was no other way when you were locked down with forty-seven other men in a pod the size of a basketball court. Everybody had to know the score if they were going to stay in the game.

Maybe it was all the speechifying he'd been doing. Last time we were in group, he was selling it like a traveling preacher, talking about how he wanted a fresh start when he got out. A couple nights before that, he even turned down a free drink. Said he was giving it up. Not that I believed him. Most likely he was just bogarting his stash for himself. Pruno takes ten days to brew, and you can't keep multiple batches going, not with the deps tossing our cells every other week. The smart guys start a new bag right after the last shakedown and figure before the next one it'll be ready.

Maybe somebody got tired of hearing his line, somebody with a lot of time coming who didn't appreciate a guy with two weeks left talking about life on the outs. Guys around here get jealous when they hear about another man's prosperity. But would that provoke a killing?

I don't know how long I sat in the dark before I heard metal scrape on metal and a stab of light pierced my eyeball. At first I thought it was the deps coming to feed me, but only the window slid open, and the face was Devere's—the pod's shot caller—a wiry, dark brother with an elastic mouth that always made you think he was clowning. Lucky for me, he wasn't into all the race hatred. So long as you followed orders, he didn't care where your people came from. Which made him the logical pick to sub for me as trustee. Not that he was worthy of trust, but everybody respected him.

"How you holding up?" he said.

"Haven't wasted away yet."

"I try to hook you up with some scraps in a minute."

"Forget the food. What's happening?"

"Nothing good. The deps rolled up Rolls Royce like he was a carpet. Now they picturing his cell from every angle and tossing everything in it. I told them they wasting they time with that.

Probably find trace of every convict slept here for the last thirty years if they look hard enough. But they ain't listening. Had us locked down all day. Said they not letting anybody out till they got a suspect to go with the victim for tomorrow's paper. If the guys don't get loose soon, they liable to start brawling with they cellies as distraction."

"You hear anybody gloating over the death?"

"What do I sound like, the cell block's songbird?"

"You want a killer sleeping next to you?"

He snorted. "Why you think they put people up in here?"

"I'm not asking you to snitch, but they're trying to hand *me* the case."

"They just paranoid. You know how cops get in the aftermath."

"You didn't see how the lieutenant was looking at me when I showed up with a busted broom handle."

"How's that?"

"Like I was the only virgin in the whorehouse."

"Don't stress, O.G. I'll dial up the radio for you."

He should have said the wireless, since all news traveled from mouth to mouth in jail, but I appreciated the effort.

Devere left the window cracked enough so I could find my way to the sink without patting the walls. The cold water felt good on my face and washed away the smegma in my mouth, but as soon as I finished, the daylight made me feel more closed in. I lay still for a while on my concrete bunk, listening to the sounds of the pod—the vacuum when somebody flushed a toilet, the ticking of the ventilation when it shut off—and waiting for Devere to return with some insight.

Maybe it was the solitude, but I started to tear up. I'd lost a friend. That's not a word you hear much in jail. Inmates have people, partners, associates, hookups, cellies, but rarely friends. Still, for me, working together half a year qualified. It's more time than I ever stay in one place on the outs. Which was why none of this made sense. If somebody had it in for RR, I would have sensed it. A look, a whisper, a word, something would have drifted my way, but I hadn't heard about him having strife with anybody.

Still, I had to admit he was acting a bit punch-drunk lately. I'd never known him to pass up free alcohol. Drinking gave his life meaning. Sure, we attended the anonymous meetings. Most guys did. It was a great way to get some good-time credits. Plus it filled up the morning. Still, even if it sometimes made me feel two-faced, I gave up on quitting way back when. The most important thing I learned in recovery was to accept my own faults.

So I like a drink? You wouldn't tell a fat person to give up eating, or a sex addict to give up screwing, so why expect a drunk to give up the thing he loves best? Without booze, life would be too dry to take. What else is there for a single guy in his fifties with no job, no house, no kids, and no prospects? Sure, in *jail* I can get work, but consider the competition. On the outs, no one wants an unabashed wino spilling into their business. Instead, I accepted that drinking always brings a hangover, whether it's getting fired or getting a stay at the county motel.

Deputy Lardsman threw open the door next, stepping aside like he was giving me back my freedom of movement. I kept quiet and tasted the air, but all he said was, "Follow me." Walking the empty corridor, with only our footsteps for company, I tried to sway him.

"All the time I've been a trustee, you ever catch me stealing?"
"You're sly about it."
"You ever hear me lie about finishing a job?"
"As little work as you all got, what's to lie about."
"You ever see me in a beef?"
"You're too docile to fight."

"Exactly! So why would I kill my partner?"

Inside the pod, he faced the cells instead of me. "I don't need to know why or how," he said, "only who."

"Then know I'm no killer. Look at my file."

"I did. You've got convictions going back twenty years: everything from possession to DUI."

"But no violence. I never had no violence on my jacket."

"If you say so."

"So if you know I'm a pacifist, why you trying to give *me* the case?"

Finally, he turned toward me just as RR's door ground open. "You walked into a murder scene clutching the weapon. You're the only guy with access to the supply closet. And you two were practically boyfriend and girlfriend." Ten quiet steps took us inside the bloody cell. "Now clean up your mess," he said.

On first whiff I wanted to run back to the iso. The dead leave a stench you can't describe. The closest comparison is water at the bottom of a flower vase after all the plants have wilted. Plus, those concrete walls held in every particle of stink, intensifying it till you cried "no more." In there, even a fart could choke you.

By then the blood had turned to tacky paste. I had to crawl through, practically scraping at the stuff with my fingernails to dislodged it. To distract myself, I eyeballed the cell for drops of knowledge.

On the wall hung magazine cutouts—the usual centerfolds and lowriders—but nothing personal. No photos, no letters, no signs of any life outside the cell. I never heard RR talk about family, and now I knew why. He was picture living.

Other clues were scarce. In one corner stood a neat stack of Ramens. Odd the killer didn't take them since noodles were the jail's currency after cigarettes got banned. Leaving them was like leaving cash in some vic's wallet, which told me that property had nothing to do with it.

Once the floors showed only dull concrete, I sprung out the door and gasped until the deputy told me to bring out the mattress, too. It was even more congealed, so coated I couldn't find a clean patch to lift it. I hoisted it by the corners, but it weighed twice what a normal one would, so heavy I dropped it, messing up my clean floor. Underneath I saw his clothes, pressed flat against the box spring. Strange that, since I never saw him looking ironed before.

I tried to hold the giant sponge at arm's length but kept bumping up against it, smearing myself with residue. Then I heard something fall: a little book, which fortunately hadn't absorbed too many body fluids. The pocket prayer guide had dog ears on a dozen pages, with the best passages underlined in pencil, such as:

1 Corinthians 6:19-20 "Do you not know that your body is a temple of the Holy Spirit, who is in you, whom you have received from God? You are not your own; you were bought at a price. Therefore honor God with your body."

I had finished only a couple passages before Lardsman noticed and said, "Give me that," like I had been trying to steal it. While he flipped through, I pretended to stand by, holding up the mattress, but really I was memorizing the marked bits. Because it didn't make sense. RR was never one of those false converts you see so often in here. He didn't go to Bible study, didn't wear a string cross, didn't have religious tats, didn't even talk about a Higher Power during meetings. He once said his dad had beaten all the faith out of him.

We marched outside to the garbage bins, with me wrestling against the mattress like it was a fighting dog. After being in that gas chamber, even the trash smelled good. It didn't last long, though. As soon as I'd maneuvered the mattress into a dumpster, Lardsman marched me right back into the iso cell. I tried to reason with him, to point out the obvious facts: "You think I could take Rolls Royce?" I said. "Look at me! I'm half as strong and twice as old. This grey hair and loose skin is no disguise. I'm an o.g. for real!"

In answer he slammed the door and closed the slider.

With nothing but darkness before me, I tried to block out the memory of the job, but I couldn't get that smell out of my nostrils: blood and death. Not even ammonia could bleach out that. I felt my way back to the sink, stripped, and used some homeless hygiene to clean up. Even then the stink stuck, so I rinsed my clothes, then lay naked and shivering while the vent overhead blew cold.

That prayer guide rattled around in the pocket of my ears but refused to fall. Despite my mom dragging me to church every Sunday, I'd never gotten much out of scripture. The Bible forbids killing, stealing, and adultery, but what society ever snuffed them? If I thought there were an ultimate reckoning, I might have cared more about kicking my own bad habits. From what I could see, the only true punishment is what we impose on ourselves.

More time passed—I don't know how long—before I heard someone scuffling nearby, someone with hard soles. At first I thought it was another guard come to tour the sights. Then I got a whiff of cologne, and I knew it was the preacher. He wore it strong enough to scare off a skunk. Probably hoped it lingered after he left, like the lessons of Christ he'd just sprayed at us. Some guys called him a sport coat. At first I thought it aped how he dressed. Instead of a robe and collar, he liked three-piece suits and broad-brimmed hats, even indoors. Later I learned the true meaning of his street name when I saw how he liked to jaw with the female nurses.

Right quick I was up, banging on the door to waylay him before he passed into the pod.

"Chaplain! I need your help."

"Who's there?"

"It's me, Andrew Viggoth."

"That's a name I don't know. You ever attend my services?"

"Haven't had the time as of yet."

"Then judgment day must nigh. What calamity is to come?"

"I need you to decode a couple verses. Like Acts 16:27.

What's that about?"

I heard him inhale and imagined him puffing up like before a sermon, then he dropped into his preacher voice, rumbling the words at the floor of his register:

"When the jailer awoke and saw the prison doors opened, he drew his sword and was about to kill himself, supposing that the prisoners had escaped. But Paul cried out with a loud voice, saying, 'Do not harm yourself, for we are all here'!"

"That's it! What's it mean? Is it about guys breaking out?"

"Hardly. It is a prohibition on self-slaughter. God forbids us from taking our own lives, which are a gift from Him, and one that only He can reclaim."

Finally the setup made sense. In Ritchie's cell nothing was out of place: the clothes, the noodles, the bed. It was how you'd leave things if you didn't plan on getting up again.

And I should have sniffed it before. Over the years, I'd seen a lot of guys bug out when their time grew short. Some would pick fights to get days added. Others would hide in their cells to avoid trouble. Rarely did I hear inmates tell anybody but their closest allies they were counting days. Talk could jinx it. So when Ritchie started speechifying about what he'd do on the outs, I should have heard the despair. After all, I was supposed to be his friend.

A while later, the window scraped open to let in a little light before it filled with the fat face of Lardsman.

"It's gonna be a while," he said.

"I can save you some time," I said. "I know who killed him."

"A little voice tell you?"

"No. He took himself out."

"You got some proof of this?"

"A while back, he told me he was tired of the video game."

"The what?"

I moved to the door so I could whisper through the crack.

"To us, that's what it's like being on the outs. You put your man in play and see how long he lasts. You're always running, dodging enemies, looking for your next stash. Only sometimes you get tired of playing and just let your player die."

"Why would a man wait till he had only a few days left to do the deed? People make a rope when they get here, not when they leave."

How could I explain it to someone who'd never seen the other side of the bars? Some of us program so well we don't know anything else. What's comfortable is what's familiar, and anything new scares us to death. "Some people can't stand prosperity," I said.

He stared at me through the slider, then moved aside so I could see a bit more light. "You sure that's the way you want to go with this?"

"It's the truth."

"It might mean more time for you. You'll probably get a violation."

"Why am I getting violated?"

"Conspiracy. Suicide is a crime, too. You should've said something."

I eyeballed him through that little window for signs of scorn, but all I saw was pity.

"Maybe I could use it. I've got some cleaning up to do."

MOTEL AT THE
END OF THE WORLD: 3 A.M.
Trey R. Barker

I can't remember her face.

The rain starts, warm and moist as subway heat. I turn my face into the mist, feel a softness that reminds me of her.

There is no neon on this street to make the rain glisten, no shiny cars throwing light into the splash, no beautiful people turning their expensive umbrellas against the rain as they hurry along on their first dates. Down here where the world ends not with a bang or a whimper but with a exhalation there are broken incandescents and flickering fluorescents that cast harsh shadows across cracked brick and shattered and shuttered windows.

The call came thirty-five minutes ago.

"Yeah, he's here. Came in ten minutes ago. Room four-oh-seven. Top floor, end of the hall, by the roof access."

"Last room in the inn?" I had asked.

"What-the-fuck-ever." Click and he was gone.

So here I am, as a skinny old man slides out of the gutter and searches for cigarette butts. He's covered in dirt and open sores but has all his teeth when he tells me to piss off and quit staring.

I'm afraid I'm going to lose her.

Inside, the night clerk nods vaguely toward the stairs. "Still there unless he went on the roof."

In the dim corner light, two men pass a small bag back and forth, one taking a long pull, then the other. In the middle of their drinking, they exchange a smaller, glassine packet and a wad of cash

"Heroin?"

The night clerk shrugs. "Whatever. Listen, Do-Gooder, ever'body here got something. Every damn room. Chumps like that don't cause me no trouble, so…"

"They pop you some product, keep you happy?"

"Mr. Skip Tracer…best in the world…getting it all figured out."

I'm not the best in the world. Not even the best in this wretched city. Hell, maybe not even the best on this mid-city block of losers and lowlifes and shitty shops with guys writing bonds on four-bit neighborhood thugs. But I am pretty good, and when I saw the notice come through on Little Johnny, I snatched the paper.

Because I can't see her face anymore.

"Everybody walks through here waiting to die. Or killing themselves, more like. Man, I'm just purgatory. You know it, I know it, hell, *they* know it. Ain't nothing left for nobody after this place."

"The land for expatiation of sins?"

He colorless-eyes me. "You gonna kill him?"

I grind my jaw. "No, I'm here to bring him back for my boss, get the court to maybe cough up the ten-grand bond."

He snorts and holds his hand out. I slap him a Benjamin and he heads toward the back door. I've pulled a lot of bail jumps out of this place and I know that back door leads to his nightly romp with his girlfriend on a mattress in the alley. He says they're in love and he's going to save her from her pimp but he says it perfunctorily and neither of us believes it. When he says it, I hear Stevie Ray Vaughan singing "Tin Pan Alley."

"Working her over with a two-by-four," I sing, and he flips me off as he leaves.

I stick to the middle of the staircase, keeping the walls with their stench of blood, piss, and the end of times as far away as I can. The carpet is worn to wood in most places and there's nothing but exposed backing in the places where it isn't completely gone. There are a few holes in the walls, ragged like missing teeth, and some spots that were patched but never painted. On the ceiling are flecks of dried brown, including more than one straight line.

Cast off.

From a stabbing? A beating? Or maybe a self-flagellant.

Purgatory or Dante's seventh circle? The circle of violence?

On the second floor, the doors to a few rooms stand open; probably the tenants trying for a river breeze to kill the summer heat. As I pass, I observe Late Poverty Modern and Skid Row Revival designs: dark and torn, nothing—furniture or people—matched to anything else. In one open room, I see a woman. She holds a well-thumbed paperback in front of her like a shield. Sits on an unadorned chair, her legs crossed, her arms close to her body, her shoulders hunched, and her eyes hard on mine.

Self-protection.

I'd seen that a few times with Abigail, hadn't I? Before Daddy threw me out and locked the door behind me. Abigail hunched and hiding from the World. Not from Mom and Dad, they had loved her dearly, but from the World and maybe sometimes from me. Ultimately, that hadn't done her a whit of good, had it? Now she waited patiently in a pauper's field for someone to find enough dough to move her to decent ground.

On the third floor, a carbon copy of the second, a man stands in the middle of his room, hands clenched, naked with a short, thick cock at half-staff. "You wanna piece'a this, bitch?"

"Too much for me, brutha."

35

He slams the door.

On the fourth floor, the lights are duller. All the lights are on, nothing is broken or burned out, but the lights aren't as bright, as though they're too weak to force their foot-candle onto the hallway. No doors open here, no one trying to seduce a cool breeze through a door or window. Locked, metaphorically, barred and boarded over, no one in or out.

Except for a woman. She barrels out of a room, three-twelve a.m. all over her, and jumps when she sees me. Her breath freezes as she stares. She doesn't back up or flex for a fight but grips her phone like it's a lifeline.

"Little Johnny?"

"Don't know him. Doesn't sound like a real name."

"Jonathon James Dormand Britton. Little Johnny. Medium guy. Skinny. Lotta miles on him."

She looks me up and down. "Could be you. Gonna fuck him up?"

"Gonna make a call?" I nod toward her phone.

"Already made my call." She inclines her head toward a door near the end of the hall. "They're coming." She leans in, conspiratorial, but her eyes are wide and scared. "He's watching. Listening, too." She looks around, though the hallway is empty. "They'll be here quick."

"They?"

"The girls." Inclines her head toward a random door. "He had 'em. They got away. Flew away like birds in the...you know...in the air, and stuff."

"Queen of the pipe?"

She glares at me. "Kiss my ass. Ain't no junkie, ain't seeing no visions. You'll see when they get here."

My vote is distilled visions, brewed hallucinations, freebased revelations and prophecies. I shove a sawbuck into her hand. For a split second she looks offended but then the money disappears into her shirt as she breathes a quiet, "Thank you," and scuttles down the stairs.

I keep moving, my 1911 pressing my side like a lover's gentle touch.

It happens quickly, a staccato heartbeat.

The door crashes open, a gun in my face. Little Johnny grabs me, a clichéd Mexican wrestler in a '50s bar in Tijuana, pins my arms tight, makes my weapon useless. Drags me into the room, the funk of a stale man making me gag. He tries to close the door while still holding onto me. I manage to free a hand and grab for the door so my fingers are on the frame when the thing closes. Pain blasts up my arm, explodes in my head like the first time I saw Abigail's death pictures.

"The fuck." But my voice is muted, his hand across my lips as he drags me across the bed and slams me onto the floor.

"Shaddup." He stomps the floor, feet around my head. "Say a word and I'll kill you."

I cover up, hands over head, wiggling to avoid his boots, heels heavy and hard.

"Johnny." My voice squeaks, metallic adrenaline thick in my throat. "Stop." This wasn't how I saw it playing. In my head, Little Johnny comes along quietly and goes to prison until someone guts him in the shower or sets him on fire in his cell. In my head, the end of this nightmare is clean and quick and allows me to make some sort of vague, barely-fulfilling peace with Abigail's death.

I'm losing her. He took her away from me.

He hits me again. And again and again. I try to dodge his blows. "Stop. I got business. They're looking for you."

The room is suddenly silent.

"Who?" A whisper.

"The cops, Johnny, the cops are looking for you." I lower my hands and finally see him.

"I'm not Johnny."

I've never seen this guy before. "The fuck are you?"

"The cops are coming. Shit." Glances at the door and for a second, maybe he'll take off, scared about cops.

"No, no." I try to calm him down. "Looking for Little Johnny. Where is he?"

"I'm Frankie. The hell is Little Johnny?"

I try to stand, angry that this idiot has pulled me into whatever is going on in his head. "Get the fuck off me, you asshole. Why'd you drag me in here?"

He jams his pistol under my chin and I hear the hammer click. Loudest sound in the world. I stop moving. His gaze darts to the door again. Closed now, the entire world a threat on the other side. "Where are the vaginas?"

I wrap my good hand around my junk. "Cock, not vagina. Take some basic anatomy, dumbshit."

His eyes bulge, his mouth spraying spittle like a firehose on inspection. "You wanna play? You wanna? Play this, bitch."

Fires and I feel the bullet. Creases my ear, shatters the window. Shards of glass raining down below.

"Easy, dude, easy. I'm not here to cause any trouble. I want Little Johnny or I want to get home, snuggle down in my little bed with a bottle of amber."

"Why you after Little Johnny? He hurt you?"

"Dude, I just track down bail jumps. That's all I do."

"Bounty hunter." Points the gun at me again.

Barrel keeps getting fucking bigger.

"No, no, nothing like that. I work for one guy and I help make sure his clients get to court. Nothing like a bounty hunter."

"Why you looking for that guy?"

"Missed a court date." I eat the rest of the answer and feel like I'm denying Abigail.

"I've never been charged with anything." He stares at his gun, at the door, at me and back at the gun. "Won't make it that far."

The silence creeps over us. If he gets introspective, maybe he'll lower that gun and I can pop him once or twice and get out.

"The vaginas are going to kill me."

"Yeah? Sorry to hear that." I inch toward the door. Pretty sure he sees but he doesn't seem to give a crap. "They can be a bitch."

"I killed four of 'em."

I stop. "What did you say?"

"Killed four vaginas."

My hands clench, my heart slips over to total ice, any sympathy I had for this fuck dies beneath my sudden cold. "Women, you asshole."

"Sure. I find 'em places. Malls or bus stations. Once at a police station when I reported a fender-bender. They're all dead."

"What in hell are you talking about?" I'm between him and the door now. He won't shoot me if I head for the door, even with the confession spilling out like an old man's drool. He's too locked up in his own world, believes he'll be dead before I can get the cops here.

"I got a basement place. Built it myself. Walls and chains and bars. I pump in some air, let 'em shit in buckets and stuff."

"You rape them."

"I use them, yeah. Only thing they're good at."

"And God lets you live."

He looks at me. "That's not how it works. Freewill, bastard."

"And yours is to enslave women."

He falls silent again, staring out the window. Rain still beats against the dirty glass, a dry, staccato tapping that reminds me of pencils dropping on a hard floor.

I turn for the door; this is not my fight, not my mess. Mine is yet to—

He shoves me aside, his eyes wide like the river at the foot of the city, and rushes to the door. He is dead silent, his chest rising and falling rapidly but his mouth is open to keep it quiet. He puts his ear at the door, then his eye at the peephole.

"They're here." Steps back from the door, raises the gun.

I throw a chair just as the bullets shred the door from the outside. The chair hits him in the backs of his knees while a bullet knocks him back toward me. A fine mist of red hangs in the air, the coppery tang heavier and thicker than the stink of his fear.

Someone kicks open the door. It bashes back against the wall. Two women. They burst through, guns blasting fist-sized holes through the outside wall. He screams, falls to the far side of the bed where he'd thrown me.

Yelping like I did when Dad threw me out, I dive into the bathroom. My gun skitters away. As I reach for it, a boot—slim, stiletto, knee-high—presses on my already-broken hand.

"Don't be stupid."

I stop when she presses the gun to my head. I can't even hear her breathing. But I do hear her smile; the sound of quiet violence.

"Or do. Your choice."

"Not moving," I say.

She puts me on my ass, bathroom light and gun blinding me. She's tall, maybe six foot, has some muscle to her, but most of it's hanging on a thin frame. If she's pushing iron, she's only been doing it a short while.

"A partner?" she asks.

I frown. "Of who?"

Cocks her head toward the other room.

"Fuck that noise. I don't even know his name."

Laughing, dismissive and condescending, she gets me up and shoves me into the room. Another woman, not as tall, not as muscular, has the guy tied up on the bed. Gagged, hands and feet bound, blood coming from the bullet hole in his leg. She's got a slit of blood leaking from her upper arm.

"Janice?"

Janice shakes her head. "Nothing. He tried to kill me."

My captor leans down to him, her smile more a snarl, her eyes those of a predator finally on top of its prey. Her voice is a stage whisper and she leans closer to him. "Zero-for-two, I guess. Couldn't kill her then, can't kill her now."

When she bites hard into his ear, jerks her head sideways, she takes a large of chunk of it with her, a low-rent Tyson v. Holyfield. He screams, muffled by the ball gag so it sounds a hundred years away. She cackles a laugh and swallows the flesh.

Janice shakes her head. "Still crazy."

"After all these years." The ear-eater leans close again, licking the blood from his wound. "Always willing to do whatever. Wanna tie me tighter? Wanna fuck my ass? Wanna beat me? Scratch me and choke me? Whatever you wanna do, booooyfrieɳnnnnnd."

She draws the word out, a blade coming slowly and silently from between the third and fourth ribs.

"I didn't love you." A scream in his face, foreheads touching, teeth at his lips and nose. "I didn't fucking love you." Hits him with the gun on his partially missing ear. Blood explodes and he yells behind the gag, rolls away from her and falls to the floor.

"Fucking survival. It was survival."

She scrambles across the bed, leans into his face on the far side. "Bet you get that now, don't you? All about survival now, isn't it?"

She hits him again and storms out of the room, slamming the door behind her.

I swallow. My death, not a bang, not a whimper, but my exhalation, will be in this room at the hands of two women.

For nearly five full minutes, an eternity when you're sitting in a theater next to your own death, the silence is bloody. Janice gently slaps the guy back to full consciousness when he flags. Eventually, Ear-Eater comes back in...different. Same woman, same face, but different body language, different walk, different breath. Homicidal rage, righteous fury, still there but subsumed into...something.

Great, I think. *Bipolar and crazy.*

"Leroy Watkins...and company," she says to me. Her voice is mid-range, emotional. Not what Leroy would call vagina-emotion, his version of a woman thing, but hard-edged emotion, personal and deep and angry.

"Not company," I say. "No part of his madness, I've got my own."

41

Ear-Eater eyes me. "I bet."

"I was just passing by."

"And ended up in his room? With this man who kept me captive for more than two years."

My mouth dries. I look at him but he's gone: eyes closed, mouth moving in what might actually be silent prayer. I've seen people in that fetal position, mouths and eyes wet and crying over whatever demon had brought them to the threshold.

"I was passing in the hallway, looking for Little Johnny." I toss the name out, hoping maybe they know him.

'Cause if they let me live, I'm still going after him. If they let me live, I'm going to be them for Abigail. Abigail couldn't take control like these two women, couldn't stand up for herself. She couldn't confront her abuser.

"He yanked me in here, thought I was with you. Kept asking me why I brought the two—"

"Vaginas," Janice says. "Yeah, it's what he always called us. Never called us women, or by our names. Always the vaginas."

"There's a special place in hell for people like him," says Ear-Eater.

"And you're going to send him there?"

Ear-Eater nods. "Yes. I'll sleep like a baby, too."

"He knew this was coming," I say.

"We've been looking for him for awhile. A friend saw him. She called us. Who is Little Johnny?"

"My own Leroy Watkins."

Janice tilts her head, confused. "You?"

"My sister. Three years younger. Booze and weed. Harder drugs. Turned her out. Let a john beat her to death."

"A whore?"

I nod. "I lost track of him. Then he got arrested on a pandering beef in some Podunk cowtown, got shipped back here to face an old aggravated battery charge. My boss wrote his paper and he jumped. I came looking for him."

"Jail or morgue?" Janice asks.

"Yet to be determined," Ear-Eater says. "Look at him. He can't decide. Murder scares him but his sister's death infuriates him."

"Yes, but—" I take a deep breath.

Ear-Eater leans in close to me, the smell of blood on her breath. I lean away, maybe scared she'll eat me, too. But her face is soft, full of anger but full of life, too. Green eyes sparkling with rage, lips bursting with ire, teeth ripping and chewing rationality. But soft to me, understanding and gentle.

She knows.

The things in this woman's face are the things I can't remember in Abigail's. My sister, three years dead but lost years before that when Daddy threw me out of the house. I have few pictures of her...the black sheep wasn't there for family days and the attendant pictures...and so details fade.

"You're having trouble remembering." Ear-Eater speaks softly. "Your memory is failing you. Guilt is pouring out of you, man, pouring out." She squeezes my shoulder. "I'm Ashlee and I can't remember, either."

"Can't remember what?"

"My father. He was old when Leroy Watkins bought me a few drinks at a bar, got me drunk, and then threw me in the basement. He died while Leroy Watkins raped me over and over. I have trouble remembering sometimes."

"I have trouble all the time."

Ashlee grins. "Not enough RAM, babe. Your RAM is full of Little Johnny. Erase him from the world and your RAM will be full of your sister. She's still there, just overwritten. Not remembering for a little while isn't fatal to them. Not doing something to get them back *is*." She punches Leroy Watkins on the missing ear, but it's a perfunctory hit. "There were days..."

"No," Janice says. "Don't."

She looks at Janice, reaches over and squeezes the woman's hand. "There were days I thought I couldn't do it anymore."

"How long did he have you?" I ask.

"Two years," Janice says.

"*More* than two years," Ashlee says. "Two years, six months, some weeks and days. Every day waiting for him to come down the stairs. Every day never wanting to see him again and desperate to see him again. I kept thinking maybe I could get through to him. If he'd just come down one more time. He came down four or five times." Her eyes are wet, her breath ragged and shallow. Her hands shake.

That's me, I think. Ashlee is me when I heard about Abigail. When I identified her body because Mom and Dad had both passed. When I realized she was gone forever.

"There were so many days I wanted to die. In some ways—" Her eyes are full of apology. "I envy your sister."

I head toward the door, unmindful of their guns and anger, ignoring the man who'd done his worst to them. They're not going to hurt me...they *are* me.

At the threshold, I look at them, "In some ways, I do, too," and leave.

In six steps, I'm at the last room on the floor. I don't hesitate. I kick the door in, my 1911 tight in my hand. The door is thin and splinters and covers me in shards. I burst into the room, see him to my left, not surprised, not scared, not armed.

Just resigned.

I grab him, shove him to the floor and screw my gun deep into his ear. Blood starts leaking.

"Little Johnny Britton?"

"Fuck you."

"Little Jonathon James Dormand Britton? Birthdate February 29, 1980? You are under arrest."

"You ain't no cop, fucking let go of me."

But he doesn't try to fight me, doesn't push against me or try and break my grip. He's a pimp and a sodomizer, he's a thief and a junkie, and he's been down this road before. He's had guns pointed at him and fists smash him. He doesn't know who I am but he knows not to fight.

Yet.

"You jumped bail. Case Number twenty-oh-five-two-eight-five. That pesky aggravated battery charge. Beating a man half to death in the alley with a pool cue. You failed to appear for court and so I—"

"You're a fucking bounty hunter? Seriously? Couldn't find any dogs to shoot? Or maybe any little kids to rape?"

I smile. "And so I am authorized to take you into custody and transport you to the cops."

"Who was shooting next door?"

"Just a little party, nothing to worry about." I lean in close. "I'm actually more interested in a friend of yours. Died a few years ago. Abigail Messer."

"Who?"

"Abigail Messer. Abigail Messer?"

"Don't know her."

"Abigail Messer."

"Repeat her name as much as you want, asshole, I still don't know her."

"Bullshit. You found her in a mall. You bought her lunch and then a movie. You dated her and got her drinking. Weed. Hard drugs. Straight down the road. Like a bad movie, man."

His head shakes but not vehemently, not as though he's trying to deny it to avoid a beating, but because—

He truly doesn't remember her.

It was a sudden, stark sledgehammer of clarity. She wasn't memorable to him; she was just another woman, another vagina he could turn out and make money on.

I pull a picture, her high school graduation picture, the effect of booze and drugs already in her face. "You told her she was beautiful, that you were going to marry her and give her everything she wanted."

He laughs. "I tell 'em all that. Are you a fucking idiot? Look, man, whatever you think it was, wasn't nothing but business. Nothing personal with any of 'em, just business." Looks at the picture and shakes his head. "Okay, some cooze. Whatever."

...RAM is full of Little Johnny. Empty it. Empty your RAM and get Abigail back...

I grab him up, the gun jammed so tight under his chin his head tilts back like his neck is broken, Abigail's picture drops to the floor. My free hand reaches around and keeps tight hold of his balls.

"Gotta thing for man-meat?" he asks.

I squeeze until tears come to his eyes, but he doesn't make a sound.

Out the door and I smash him through the roof access door. We take a half-flight of stairs up to the roof. Rain pelts us, driving into our faces. I shove him to the edge of the roof.

"Nothing personal, man, this is just business. You're too big a risk for my boss. He just lost ten thousand dollars on your failure to appear. Man, it's just business."

"Fuck you, this don't scare me. You gonna make a threat, make it real."

I whisper, "I don't make threats."

He falls gracefully, never making a sound, silent until the moment his skull shatters on the sidewalk in a red puff that the rain immediately dilutes. His right arm is behind his back at an odd angle and his pelvis seems sideways.

After retrieving Abigail's picture, I stop at Leroy Watkins's room. The women have him spread-eagle, tied to the bed. They haven't started working on him yet.

"I think I caused you a problem," I say.

"Yeah?"

"Little Johnny is on the sidewalk. Cops are probably coming. You might want to move your project."

Ashlee steps up to me, slides her arm over my shoulders. "Can you see her again?"

I take a deep breath. "No."

Then I leave, passing the night clerk and stepping back into the rain.

ONE WAY OR THE OTHER
J.L. Abramo

The old man looked directly into my eyes.

"You know what your problem is?" he asked.

"Which one?"

"You always bet on the wrong horse."

"What can I say? The ponies have minds of their own."

"I'm speaking figuratively. I'm speaking of your decision-making."

"Making a decision necessitates a choice."

"There is always a choice."

"I've used up all my choices."

"If it's about money, maybe I can dig some up. I still have a few friends outside."

"No offense, but you would need a bulldozer to dig up what I need."

"Do you know these people?"

"They found me. Said I was recommended."

"How do you know you can trust them?"

"I don't trust anyone."

"If you're convicted of a felony again, they'll throw away the key."

"It would be free room and board, and keep me out of trouble.

Looks like it's working for you."

"Are you trying to hurt my feelings?"

"No, not at all."

"Is there *anything* I can do for you?"

"Yes. Forget we ever had this conversation."

I stood up, turned, and headed for the visitors' hall exit.

"Matthew?" the old man called from behind.

"Yes?"

"Will I see you again?"

"One way or the other, Dad. One way or the other."

We met at Swift's Coffee House on West Colfax.

To iron out a few details.

I had to admit they were a smart-looking couple.

Mid-thirties.

Simon. Clean-shaven. Hair cut short and neat. Button-down shirt. Black slacks. Black laced shoes.

Amanda. Not Mandy. Long brown hair tied back. White blouse. Maroon skirt. Sensible brown flats. No make-up. None needed.

No tattoos. No piercings. Nothing alarming.

"One-hundred-fifty grand. Minimum," Simon said. "Three-way split."

"Doesn't sound like a three-person job."

"I'll be entering alone," he said. "I'll need twenty minutes inside. I need cars and eyes, front *and* back."

"I don't have a car."

"You'll have one."

"So, we get equal shares for sitting in cars?"

"We get equal shares for giving Simon peace of mind," Amanda said.

"When?" I asked.

"One week from today. We meet here at seven-forty-five in the morning. We're in place at eight-fifteen. The mark is out of the place by eight-thirty. He leaves, I go in."

"And you're sure you can get into the safe?"

"It's what I do. Twenty minutes, thirty tops. Look, if you don't feel right about it, I understand. We were told you were reliable and could use the bread. But we need to know *now* if you're in or out."

"You never mentioned who pointed you in my direction."

"Is it really important?"

"Probably not," I said. "I'm in."

I'd managed to put off the inevitable for months, scraping up minimum interest payments and late penalties—which ate up nearly all of my paycheck from part-time work at a car wash on Lincoln.

The latest correspondence from the bank suggested I would be out on the street by Labor Day.

My father's small, one-bedroom cottage had been my home since my release.

The home where I had been raised was long gone—as long gone as my mother.

Sold to pay for lawyers who did my father no good.

With what remained, the old man had made a down payment on the cottage and set up an account to cover mortgage payments for a few years.

Then he was locked up.

Two years after he was moved to his all-expenses-paid, state-operated residence, the money ran out and payments to the bank stopped.

Before long, the cottage would be off-limits to me as well.

Two days before my next meeting with Simon and Amanda, I left the car wash at two in the afternoon and rode a bus downtown to meet with my parole officer. A once-every-two-weeks affair.

* * *

Leon Harris was not one to waste words.

"Still working?"

"Yes," I said.

"Part-time?"

"It's all they have."

"Is that cutting it?"

"I put in an application with Leprino. I should hear this week."

"Leprino?"

"Cheese-makers. They're looking for a driver to deliver to supermarkets and restaurants. They're the largest producers of mozzarella in the world."

"Good to know."

"If I get the gig, I should manage. It's early mornings, weekdays, and I can still work afternoons and weekends at the car wash."

"And if you don't get the job?"

"The prison counselor gave me lessons in positive thinking."

"You know what happens if you have no place to live."

"Too well."

"Let me know what you hear."

"You'll be the first."

"Good luck," Harris said, and the session was over.

The next day, Leprino offered me twenty hours a week at ten dollars an hour. Monday through Friday, six until ten in the mornings, beginning a week from the following Monday.

I neglected to call Leon Harris with the good news.

On Friday morning, I woke early with a head full of questions.

Who was the mark? What was the mark doing with at least one-hundred-fifty-thousand in cash in a house safe?

Who the fuck was Simon, and how did he know about the cash?

But other questions made those irrelevant.

Could two part-time minimum-wage jobs keep a roof over my head—in a place where I felt less at home than I had in the joint?

And how soon could I get the fuck out?

I dressed and took a bus ride to find some answers.

When I walked into Swift's at seven-forty, Amanda and Simon were sitting in a booth at the window.

I settled into the bench opposite.

There was an empty mug and a pot of hot coffee waiting for me.

Simon slid a key across the table as I poured.

"It's the blue Camry out front. The house sits on a large lot, northeast corner of Thirty-Eighth Avenue and Cody Street. Park on Cody, just south of the avenue, where you can clearly see the front of the house. When he leaves, Amanda will drive me around to the back where I'll enter. She will stay back there to watch the rear. If you spot anyone coming anywhere near the place, hit your horn three times. When you see us drive out, take off and meet us at this address for the split," Simon said, handing me a small slip of note paper. "Questions?"

"None."

"Good," Simon said, dropping a ten-dollar bill on the table.

He and Amanda headed for the exit.

I followed.

I watched them pull out of the parking lot and slipped on a pair of leather gloves before climbing into the Toyota.

As I drove, I imagined all of the places I might possibly reach with fifty thousand bucks.

I parked at the southeast corner of Cody, across Thirty-Eighth, facing the house.

It was fifteen minutes past eight.

Moments later, the other car pulled alongside.

Amanda at the wheel.

"He left a few minutes ago," Simon said, from the passenger seat.

"You said he leaves at eight-thirty."

"Guess he had an early date. Who fucking cares? Means we get out of here sooner is all. Keep your eyes open and your hand near the horn."

Simon put the window up and they pulled away. Their car disappeared around the rear of the house.

I sat.

Fifteen minutes later, Simon stepped out of the front door of the house.

He waved me over with a few sweeping arm gestures and went back inside.

I started the car.

Every rational instinct told me to beat it.

I was officially known as a two-time loser.

Although the loss column was actually as long as my arm.

But as they say—you can't win if you don't play.

I killed the engine, pulled the key, stepped out of the car, and crossed the avenue.

The front door was wide open.

I stepped across the threshold.

The body was on the floor. Male. Gunshot to the head. DOA.

I went to the back door.

The other car. Simon and Amanda. MIA.

Police car sirens.

I went out the back.

West one block, then south one block, west and south again.

Dropped the car key down a sewer grating.

Ducked into the Wendy's on Wadsworth.

Took a coffee and a bacon and egg sandwich to an empty table and considered my future.

I needed a vehicle.

Pulling out my cell, I wondered how soon the phone would be as dead as the guy on Thirty-Eighth.

I called the only name on my long list.

"Sammy, it's Matt."

"Hooker. What's up?"

"I need a car."

"For how long?"

"Not sure. A few days."

"I have a beater out back. It should fire up. It's registered, but it's not insured."

"Works for me."

"Where are you?"

"Wendy's. Fortieth and Wadsworth."

"I'll pick you up. Twenty minutes."

"I'll be here."

Sammy was righteous.

He had filled the gas tank.

I dropped him off back at his place.

"I appreciate your help, Sammy."

"No problem. Try not to get pulled over. By the way, did Jimmy reach you?"

"Jimmy?"

"Doyle. He asked if I knew how to find you. I gave him your number. Sorry if that was out-of-line."

"Never heard from him. Did he happen to mention what it was about?"

"He didn't say. I didn't ask. I can give you his number."

"I'll take it. Do you know where he lives?"

"I do."

"Give me an address also."

I imagined I would have better luck finding Doyle at home in the evening.

Time to kill, and washing cars wouldn't cut it.

I called in sick. Said I'd be back for my next shift on Thursday.
Simon had given me the location for the split.
Fat chance, but I drove over anyway.
No such address. Fucked over. Any doubt erased.
I headed home.
Back at the cottage, I picked up the cash I had put away for
the next useless bank payment and I went shopping for a gun.

I parked on Broadway in front of the pawn shop.
I went in, setting off the loud buzzer.
"Is Don here?" I asked the guy behind the counter who
wasn't Don.
"He walked over to the Seven-Eleven."
I left the shop and went looking for Don.
I found him watching a microwave heat up a burrito.
"Those things are not good for you."
"What is?" Don said. "I would say *fancy meeting you here,*
but I have a hunch it's not accidental."
"I need a gun."
"What do you have to spend?"
"Three hundred."
"Are you driving?"
"Yes."
"Pull around to the rear of the shop. I'll meet you there in
ten minutes. Want a donut?"
"I'm good."

Don came out the alley door of the pawn shop and waved me
over.
"Is that Sammy's piece-of-crap Chevy?"
"It is."
"Still running."
"So far."

He ushered me through the door into the back of the shop.

"How is Sammy?" Don asked, as he opened the floor safe and pulled out a .38 Police Special.

"He's Sammy."

"This is the best I can do. I'll take two-fifty."

"Is it clean?"

"You could eat off it."

I gave him the cash and took the weapon.

I rapped on Jimmy Doyle's door just after seven-thirty.

"Matthew Hooker. This is a surprise."

"Can I come in?"

"Sure. Want a beer?"

"Sure."

Jimmy led me into the kitchen, offered me a seat, pulled two cans of PBR from the refrigerator, and joined me at the table.

"So?" he said.

"Sammy said you were asking for me. I'm curious."

"Didn't Jill contact you?"

"Jill?"

"I'll take that as a no."

"Tell me about Jill."

"Something like a friend. Did a few scores together. She came to me with a proposition. I passed. Not my cup of tea."

"What kind of tea was it?"

"The kind that's too hot to handle and takes too long to brew. Paintings."

"You lost me."

"This cat hits on Jill at a bar. Put her in the right outfit, she can be very alluring. He buys her a few drinks, he has a few too many himself. He invites her to his place to *see his paintings*."

"Seriously?"

"Guy has a pair of Monets on the wall. While he's mixing more drinks, Jill snaps a few shots with her phone. She sends me the photos to entice me. But I don't do art heists. Too hard to fence and too long to wait for a payout. And, far as I know, there's no one in Denver who could handle it. They would need to travel. San Francisco. Chicago. Jill asked if I knew anyone who might be game, I thought of you. I called Sammy, I got your number, and passed it on. I have to admit it was tempting. Even at thirty cents on the dollar, those two paintings could bring in more than a half-million."

"How can I contact her?"

"I can give you a phone number."

"How about an address?"

"It's not a good idea to drop in on a stranger uninvited."

"Good ideas are not my strong point."

With some coaxing, Jimmy gave up Jill's address.

Amanda's address.

I figured the chances of finding her or Simon were slim to none, and that slim had probably already left town.

But, I had a full tank of gas and nowhere else to go.

I found *Amanda*.

When I turned onto her street they were wheeling her on a gurney to a waiting ambulance.

A uniformed cop ushered me past the house.

I saw a medic covering her face with a sheet.

I drove a few blocks, called Jimmy Doyle, and left six words in his voice mail.

Jill is dead.

Watch your back.

I drove back to the pawn shop on Broadway.

Don was behind the counter this time.

"Run out of bullets already?"

"I need some more help."

"I was just about to lock up. Meet me at Stoney's on Lincoln. Give me twenty minutes, I'll buy you a drink. Feel free to start without me."

"What?" Don asked, as he sat beside me at the bar.

"Where would you try to sell two Monets?"

"Like the two Monets that went missing from the dead guy's house in Wheat Ridge? Heard it on the news. Were you in on that?"

"Just until I was out. I was told there's no one here in town who could handle the paintings."

"Only one. Runs an antique shop on South Broadway at Arkansas. Lives above the place."

"Man have a name?"

"They call him Einstein."

"Some kind of genius?'

"I don't know anything about his I.Q., but he's the spitting image of the original."

"Do you have handcuffs in the shop?"

"I have a few pairs in my car."

"What's that about?"

"About thirty bucks a pair."

The antique shop was closed, but lit inside.

There was a door to the south of the storefront.

I knew the setup.

It would open to stairs leading to an apartment above.

The light in the shop died.

When he came out and turned to lock the door, I left the car.

When he moved to the south door, I crossed Broadway.

He unlocked the door, started inside, and I came up behind him.

I pressed the gun against the back of his head.

"Who are you?" he asked.

"Claude Monet. Step inside. Put your hands back."

"Are those really necessary?" he asked, as I cuffed him.

"I don't know, Einstein, you tell me. Move."

I followed him up the stairs and sat him in the living room.

He didn't resist.

Answered every question without hesitation.

He could have won the Nobel Prize for Cooperation.

He already had the paintings. Told Calley he would need a few days for authentication.

Calley would be back on Monday night to pick up the cash.

Five-hundred-sixty thousand dollars.

"Calley?"

"That's what he called himself."

Amanda. Jill. Simon. Calley. Einstein.

What's in a name.

"I'm guessing you don't know where to find Calley."

"Here. Back door of the shop. Monday evening at eight."

"Where do you come up with that kind of cash?"

"A safe-deposit box. A bank downtown."

"And this *authentication*?"

"Done. Not that I had any doubts. Just a formality."

Protocol among thieves.

I was about to ask what he could get for the two Monets.

I decided I really didn't give a fuck.

"Where are the paintings now?" I asked instead.

"The storage room, in back of the shop. Would you like to see them?"

"I believe you."

"They're beautiful."

"I'll take your word for it. Here's the deal. I let you keep the paintings for a quarter million," I said, liking the sound of it. "Less than half price. Or, I call the police right now. They take the paintings and bring you in for accessory to grand larceny, maybe murder."

"And Calley?"

"What about him?"

"If I don't pay him, he'll probably kill me."

"If you *do* pay him, he will *definitely* kill you. I'll take care of Calley."

So, the deal was struck.

Einstein would hand over two-hundred-fifty-thousand in cash at six Monday evening. Then he would make himself scarce. I'd wait in the alley behind the shop.

Wait for Calley. Or Simon.

Or whoever the fuck he thought he was.

I've been a thief for as long as I can remember.

It's been like a hobby since I was a kid.

If I wanted something, I took it.

Whether I really needed it or not.

The first time I was caught at it, I was nineteen.

I had planned diligently.

A small convenience store off the beaten track in Arvada. I visited the place a few times before going in. No outside cameras, one inside behind the cash register. Closed for business at eleven, locked up by the last remaining employee by midnight. A college kid, a year or two older than I was.

I stopped him as he came out, forced him back in at gunpoint, emptied the register, five-hundred-eighty-four dollars and change, tied him up after he handed over the security camera tape.

I slipped out the back door and walked two blocks to my car.

The fucker intentionally gave me the wrong tape.

Since it was my first *known* offense, and the gun was a black plastic number, I got two years followed by two years' probation.

My second arrest and conviction was dumber still.

Went into a liquor store just before closing. This time with a modest disguise—three days' growth, dark-rimmed glasses, long blond wig under a New York Mets cap. That clerk looked like a college student also, only a lot younger than I was by then.

I carried a bottle of Scotch over to the counter.

Twelve-year-old Macallan.

It looked like a good one, if the price was any indication.

"Is this the best you carry?" I asked.

"Personally, I think the fourteen-year-old Balvenie is a lot better."

At that point I pulled out the gun, a real one this time, had him lock the front door and turn the sign over to *Closed*, tied him up in back, and emptied the register. Two-thousand-five-hundred-seventy-six dollars.

I left the change.

Before I walked out, I grabbed a bottle of Balvenie off the shelf.

They lifted my prints off the bottle of Macallan I'd left at the counter.

There had been a time when I tried to lay it on the old man.

The clichés rolled off the tongue:

A chip off the old block. Like father, like son. The apple doesn't fall far from the tree. It's in the genes.

It was bullshit. There was no comparison.

Our motivations were totally different.

My father robbed what he needed, not what he wanted.

All he *wanted* was to keep food on the table and a roof over our heads.

He came back from a war and was greeted like a villain, when he should have been hailed a hero.

Doors were closed. Slammed.

Right or wrong, he had reasons to overlook the law.

I had no excuses.

For me it had always been a game.

Pick a pocket, bet a nag, mug a sap at an ATM, go all-in at a poker table, shoplift a piece of jewelry, buy a fistful of lottery tickets, enjoy the rush.

For the old man there had been necessary gambles.

And he had much more to lose—a wife, a kid, a home, his dignity—and he lost it all.

And I had never helped.

I tried to remember when the old man was scheduled to get out.

I thought about what two-hundred-grand could do to settle the score.

Funny the things you think about while you're waiting for the next thing to go wrong.

I was in Sammy's car behind the antique shop when Don arrived.

Einstein let us in the back door.

He handed me a small Colorado Rockies gym bag.

Twenty-five neatly bound bundles of one-hundred-dollar bills.

One-hundred C-notes each.

"What now?" Einstein asked.

"Go somewhere and hide."

I gave Don the bag to lock up in the pawn shop for safekeeping—and a ten percent cut.

Once they both left, I sat in the car.

I checked my wristwatch.

It was almost time for Simon says.

As I waited, it became perfectly clear.

There was nothing Simon had to say that I needed to hear.

Nothing I couldn't guess.

He knew the cat with the paintings would be at home and had planned to kill him from the start.

He probably left the weapon there, somewhere, called the cops, and then waved me in to take the fall.

Killed Amanda because he was that much more greedy and evil.

I picked up the baseball bat, another thing Don had handy, and stepped out into the darkness.

When he pulled into the parking area behind the antique shop, I moved.

I cracked his skull as he was climbing out of his car. He hit the ground.

I heaved him into the back seat and threw the Louisville Slugger in after him.

I got behind the wheel, headed over to Santa Fe Drive, and parked at a deserted railroad yard.

The back seat was drenched in blood.

I thought about checking if he was still alive. I tried estimating how long he would last if he *were* still alive.

I decided it didn't matter and I shot him twice in the head.

I left the weapon, trusting Don's assurance that it was untraceable, left the baseball bat, and walked back to the antique shop and Sammy's Chevy.

I drove home to the old man's cottage and slept like a baby.

Tuesday morning.

First thing, head to the pawn shop for some spending cash.

Don handed me a bundle from his safe. Ten grand.

"Plans?" he asked.

"Find a place where I don't need to report to Leon Harris twice a month. Preferably, someplace with sand and surf."

"You won't be able to fly out of here with more than ten-thousand dollars in cash."

"Any suggestions?"

"Bearer bonds."

"I thought they went out of fashion with *Beverly Hills Cop*."

"I know a guy. He'll sell me two-hundred-thousand in bonds. Cost you twenty."

"Do it."

"Do you have a passport?"

"No."

"I would get right on that."

"How long will that take?"

"Six, eight weeks."

"I guess it is what it is."

"Yes, it is," Don said.

I drove out to Sammy's place to return the Chevy.

He drove me up and down Federal Boulevard to shop for wheels of my own. I paid five-thousand cash for an eight-year-old Subaru Outback. Came with five good tires, a new battery, and a temporary cardboard license plate.

We parted at the car lot, and I found a Walgreens where I had my photo taken.

Then off to the post office to apply for a passport.

Don had nailed it—six to eight weeks.

I decided to play the game until the document arrived. Wash cars, haul cheese, make a few token bank payments, visit Leon Harris every two weeks.

I spent the rest of the afternoon in bookstores, gathering travel guides.

South America, Central America, Costa Rica, Dominican Republic.

Maybe I could make use of the Spanish I had picked up inside.

I ended the day with a T-Bone at Elway's and a jazz combo at Dazzle.

On Wednesday, I was determined to celebrate one last day before having to return to a pair of pointless jobs.

I decided gambling and drinking in Blackhawk would fit the bill.

After too many lost blackjack hands and far too many bourbon and Cokes, I knew it was time to leave the casino floor.

I knew that much.

The old man had questioned my decision-making ability.

I had blamed the lack of options.

But that evening, as I walked away from the card table, there were two clear choices: Drive back to Denver or get a room.

The State Trooper who pulled me over had me at twelve miles per hour over the speed limit.

He didn't need the standard tests to determine I was DUI, but he ran me through them anyway.

When he discovered I was uninsured, he deposited me in the back of his cruiser.

Handcuffed.

Three offenses.

All parole violations to boot.

Leon Harris was going to be impressed.

I was immediately bounced back in.

Do not pass go. Do not collect two-hundred grand.

I spotted my old man the next day.

I carried my tray across the dining hall and sat at the table facing him.

He was busy playing with the food on his plate.

He raised his head and looked directly into my eyes.

I wasn't surprised that he wasn't surprised to find me there.

After all, I had told him he would see me again one way or the other.

THE MAILMAN
Andrew Welsh-Huggins

They were just north of Martinsville when he made the van. He'd had his suspicions three or four miles back, but traffic was heavy and a pair of Marsh tractor trailers kept blocking his view as they jockeyed back and forth on the highway, passing cars on the downhills and losing ground on the long inclines. Those kinds of conditions, you can't always be sure. But there was no question about it now, even as the evening shadows lengthened and merged into the coming of night. Consistent but not blatant, which meant professional. A hundred yards back, then a hundred and fifty, then fifty, sometimes letting a car or two or even three fill the gap, but always right there. White, no side windows, possibly a commercial vehicle. As obvious now as if it were a sheriff's cruiser with strobes flashing and siren howling. Obvious to him, anyway.

He held his speed at sixty-seven, staying in the right lane. At this point it probably didn't matter if they knew he knew, but every little bit helped. He patted both sides of his utility vest, a nervous habit. He glanced in the rearview mirror. The woman in the back seat appeared to be dozing. He couldn't blame her. She'd seemed exhausted from the moment he saw her this morning, and the long ride hadn't helped matters. Beside her, strapped in a car seat, the child stared back at him. Wide awake, eyes bright, watching him watch her. He cleared his throat.

"Jenna."

The woman stirred. The girl looked over in interest, hearing her mother's name.

"Jenna," he repeated.

"Mmm," the woman said, lifting her head and opening her eyes.

"Are you awake?"

"Yes." She sat up straight. "Is everything all right?"

"Do you have a cell phone on you?"

She hesitated. He watched her glance at the girl, then glance outside at the countryside rushing past. Took in the guilty flick of her eyes at the purse beside her, between her and her daughter.

"I—"

"Yes or no."

Another pause. He raised his eyes, finding the van in the near distance. Steady as she goes, a hundred yards back.

"Yes," Jenna said, face tightening.

"Is it yours? Or a loaner?"

"Mine," she said after a moment.

"Could I see it please?"

"I'm sorry...I know you said. But she was insistent. And I didn't see the harm. It wasn't for me. It was just, what if something—" She stopped and looked at the girl.

"The phone, please."

A second later she nodded as if assuring herself of the answer to a quiz and dug into the purse, the girl watching her intently. She retrieved the phone and stared at the screen.

"Please take it out of the case."

She fumbled for a minute, clawing at the back, and then freed the phone. She handed it forward. He took it, looked at the screen, frowned, and set it face down on the seat beside him. He reached over and opened the Suburban's glove compartment and moved his hand around, searching the items inside by feel, one by one. Satisfied, he closed his hand around heavy-duty pliers and pulled them out. He closed the glove compartment and reached for the phone. Watching the road ahead of him carefully, he fit the top half of the phone between the pliers' jaws, squeezed, and pulled the bottom half down until the phone snapped. Behind him Jenna gasped. Setting the top half of the phone on the seat beside him, he used the pliers to dismantle the bottom half, removed the battery and tossed it into the passenger seat wheel well.

"Did you really have to do that?" Jenna said. Even her voice sounded exhausted, as if she'd gone several hours in the sun without water.

"Yes," he said.

He took the consult in person, which he did whenever it was feasible, prior to assuming ownership of cargo. Same time-zone pickups, almost always. Farther afield but still domestic delivery, when he could swing it. International shipping, rarely. They met in the cafe of a Wegman's in a suburb of Rochester that might have been any bedroom community between Albany and Erie. He and the Rochester contact. He could tell right away she might be a problem. She refused to give her name, which seemed silly since he already knew it. Her outfit didn't help matters: black jeans, black sneakers, and black T-shirt with "#metoo" emblazoned across the front. She wore silver-rimmed wire glasses and her gray hair was short and spiky.

"I want you to know up front I don't approve of this," she said.

"Of what?"

"Any of this. Why can't I just drive her myself? Why does it have to be a stranger—and, I'm sorry, a man?" She glared at him. "Why do we have to meet out in the open like this?"

"I like Wegman's," he said. "I always stop in when I'm in Rochester. We don't have them in Ohio. Their pho is good—

you should try some." He gestured at the steaming bowl before him.

"Oh, for God's sake—"

"As for my role, that was set by the clients. You'd have to check with them."

"I did, believe me."

"What'd they say?"

She frowned. "That it was you or no deal."

"Okay."

"But what about, you know, in case."

"In case of what?"

"You know what I mean. Do you have a gun?"

"A gun?" He got this question a lot, actually. "I have a gun, but it's not something I carry on long trips like this. They tend to complicate things."

"What then?"

"I can take care of myself, if that's what you're worried about."

"Really?" She looked his slight frame up and down. "No offense, but you're not exactly a big guy."

He shrugged. "Big guy, big target. So listen. There's a few things I need to go over."

"Like what?"

"No suitcase, for starters. For either of them. No toiletries, no keepsakes, nothing. Nothing to indicate they've done more than run up the street to the grocery."

"He barely lets her do that now," the woman said.

"Same for the girl. Whatever she's wearing that morning, that's it. No toys, no favorite book, no backpack."

"But—"

"And no electronics of any kind."

Reluctantly, the #metoo woman nodded. "They already told me that. I'll make sure she turns her phone off—"

"Absolutely not. No cell phone."

The woman stared as if he'd catcalled her on the street.

"Like I'm going to agree to that. You have no idea what she's been through. What her husband is like. The power he wields. The people he knows. What if something happens? What then?"

"Nothing's going to happen."

"How can you be so sure?"

"I've never lost a package. I'm not about to start."

"A package? Jesus Christ, we're talking about a woman. A mother and child. Human beings. You make it sound like you're some kind of mailman."

"No cell phone," he said, slurping another spoonful of pho.

He should have known when he saw Jenna lift her sleepy daughter from the #metoo woman's car in the gray light of dawn that morning. The parking lot was a prearranged rendezvous, the husband already at work, his goodbye a warning to Jenna to watch herself. The girl had been clutching a much-loved stuffed rabbit, one rule already broken. Too late to do anything about it at this point; taking it from her now was pointless and the fuss she'd kick up could draw attention. True, he'd asked to see Jenna's purse before they started off, satisfying himself it contained nothing beyond the usual jumble of belongings: wallet, tube of lipstick, tissues, individually wrapped mints, make-up compact, travel package of tampons, keys. As if she had just gone out for a bit. Hard to say where she'd hidden the phone at #metoo's instructions, though he figured bra cup was a decent enough guess. Not that it mattered now.

"Is something wrong?" Jenna said.

"There's a slight change of plans."

"What do you mean?" she said, panic in her voice.

"We have to make a stop."

"Where?"

"When we do, I'm going to need you to do exactly what I say. Follow my instructions to the letter. Without question. Is that clear?"

"I don't understand—"

"I said, is that clear?"

She didn't respond. Their eyes met briefly in the mirror before he dropped his to look at the child. Jenna raised her right hand to her mouth and nodded.

Five minutes later he exited Route 37, drove up the road and pulled into the last parking space on the right outside the Hoosier Cafe, an all-night diner attached to a truck stop. Moths danced like swirling ash around sodium lights turning night into day. It wasn't perfect but it would have to do. Jenna's cell phone had changed everything. The fact he made it from Rochester to south of Indianapolis without detection told him all he needed to know about who he was dealing with. The husband, or his people, tracking Jenna electronically for hours but waiting to set the tail here. Smart; it was exactly what he would have done. There was little he could do about it except the obvious, once he was detected. Deliveries occasionally encountered hitches and now he'd have to wing it.

He stepped down out of the Suburban, closed his door and opened the passenger door. He waited while Jenna unbuckled the girl, stepping back as the mother lifted the daughter free.

"Mommy where we are?"

"I'm not sure."

"Why is the man with us?"

"He's helping us."

"Helping us what?"

"Helping us take a trip."

"A trip where?"

"Someplace nice."

"Why isn't daddy here?"

"He's busy."

He shut the door firmly but not loudly behind them. He'd heard a version of this conversation at least four times so far today. He admired Jenna for her patience, given everything she'd been through. At the toll booth at the Pennsylvania line that morning, as the girl fussed and whined, Jenna explained apologetically that they always traveled with a tablet so her daughter could watch movies. Otherwise, trips were almost impossible. Her husband didn't like it when the girl complained. He just nodded, listening. He realized he'd missed the transition in long distance trips from the license plate game and coloring books to the hypnosis of screens. He thought of some long childhood stretches in his parents' station wagon that could have been mightily improved by a movie or two.

He said, "We're going inside. Get something to eat. Maybe some dessert."

"I'm not hungry," the girl said.

"They have pie," he said.

As he held the door and felt the kiss of air conditioning he watched out of the corner of his eye as the van pulled into the truck stop and parked on the opposite side, along a line of cars next to a dumpster.

"I don't like pie," the girl said.

"Inside," he said.

Standing by the cash register beside the hand-lettered *Please seat yourself* sign they caught a break. A big guy rose from the booth at the far end, extricating himself with difficulty, threw a bill on the table and stumped toward them. Long beard, olive green T-shirt the size of a small tent, what he guessed were size forty-eight or fifty jeans. Peterbilt ball cap. He nodded at the man as they passed. He sat them down in the booth, the girl and Jenna opposite him, against the wall, the two of them visible to everyone in the place. He sat down himself, patting his vest pockets again, his back to the other booths and stools running along the counter. He piled up the man's salad plate and soup bowl and gravy-smeared dish and coffee cup and pushed them to the edge of the table.

"Here, hon, let me get those for you." Their waitress materialized before them, handed out menus. "Sorry about the mess. We're a little short-handed tonight."

"Not a problem," he said.

When she was gone, he opened his menu and scanned it. He shut it, placed it between the ketchup and mustard bottles and the napkin holder at the edge of the table. He said to Jenna, "Please listen carefully."

"Okay." Her face was even paler in the diner light, the circles under her eyes dark as inky thumbprints. You'd have to be blind not to notice the bruises on her cheek.

"Did two men just walk in?"

She looked down the length of the diner. She nodded.

"Do you know them?"

She shook her head.

"You're sure?"

"Yes."

"Have they seen you?"

Whispering. "Yes."

"What are they doing?"

"They're just standing there. They're—no, wait. They're sitting down."

"Where?"

"In a booth on the other side."

"On the other side of the restaurant from the counter?"

"Yes."

"Can they see you?"

"One of them can."

"Can you describe him?"

She started to, in a faltering voice. As she spoke the waitress returned, set down three glasses of iced water, and wiped the table clean. He asked for coffee for himself and Jenna, and apple juice in a takeout cup with a lid and straw for the girl. He ordered three cheeseburgers and an order of fries to split. When the waitress left he nodded and Jenna finished describing the man. She did a good job.

"Do you know who he is?" she asked.

"No."

"What do they want?"

"Nothing good, I'm guessing."

"What are we going to do?"

"I'm going to go talk to them."

"But—"

"I won't be long. You'll see me the whole time."

"I'm frightened."

He didn't reply. Fact was he was frightened too. He waited until the waitress returned with their coffee and the juice. When she walked back down the aisle he took his coffee cup and followed. He walked without hesitation, passing the booths on his right and the counter stools on the left. To the right of the cash register was a Plexiglas cabinet with three shelves holding whole pies. Taped to the bottom was the upcoming schedule for the men's and women's Indiana University basketball teams. To the right of the cabinet sat a Kiwanis can for donations to a summer baseball league. A moment later, he reached the booth where the men sat, registering the look of surprise in the eyes of the man sitting on the opposite side, the man Jenna had described to him. He sat down without being asked, which required the other man to shift to his right. Both men were bigger than he, and more than a few years younger. Both had more hair.

He cleared his throat. "Gentlemen," he said. "We have a little problem."

"The fuck are you?" the man opposite him said.

"I'm nobody, trust me. But what I need to know is, what will it take to make the problem go away?"

"Meaning what?" said the man next to him, the flat tone of his voice making him understand he was the one in charge. Eyes the bright blue of roadside chicory.

"Meaning I don't want any trouble. Meaning I just want to go on my way. I'm hoping there's something I can do to persuade you to let me do that."

"Are you threatening us?" said the man opposite him. He had a bristly black goatee, an off-kilter nose, like a door sagging on its hinges, and not much of a neck.

"Hardly," he replied, allowing himself a smile. "I'm not stupid. It's just me, and, well…" He spread his hands flat on the tabletop, palms up. He guessed each man had, at a minimum, thirty pounds on him.

"We don't want trouble either," Blue Eyes said. "I think you know what we want. The fact you're sitting here tells me that much."

"In that case, maybe we could reach a mutual understanding."

"Understanding?" Goatee said.

"I'm wondering if I could offer you an inducement to let us continue. I'm not sure I can match what you're being paid for this trip. But maybe I could make it worth your while."

"To do what?" Goatee said.

"To turn around. To let us pass. To go home and forget about tonight."

"How much?"

He told him.

Blue Eyes took a sip of coffee. "That's not going to be possible."

"Why not?"

"We have strict instructions. We can't return empty-handed. We face a penalty if that happens."

Goatee looked surprised by this. "A penalty? Like what? You didn't say nothing about—"

Blue Eyes waved him off. "It doesn't matter what the penalty is because we're not paying it. It's not an option. We have a job to do, and it's getting done. And that's just the way it is."

Eyeing the two men, he took a sip of his own coffee and

considered his options. He had to admit there weren't many. He thought of Jenna's cellphone, courtesy of #metoo. How much aggravation it was costing him. How they'd disobeyed his instructions by letting Jenna's daughter bring the stuffed rabbit. How much he could do without any of this.

He said, "In that case, could I offer a counter-proposal. In the interest of none of us wanting any trouble."

"I'm listening," the man beside him said.

He explained what he had in mind. The amount he desired.

Goatee guffawed, the sound like someone clearing phlegm from his throat on a cold winter morning. "Now you want us to pay *you*? The hell kind of deal is that? You know we can just take them, right?"

"I've no doubt. But I've incurred certain expenses. And what I'm proposing requires no trouble at all on your part. No effort. A quick fix."

Goatee started to speak when Blue Eyes interrupted, naming a figure considerably less than the original proposal. He counter-offered. Blue Eyes countered that. It went like that for another minute, the two of them speaking in hushed tones, the look of exasperation on Goatee's face growing by the moment. Finally, they reached an agreement. He sat sipping his coffee while Blue Eyes took out his wallet and handed him five bills. They discussed meeting places. He rejected the first two, listened to the description of the third option and nodded.

"See you there," he said, standing up and walking back down through the diner.

"What are we doing?" Jenna said.

"We need to get on the road."

"She just brought our food."

"We have to leave it, I'm afraid."

The girl started to whine, face smeared with ketchup. Before he could respond Jenna grabbed her daughter's cheeseburger defiantly, wrapped it in napkins, and stuck it in her purse.

"What did they say? Those men?"

"Not much. I worked it out."

"The one next to you handed you something. What was it?"

"Like I said, I worked it out. But we need to get going."

"I'm really confused," Jenna said. "I don't know what's happening."

"I'm sorry about that." He placed a five-dollar bill under his coffee cup and walked behind them to the counter. He added the largest cup of Coke they had to go, ignored Jenna's glare at the purchase, paid in cash, and followed Jenna and the girl outside.

He filled the tank before driving out of the truck stop. He watched the men in the van do the same. A good thing, considering what lay ahead. He watched them turn onto 37 and followed a minute later. Now he was following them. They headed south, past the turnoff for Martinsville, past a jumble of used car places and fast-food restaurants. In a mile or so the landscape returned to fields and rolling hills. Two miles farther on, the van's right turn signal winked. He made the same turn.

"What are we doing?" Jenna said. "Is this it?"

"Almost," he said.

The road they were on now was narrow and twisty, and in a couple of places the first wisps of late August night mist rising from a nearby creek drifted across the pavement. The van a couple hundred yards ahead, out of sight only once or twice around a bend. He crested a hill and encountered a long, slow decline. Trees towered overhead on either side and farther out fields stretched to what would have been the horizon during the day. The glow of the lights of town faded away. Three hundred yards up, the road T-boned at a gravel lane. He turned right and followed the cloud of dust ahead of him. Two minutes later he pulled into a farm drive, an old, abandoned barn ahead of them, the white van parked beside it.

"What's going on?" Jenna whispered. His stomach tensed at the fear in her voice, but he forced himself to set the feeling aside. Deliveries and hitches, he reminded himself. He unbuckled, turned off the engine and darkness enveloped them.

"Oh my God," Jenna said, twisting in her seat.

"Relax," he said.

"You sold us out, didn't you?" she said. "That's what's happening. Jesus—she was right."

"Please don't move, and whatever you do, don't get out of the car. That's an order."

"Like hell I'm not—"

Ignoring her, he reached into the glove compartment, searched by rote, passed over the pliers, found the items he wanted, took and placed each in opposite deep pockets of his vest, and clicked the compartment door shut. He picked up the cup of Coke and opened the Suburban door quickly, got out, and hit the fob to lock the doors. The child-safety locks were set, though he didn't need the car's *meep meep* to tell him that. Jenna's scrabbling at the door handles and her weeping pleas for mercy told him everything he needed to know.

He walked toward the van, stopping ten feet short. He nodded. Both doors opened and the two men got out, Goatee from the passenger side. He took two steps closer.

"Keys," Blue Eyes said. "We'll take it from here."

Behind him the muffled sounds of Jenna's sobs and the pounding of her fists on the windows of the car. A moment later a keening from the girl joining the cacophony.

"Sure thing," he said, taking three steps forward. He tossed the cup of Coke on the ground, reached into the pocket on the right side of his vest, and withdrew the knife. In one swift motion, like a teacher drawing a parabola on a chalkboard, he drove the blade deep into Blue Eyes's throat. He jerked it with practiced ease back and forth as the blood gushed, cutting through tendons and cartilage and bone, letting the deep serrations along both edges of the blade do their work.

"Hey," Goatee said weakly, raising the semi-automatic in his right hand.

He turned without hesitation, tugging the blade free and bringing it down in a single, fast slashing motion on Goatee's wrist, ignoring the guttural gasps of Blue Eyes collapsing to his knees beside him. Goatee yelped in pain, dropped the gun, and took a step back. His assailant stepped forward and clamped his left hand onto Goatee's right shoulder and thrust the knife into his belly, just below his sternum. Ignoring the man's surprised grunt, he held the shoulder tight as he pushed the knife in deep and then jerked it up, once, twice, a third time, hard, feeling the warm spray of blood on his hands. Finished, he withdrew the knife and stepped back and waited for Goatee to fall onto the ground beside Blue Eyes. It didn't take long. He glanced at the Suburban, realizing its occupants had gone quiet. He saw Jenna staring out the rear window, hands pressed against the glass, eyes wide, face as white as a birthday balloon.

Hearts pump longer than you think, even at the end, and so he waited a full two minutes as the last of the blood pooled onto the Queen Anne's Lace and butter-and-eggs encroaching the barn from the overgrown field. When the bodies of the men went still, he set the knife on the ground, leaned over, picked up Blue Eyes's legs, and dragged him to the van. He opened the rear doors and with a bit of effort set him inside. He repeated the task with Goatee, which took longer because of how big and muscular he was. Everyone knew muscle weighed more than fat. When they were both inside, slumped against one another like sides of beef pulled from a cooler, he reached into his left vest pocket and retrieved a coiled rubber tube. He found the Styrofoam cup of Coke and shook the dregs onto the grass. He walked to the rear of the van, popped the gas cap, and snaked the tube down. It took a couple of tries because he wasn't as good at this as he should be, but five minutes on he'd filled the cup to the top. He retrieved the tube, rolled it up and pocketed it. Spitting several times to clear his mouth of the taste, he poured the gasoline out carefully, onto the bodies first, then the driver's and passenger seats, then the console, then the back seat. Finished, he tossed the cup inside. He reached in and tore loose Goatee's shirt, which wasn't hard because of how thoroughly the knife had shredded it. He twisted it up tight, like a giant hand-rolled cigarette, returned to the gas tank and worked the end of the shirt down as far as he could. He pulled it back a moment later, sniffed in satisfaction, and reversed the process, this time leaving five inches free, the shirt hanging limp from the hole. He retrieved the knife and walked back to the Suburban.

He stopped two feet from the rear and unlocked it with the fob. He opened the trunk and raised the door.

"Please," Jenna said, as she reached for her daughter. "Oh God, please don't hurt us."

"Shhh," he said.

He slipped off his shoes and socks, then his pants and underwear, and finally the vest and his short sleeve shirt beneath it. Now wearing nothing, he reached into the rear of the Suburban and located a box of scentless baby wipes. He opened it and pulled out first one wipe, then another, and cleaned his hands and forearms, dropping the wipes one by one onto his pile of clothes. He reached back into the car and tugged a thirty-nine gallon black plastic garbage bag from its box, knowing from experience that thirty gallons was never enough. He placed his shoes and socks and pants and underwear and vest and shirt and knife and the wipes inside the bag, looped it shut and placed it beside the box of wipes. Next, he pulled out a small gym bag and removed the identical set of clothes inside, dressing quickly because a chill that signaled the coming of autumn was beginning to descend. Without speaking to Jenna, he pulled a remaining item from the gym bag and walked toward the van.

Halfway there he stooped and picked up Goatee's gun. Reaching the van he tossed it onto Blue Eyes's lap. He stepped to the side, lifted the lighter, ignited it, and set the flame to the soaked T-shirt hanging from the gas tank filler tube, hopping away quickly and trotting back to the Suburban. He got inside and started the engine and drove off slowly but deliberately. He turned left onto the gravel lane. They made it as far as the first bend in the road when the fireball, angry as a dying sun, lit up the countryside.

Twenty minutes later they were back on 37. Five minutes after that he watched in the mirror as Jenna shifted into the middle seat behind him. The girl, surpassing all expectations, was asleep in her car seat.

"What just happened," Jenna whispered.

"What do you mean?"

"Those men…"

"What about them?"

"I thought you, that you had…"

He drove on, speed set at sixty-seven.

"It's my fault, isn't it? Because of the phone."

"What's your fault?"

"What just happened."

He sighed. "To be honest, the phone complicated things. It would have been better not to bring it. But what happened to those men had nothing to do with that. They made a choice."

"I feel responsible."

"Please don't. It might be better to get some sleep. It's not much farther, and it could be a long night still."

"Is this what you do?"

"What?"

"Your job. Taking people like me places. Safe places."

He considered the question. "I deliver a lot of things. Sometimes people, sometimes not."

"Like what?"

"Like try to get some rest."

He took the Bloomington overpass across the top of the city, followed it west and continued driving for another hour or so. When they were deep inside Owen County he consulted the map on the seat beside him and made the turn. Ten minutes down the dark road, the velvet sky carpeted with stars, he pulled down the long drive to the farmhouse and parked the Suburban.

"Any problems?"

The woman approached from the porch, rocking chair still tipping back and forth from where she'd been sitting. A tall man trailed her, lean and lanky.

"Not really. It might be better to leave sooner rather than later." Their ultimate destination Seattle, he thought, but it didn't really matter. He'd only been engaged for one leg—admittedly the most dangerous—of the journey.

"Understood," the woman said, nodding at the man. He was already moving to the Suburban, signaling to Jenna to get out. A minute later she approached on shaky legs, clutching the girl in her arms.

"Here," he said. She flinched as he extended his hand. It held the five bills that Blue Eyes had handed him in the diner.

"What's that for?"

"For whatever you need."

"Isn't it yours?"

"No."

She hesitated, took the bills at last and tucked them into her purse. "Thank you," she said.

"For what?"

"For bringing me here."

"You're welcome," he said, and left it at that. It had grown late, later than he was counting on. And the trip wasn't over. He needed to be in Evansville by ten the next morning, picking up a gold locket confiscated from a stately Berlin apartment in 1940, not to be seen since. Delivery to a Lake Avenue residence in Chicago by six, so it was going to be close. Maybe not as eventful as tonight, but you could never tell. One thing the mailman had learned over the years, he reflected as he walked toward his Suburban, was his deliveries tended to follow a certain pattern, except when they didn't.

RED NOCTURNE

Ann Aptaker

This is what happened.

We walked along the shadowy hallway from her apartment to the elevator, her blond hair, the color of moonglow, catching stray bits of light from the only two working lamps along the blood-red walls. When she tossed her hair back from her cheek, I marveled at how a simple tilt of her head created a halo around her, turning the dust motes in the air into tiny floating jewels. Then she smiled at me. The way she looked at me through those long green eyes of hers pumped me up plenty, made me feel as if I were the only guy in the world worth her time.

The elevator came, we stepped inside, and then she pressed her body against me, didn't even wait for the doors to close. She was playful, flirtatious as a fairytale nymph as she ran her hands up my bare arms, traced my muscles with her fingertips and tugged at the shoulders of my sleeveless T-shirt. As if I wasn't already a tingling nerve, she looked up at me and gave me that *Lady and the Tramp* smile again before she kissed me, a full, unending kiss of such insatiable craving she sucked up my juice, my air, making me dizzy, while she nearly devoured me. I never felt the elevator stop its descent, didn't see the doors slide open. I didn't want to untangle from her, not then, not ever.

But I obeyed when she pulled me out into the lobby, her fingers tugging at my belt. Of course I obeyed, and stumbled out like a drunk.

The lobby's dusty floral carpet silenced our footsteps. The dark red marble walls, dulled by decades of the city's grit, echoed our every breath.

I held her hand as we walked out into the noisy, crowded street.

Even on steamy summer nights like that one, when the air is nothing but a slab of rubbery heat, city people go places, maybe take in a show, grab a bite, keep on the move. We were going someplace, too, but I hadn't mentioned it. As far as she was concerned, we were just a couple of lovers out for a leisurely walk on a summer's night under a starry sky and a sultry moon.

The hellish heat didn't stop me from holding her hand. She didn't pull away, not even when a hot bead of sweat rolled down my wrist and seeped between our palms and through our fingers. We gave each other sidelong smiles, sidelong looks. Something in her green eyes came at me with the beguiling allure of swaying snakes. Her eyes slithered down my body, finding every bone and nerve, obliterating any consciousness of anyone else on the street. I saw only her. She was so beautiful, so darkly sparkling beautiful, a delicate beauty but with that hint of dangerous power, like one of those ancient goddesses you see in old paintings. Looking at her was like looking at fire through mist.

I don't know what she saw when she slid her eyes to me. I don't know if she'd figured out that I was going to arrest her for murder, pull her arms behind her back and cuff her, that it was something I had to do, was under orders to do, something that made me sick to do.

I'd never told her I was a cop, an undercover plant to get the evidence that would lock her up for life. If she'd asked me what I did for a living, I had a story ready, but she never asked. For a while I thought it was strange, her not asking how I made my dough. It's often the first thing out of a woman's mouth after she's looked a guy over. But she wasn't the usual sort of woman. Nothing mattered to her except whatever she was doing at the moment she was doing it.

So we just kept walking along, strolling easy in the hot, humid night, moving with the crowd. We were quiet, we didn't need to bother with conversation, just let our entwined hands do our talking until she suddenly said, "Lucky me to fall for a sweet guy like you. That's what you are, you know. A sweet, delicious hunk of a guy." The way she said it, with a teasing sincerity inside a voice that rolled out like fog, she gave me the shivers.

I managed, more or less stammering it, "I guess you bring out the best in me."

"We bring out the best in each other." Her whisper could dissolve my bones.

She finally slipped her hand from mine, but what she did next made up for the loss. She slid her hand up my arm the way she did in the elevator, knowing damn well how much I liked it, which made it twice as seductive. The slide of her hand along my arm roused every nerve and muscle in my body right down into my jeans, igniting every inch of me with need of her. It didn't matter that her palm, her fingertips, were even hotter than the steamy sweat on my skin. I still shivered.

God, I loved her.

I was in hell. My own private hell. A hell as brutal as the one the law wanted me to lock her away in.

We neared the little neighborhood saloon that had become our bar. She asked if I wanted to stop in for a drink.

"Not tonight," I said. "Let's keep tonight to ourselves."

She gave my arm a quick squeeze, made my blood pump hard and fast under my skin.

I agonized over sending her to prison for life, wondered how I would live without the touch of her, without the earthy scent of her skin, the dizzying wine-taste of her kiss, the wild nights of lovemaking in her bed. And I wondered what kind of nut case I'd become, a cop crazy in love with a woman who murders.

If I was going to get through this night's business I knew I had to kick my cop sense into gear. I had to settle down, force myself to ignore the heat of her fingers on my arm, not get distracted by the way the light of the moon and the light of the streetlamps slid along her red polished nails. I had to forget about the hypnotic sway of that red leather handbag swinging from her shoulder and the way it brushed against the red polka dots on her pink summer dress. I had to ignore how the low-cut dress clung to her, found every curve of her. To ignore all that, I had to clamp my jaw so tight I felt my teeth could break.

She said, "I thought about you after you left this morning."

"Only *this* morning?" I said, making an effort to tease, keep things light. With my senses on fire, my cop's nerves stretched tight, it wasn't easy. "You wound me, woman."

She really did, too. Her tinkling laugh twisted into me like a screw biting through a wall.

"Not *only* this morning, silly," she said. "But especially this morning, because it's our anniversary. You came into my life six months ago today." The day after she'd put a bullet into the head of the Joe Schmo who'd been in her life before me. The day I knew in my cop's bones that she'd cooked him. It came from something chilly that floated from her, seeped through her erotic heat, something in those gorgeous eyes—a hint of darkness? A too-sharp pinpoint of light?—that cops know are the eyes of a killer. It took me and my squad all these months to get the goods on her, for the forensics mavens to tickle out the evidence she so skillfully smeared up, but we finally locked everything tight. It might've taken less time if I didn't need to be on my guard every minute in case she had a notion to kill me, too. I'd long ago stopped looking for a motive for why she killed. She didn't have a motive. She didn't need one. Her bone-deep compulsion to kill the men who loved her took care of that. I've arrested my share of such women before. The prisons are full of 'em.

But I'd never fallen in love with one.

I knew there was a gun in the red handbag that hung from her shoulder like a blood drop. It wasn't the same gun she'd used to kill the guy six months ago. She was smart enough to get rid of that one. Anyway, it was never found. All she'd told me about the .38 snubnose she kept in her handbag was that she carried a gun because of some incident she didn't name that happened to her when she was a kid growing up in the rotten luck part of town. The weapon made her feel safe, especially at night, was all she'd said, the look in her eyes blank, her face hard as stone.

I didn't have my gun. Walking around with a gun wouldn't fit with my cover in case she asked, but as I said, she never did. The steel bracelets warming up in my jeans, well, they were another story. Fooling around with my jacket one night, putting it on over her naked body, she found them in a pocket. I wanted to kick myself for forgetting to leave them in my locker at the precinct house where I'd stashed my shield and my gun before going to her place. But she'd smiled when she handled the bracelets, a slow, curling smile. Then she put them on. She wore them all night. A cop's wet dream.

We neared a street corner. She tossed her head back, closed her eyes. "Do you feel it?" she said. "The little breeze coming off the river? Let's walk over to the old docks. It'll be cooler there. Darker, more romantic."

The docks. Not the direction I'd planned.

And then I warmed to it, figured how the setting could work for me. Those old docks hadn't been used in years, not since the last of the warehouses was boarded up and left to die in peace. There'd be no light from windows to shine on my miserable doings. No snooping citizens around who'd rubberneck or panic, ruin a good arrest. I could lock the bracelets on her without interference, pull my cell phone from my back pocket and call for my squad to pick us up.

Romantic.

I said, "Baby, look there," and led her to the curb where a

pimply kid was selling flowers from a bucket next to a newsstand. "Gimme the red one," I told him, "and shorten the stem." I gave the kid a couple of bucks. He clipped the stem of the rose or whatever the hell that red flower was. I only remember it smelled sweet and looked terrific against her heat-flushed face when I slid it behind her ear. The bright red petals against her blond hair made her green eyes seem even greener. I stroked her cheek. I couldn't help myself. And then I pulled her to me and kissed her. I couldn't help that, either.

The pimply kid snickered, spoiling the moment, killing the kiss.

I took her hand again and walked us along, got us away from the sneering kid. A few steps later, we turned the corner, headed for the river.

I didn't catch any of that breeze she'd said she felt. The night was still hot as a steam iron. My T-shirt stuck to me, trapping my sweat, cooking my skin. And that's when I started thinking about cooler climates in faraway places where I wouldn't have to be a cop and nobody would have to know she was a murderer. Maybe even I could forget it. All I wanted to do was hold her in my arms all day and roll around in her arms all night. And if she decided to kill me, shoot me quick or cut me up slowly, hell, I'd die happy.

I said, "Listen, since it's our anniversary, why don't we celebrate it with a nice long trip?"

"A vacation? Oh yes, that's a wonderful idea! We can find someplace special, somewhere I've never been."

"Okay, where haven't you been?"

"Oh, lots of places."

"Then you pick the place. Just make sure it has cooler nights than this one."

"I thought you liked the heat."

"Yeah, I thought I did too. I guess it's time for a change."

We'd arrived at the waterfront. The crumbling brick warehouses looked almost delicate in the moonlight. Romantic, sure, just like she'd said. The silvery light drifted across her face, touched the red flower, gave her eyes a sheen.

We walked out to the end of one the old piers. Moonlight glistened on the river, its reflection from the red brick warehouses turned the water the color of old blood.

She gave me a wistful smile, and when she spoke it was nearly a whisper. "Yes, a little vacation, a week or two in some romantic spot. It sounds...perfect."

"Well I—actually, I was thinking about something longer."

"Like a month? How wonderfully extravagant!" She hugged me with the sort of sweet embrace a kid gives someone who just gave her a terrific birthday present. But when my arms wrapped around her, I couldn't prevent my hug from being stiff and awkward. Sensing it, she pulled away, her eyes narrowing, a little sadness in their sparkling green, a little suspicion. "Or maybe you're talking about a permanent trip, about leaving here altogether," she said.

I couldn't tell if she was on to me, if she'd figured I knew about her murdering ways or if it was just an insightful guess, but chasing either of those ideas was a dark and dangerous alley I didn't want to stumble around in. So with a shrug as easygoing as I could fake it, all I said was, "How about it? Make a home somewhere, a fresh start," but meaning every word.

She lingered over it, looked out to the water, stared at the river for a while. So help me, I really believed we might stand a chance.

She said, "Well, I don't know. This city is my home, after all. I have a life here."

"Yeah, but—" I wanted to choke on my own tongue. How could I tell her what was in store for her if we didn't make a run for it? How could I tell her that she'd spend the rest of her life walled into a hell house where she'd be beaten—and worse— without end?

She rummaged through that red handbag. My cop sense, that stealthy animal who slumbers in my bones, woke up fast, leapt through my marrow and clawed into my brain, preparing me to break her wrist if she brought her gun out.

Her hand slid a pack of cigarettes from her bag. "I'm out of matches. Do you have a light?"

That was the moment; her right hand holding a cigarette, her left hand arranging the strap of her purse on her shoulder, both hands busy, at their least resistant or quick, defenseless against any move I'd make to grab her wrists, lock her down, turn her around and put the cuffs on her. I slid my hand into my jeans pocket. My fingertips moved past my car keys, the keys to my apartment and my police locker, past the keys to her place, slid along my lighter, and rubbed the warm steel bracelets.

My fingers curled.

I slid my lighter out.

"Thanks," she said after I lit her cigarette.

I thought about lighting a smoke for myself. There's nothing like tobacco to cool the moment. But I needed my hands free, needed them ready. I slid the lighter back into my pocket, hooked my fingers through the steel cuffs.

She took a deep drag on her cigarette, exhaled slowly, the smoke tinged red as it blew across her lipstick, drifted up along her cheek and curled in the air. Smiling a small, flirtatious smile but with enough smarts behind it to flatten a university professor, she said, "You know, it's okay that you're a cop. I don't mind."

My breath stopped, my chest knotted tight. Even the hot night couldn't prevent my blood from suddenly running cold, while my skin, already slick with sweat, turned chilly and clammy.

No wonder it took my squad so long to trap her. She was the hardest type of killer to catch: a smart one. A smart one who'd figured me to my bones.

She took another long pull on her cigarette. As she exhaled, a soft breeze came up, the lipstick-tinged smoke gently billowing around her face like a lacy red tinted veil. She looked so beautiful I could have fallen to my knees. When she put her fingers on my face and slowly stroked my cheek, I swear I almost cried.

She said, softly, "Really, you could have told me you're a cop. It wouldn't have made any difference. I fell for you the first time I saw you, when you sat on the stool next to mine at the bar. I fell for your puppy-dog eyes. They're so sweet and soft, but with something stony and in command underneath. It was that secret hardness that made me think you might be a cop, that it wasn't just coincidence that you sat next to me. But I fell for you anyway. I couldn't help it. You're my type of guy, handsome and tough. And I'm still in love with you."

"Then come away with me. It's our only chance. *Your* only chance."

Her fingers slid from my cheek to my lips as she brought her face close to mine, her eyes piercing, her breath oddly cool through the hot night air.

She whispered, "We don't have to run. You won't turn me in."

I pushed her hand away with a harsh snap, a cop's bone-deep reaction to being challenged. It didn't faze her.

I was the one who was desperate. "I'd have no choice," I said. "Don't you get it?"

She did, slowly. I saw it take hold in her eyes, a look helpless and feral at the same time.

"Listen," I said, "I'm nuts about you, but if we stay in this town, I'd have to be a cop, bring you in because I'm a cop. We can't stay here together if you want to avoid...want to avoid..." I couldn't say it. But I could see it, all of it, in the back of my mind, the horror of caging her, a terrible thing to do to a wild animal, which is what she was. I grabbed the cigarette from her hand, tossed it away, pulled her to me.

She came at me with more hunger than I'd ever felt in a woman. She covered my mouth with hers as if she wanted to chew me up and swallow me. I wished more than anything that she could, because then I wouldn't be around to hand her over. She could go on enjoying the ferocious, predatory life she'd been created for.

I kissed her and drank her and knew I'd *never* let them cage her.

My hands cupped her face. The heat of her skin seeped into my palms. I pressed my mouth deeper into hers, still hoping she'd swallow me even as my hands slid slowly down to her neck. *I won't let them cage you, I can't, I can't,* kept running through my mind, the words repeating like a drumbeat as my hands tightened around her throat. I let my hands do the grisly work because I loved her and I couldn't live with the idea of her body being used for brutal jailhouse pleasure.

She didn't try to pull away. She just kept on kissing me while my grip around her throat grew tighter. She kept right on taking as much of me as she could, groaning softly in long beautiful moans that grew shorter, coarser, until breath and life finally died in her, her mouth still on mine.

I held her a little while longer, not ready yet to give up the feel of her, the last warmth of her. In time, her mouth fell from my lips, her head lolled back, her eyes staring up at the night sky. Sweat coated her face, her neck. In the moonlight, the red band of bruises my hands made around her throat shone like a collar of rubies.

She slid down to my feet. The red flower fell out of her hair. It crushed under her cheek.

I'd just committed murder, and it felt like a dream, a dark nightmare dream.

And then my cop sense woke me up. That good ol' reliable, stealthy cop sense. It told me to play it smart, don't let the law figure me, cage me, maybe even fry me.

Still…

What a coward I was. I should have died with her, should have…

But the grip of love loosened and slipped away, the instinct to live took over. And not live a caged life, either.

I pushed the panic down, that trustworthy cop sense stiffening my spine. I took stock of my situation, my surroundings. Neither were too bad. My situation, my status as a gold-shield cop, would make my word believable *if* I handled things right. Which is where my surroundings came in. The warehouse piers along the old waterfront were chock full of loose bricks and leftover lines of rope. I gathered a few bricks, tied them together, wrapped the rope around her ankles. I did the same to her arms, then stuffed a brick into her handbag, right on top of her gun.

Even as a trussed-up corpse she was still beautiful. Her silvery blond hair, her red lipstick and the rubies of death around her neck all caught moonlight. I kissed her one last time, savored her lips, the last of their warmth and softness, then shoved her over the pier and into the water. The splash she made was more delicate than I'd expected. It gave me the creeps. So did the way her wet dress rippled along her body, the way her red handbag gleamed in the water before it sank with the rest of her.

Sooner or later, though, she might surface, even with the bricks that were now pulling her to the bottom. Sooner or later Mother Nature might try to have her way with her, bloat the body with gasses that could send her floating to the surface. By then, fish would have gnawed at her flesh, nibbled away her beauty.

A chilling thought crept through me: what if I'm the cop called in to I.D. the body? *I'll handle it,* I told myself, *I'll handle it.*

I knew I'd better start handling things right then and there. I couldn't let too much time get away from me, not if I wanted my story to stick.

I headed back to her apartment, walked fast past our bar, didn't even glance at it, though from the corner of my eye I saw the bartender step outside for a smoke. He started to give me a wave. I didn't acknowledge him, kept moving, let him figure maybe I was someone else.

I finally made it to her apartment building, unlocked the street door and walked inside. The red marble walls of the lobby echoed my breathing, just as it had echoed her breath and mine a little while ago, but the sound wasn't romantic anymore. It was a punishing sound, tightening around my head like a band of nails. I bypassed the elevator and the romantic memories it could trigger, ran up the four floors of stairs to her apartment, let the exercise pump me, harden me.

Panting, I put the key into the lock, but didn't turn it. I just stood with my fingers around the key for a few seconds, steadied my breathing and steeled myself against the emptiness that might attack me and tear me apart on the other side of the door. Finally trusting my cop sense to hold me together, I opened the door, stepped inside.

I didn't dare look around as I walked through the living room, didn't dare let anything trigger lovesick memories that could cloud my thinking, cause me to stumble through my story. I just walked straight ahead to the phone on the little table next to the sofa, tried to ignore the upholstery pattern of red and pink flowers that suddenly looked like smudges of blood.

I used her phone to call my precinct so there'd be a tag back to this number, evidence that I was here, strengthening the story I gave to the detective on my squad who took the call, a guy I'd worked with for years. I told him she wasn't here, she'd skipped, told him the planned arrest was dead. He said he'd put out an APB. I said, "Sure," with an Academy Award-winning sigh of disappointment and resignation. Then I lit a cigarette and left the apartment.

That was three months ago. Her body still hasn't surfaced, might not after all. I'm on another case, another beautiful dame who'd offed another poor schmo.

As for what happened on the pier and the woman at the bottom of the harbor, the only other person who knows about it is you.

BETTER NOT LOOK DOWN
Josh Pachter

As I stand here on the narrow ledge on the outside of the Bradbury Building, five flights above the rumble and honk of the midtown LA traffic, a line from an old B.B. King song floats across my mind.

Better not look down, if you want to keep on flyin', put the hammer down and keep it full speed ahead.

My eyes are squeezed tightly shut, so there's no danger I'll look down, B.B., no need to worry about that.

Instead, I look *back*, twenty-four hours into the past, to a time when all I had to worry about was whether I wanted another cup of coffee with my breakfast...

Millie stood on the other side of the counter with the carafe in her hand, her face a vision of Hollywood loveliness, her scarlet fingernails tapping on the glass. The nails were carefully manicured, much too nice for a waitress in Jerry's Diner, and they distracted me from the question of coffee.

Millie snapped her gum, and I blinked out of my reverie.

"You was sure out there somewhere, Mr. Taylor," she said, the New York not yet bleached out of her voice by her years in

La La Land. Her lips were the exact same red as her nails, their bold color contrasting attractively with the pastel pink of her uniform. "You want a refill or not?"

"Sure, hit me again," I said. "But cut me off after this cup. I don't want to show up for work with too much of a buzz."

She topped off my coffee, and as she turned away to replace the pot on its burner I scanned the sleekness of her afterdeck. Then she swiveled back to face me, and once again I admired the warm curves of her superstructure.

"What are you doing in a dump like this, Millie?" I asked her, not for the first time. "With your looks, you ought to—"

"I ought to be in pictures, I know," she completed our daily ritual. "Just like a million other girls in this town. If only you was a producer, Mr. Taylor, maybe you could do something about it."

"I'm working on it," I smiled. "I might be just a crummy claims adjuster today, but I'm making headway on my script, and someday I'll—"

"Someday, yeah. You and a million other guys in this town. Except by then I'll be too old to play anything but grammas."

She went off to take an order from an elderly couple who'd just settled into a booth, and I shoveled the last of my Western omelet down the hatch and chased the eggs with a swallow of hot java.

I was sliding my check from beneath my saucer and reaching for my wallet when she called, "Adam and Eve on a raft, whiskey down, and flop two with a brick," through the pass-through into the kitchen, then came back to where I was sitting. "Hey, Mr. Taylor," she said, frowning slightly, "maybe you could help me out with something, after all?"

"If I can," I said, wondering how in the world a schlub like me could possibly be of assistance to a knockout like her. "What's on your mind?"

As I balance precariously on the ledge, B.B. King goes on singing that damn song inside my head.

An old girlfriend of mine showed up the other day. That girl had lived in love and for love and over love and under love all her life.

My fingertips and the right side of my face are pressed tightly against the Bradbury's rough exterior brickwork. My toes are beginning to cramp. I ease my eyes open a crack. About eight feet to my left, a uniformed cop is leaning out of my manager's office window, forcing a friendly smile, waving encouragingly for me to come on back inside.

I swivel my head and look the other way. Eight feet to my right, a boulder in a cheap suit leans out *my* window, his ugly mug wearing an expression that is neither friendly nor smiling.

"What do you think you're doing out there, asshole?" the boulder growls. "Get the fuck back in here and take what you got coming."

I lick my lips. My throat is bone-dry. It's maybe a quarter past nine and the sun is hidden behind a bank of gray clouds, but the day is already hot, and inside my jacket and tie I'm sweating like a pig.

Better not look back, B.B. sings, *or you might just wind up crying.*

Ignoring his advice, I look back, back thirteen hours, though it seems like it all happened years ago…

Just after eight p.m., Millie and I strolled into Barney's Beanery on Santa Monica and managed to snag a booth by the window. This was the first time I'd ever seen her out of uniform, and she looked even more shipshape in a sheer white blouse and short sea-green skirt than in her waitress outfit.

At the diner this morning, she'd explained that she'd been dating some guy named Terry d'Agosto for a couple of months. He was a decent young man, but it wasn't serious between them, at least not as far as Millie was concerned. He was more a friend than a boyfriend, someone to catch a movie with, go to the zoo on a Saturday afternoon, drive up to Griffith Observatory and gaze out at the view.

Then, two weeks ago, Terry'd invited her to Sunday dinner at his parents' house in Reseda. That seemed a little premature to Millie, but she didn't have any other plans for the day, so she agreed to go. Mom and Pop were pleasant folks, but Terry's brother Tony showed up halfway through the meal and put a damper on things. He was a thug, a creep, "sort of, I don't know, Godfather-y, you know what I mean?"

And that tore it for Millie. In Terry's car on the way back downtown, she told him she was uncomfortable about his brother, and she thought it would be best if the two of them didn't see each other anymore. Terry was disappointed, but he seemed to take it well enough, and when he dropped her off at her place in Central-Alameda they shook hands and parted, she thought, on friendly terms.

Except that wasn't the end of it. Terry started sending her emails and texts, calling her at home and at work, begging her to get back with him, and nothing she said seemed to penetrate his dogged determination.

Which is where I came in. Once Terry saw she'd moved on to another guy, she explained, he'd have to get the message and leave her alone. She hated to put me out, but would I be willing to…?

Barney's Beanery was pretty much a busman's holiday for Millie, but it was a place she knew Terry and his pals frequented, so there was a good chance either he'd see us himself, or some-one else would and would pass the word along that she'd found herself a new beau.

We'd both already eaten supper and neither one of us was hungry, but for the sake of appearances we ordered a plate of Irish nachos and a chocolate milkshake with two straws. We nibbled nachos and took turns sipping the shake and talked. Somewhere along the line, I convinced her it was okay to drop the "Mr. Taylor" and call me Al.

Right at nine, they dimmed the lights for some reason, and it took a few seconds for my eyes to adjust to the different illumination...

The sun comes out from behind the clouds, and my eyes adjust to the sudden glare.

"We can work this out, Al," a voice says, and I turn back to my left and see my boss, Ira Steinmetz, leaning over the cop's shoulder. "Whatever this is, it can't be as bad as you're thinking. Come back in, and we'll figure it out, I promise."

"Butt out, shitheel," the boulder on my right rumbles. "You got no fuckin' *idea* what kind of trouble this dick is in."

I keep my attention focused on Mr. Steinmetz and the cop, so the boulder jacks up the volume. His voice pounds inside my skull.

"I'll give you exactly thirty seconds to haul your sorry ass back in here, Taylor. Don't *make* me come out there and get you."

If the arrows from Cupid's bow that had passed through her heart had been sticking out of her body, B.B. sings inside my head, drowning out the angry howl, *she would have looked like a porcupine.*

I force myself not to think about the boulder or Mr. Steinmetz or my situation. Instead, I cast my thoughts back eleven hours into the past...

It was about ten p.m. by the time Millie and I stepped out of Barney's onto Santa Monica. I'd left my car on the upper deck of the Kings Road Municipal Parking Structure, and while we waited for the light at North Olive to change, she put her arm through mine. I glanced down, surprised. "Just in case he's watching," she whispered, and I half relaxed but felt a twinge of regret that the physical contact was only an act. I think by then I was beginning to believe the whole story of Terry d'Agosto and his hoodlum brother was just a story, an excuse to give Millie and me some time to get to know each other as something more than waitress and customer.

There's a narrow alley halfway between Olive and Kings, and as we walked past it a hand shot out and grabbed my collar and hauled me into the darkness. Millie, her arm still linked through mine, staggered in on my heels.

"So this is the scumbag you dumped me for?" a reedy voice spat. I was confused for a second, since the voice was a good six feet away, too far to go with the hand still clamped on my collar.

"Terry!" Millie gasped. "What do you think you're—?"

A cellphone flashlight blinked on and lit up a sliver of the alley, revealing two guys I'd never seen before. The scrawny one holding up the phone, six feet away, was apparently Terry d'Agosto.

And the gorilla who had me tight in his grip was apparently Terry's brother Tony.

The hulk to my right disappears from my office window, and for just a second I feel relief wash over me.

Then a weathered brown brogan comes into view, and I realize the guy is about to do exactly what he warned me would happen next: he's coming out to get me.

I shuffle a careful step to my left, lengthening the distance between me and the boulder but bringing me that much closer to the cop hanging out of Mr. Steinmetz's window.

What difference does it make which way I go? They've got me surrounded.

Inside my head, B.B. King sings, *Do you think I've lived my life all wrong? And I said, "The only advice I have to pass along is concealed in the chorus of this song."*

This is too goddamn much for me to handle, so I disconnect from the present moment and let my thoughts go back…

"Here's how this is going to work," Tony d'Agosto growled. *"You,"* he nodded at Millie, *"are gonna get back with my brother. And* you*"—he shook me like a maraca to make sure I was paying attention—"are gonna go on about your business and forget you ever met this young lady."*

"Are you crazy?" Millie exploded. *"What makes you think you can order us around like that?"*

Tony's free hand slipped inside his jacket and came out holding the biggest gun I have ever seen in my life.

"This does," he said.

As I inch farther to my left, away from the boulder and closer to the uniformed cop hanging out my boss's window, I see that the forced smile is gone from his face and he's holding a matte-black gun in his hand. It might be a pistol, a revolver, a Glock, a Sig Sauer, I don't know anything about guns. I'm not sure I ever *saw* one in real life before last night.

I've been around, and I've seen some things, B.B. King sings inside my head. *People moving faster than the speed of sound, faster than a speeding bullet.*

Right here, right now, my thoughts are moving faster than I can process, so I let my mind drift back to that alley between Olive and Kings Road...

I am not a man of action. I'm a claims adjuster, for God's sake! I haven't been in a fight since I was ten years old, and I lost that one, wound up with broken glasses and a bloody nose.

But at the sight of Tony d'Agosto's gun some primal instinct kicked in, and I grabbed for it with both hands. If Terry's brother had been thinking rationally, he would have backhanded me the hell out of the way, but I guess my sudden shift onto the offensive sent him into instinct mode, too, and before I knew what was happening, I was wrestling him for control of the weapon, so focused on the moment I barely heard Millie's screams and Terry's shouts in the background.

And then an enormous blast knocked me on my ass and the air was heavy with the acrid stink of gunpowder and the world went completely silent.

It took a while for my hearing to come back, and all I heard when it did was a horrified whimpering. I looked around and saw Terry's iPhone lying in the dirt, the flashlight still on, its harsh glow leaking from around the edges of the case. I managed to crawl over to it and pick it up and pan it around the alley.

All four of us were on the ground. Millie was shaking convulsively and sobbing. Terry had a hole the size of a baseball ripped out of his chest.

"Jesus God," Millie was whispering, over and over again. "Jesus! Jesus God!"

The gun lay in the dirt at Tony's side. His head was covered in blood, and he wasn't moving. The recoil from the gunshot had apparently flung him backward, hard enough to smash his skull against the brick wall of the building that ran along the side of the alley.

I stare at the gun in the cop's hand. It's pointing downward, not at me, and B.B. King reminds me *You can keep it moving, if you don't look down.*

But where else is there to look? I've got an armed cop to my left, a raging boulder coming at me from my right. Where else *is* there?

So I press my forehead against the Bradbury's brick wall and look back, of course, back ten hours in time...

Millie and I sat there in the dirt, holding hands, expecting at any moment to hear the wail of approaching sirens.

But there were no sirens. No one seemed to have heard the gunshot but us, and after a while her weeping tapered off and she wiped her runny nose with a tissue from her purse and we had to decide what to do.

"It was an accident," she said. "And it was their fault, Al, not ours. We have to call the police."

"No way," I said. "We're sitting here with two dead bodies for company, there's no way the police don't arrest us. Me, at least, and maybe you, too."

"Then what?" she said, and I could see fear growing in her eyes.

I thought furiously. "Nobody knows a thing about this except us," *I said at last.* "You got any more of those tissues?"

She handed me the packet, and I picked up Tony's gun and wiped it clean, then worked it back into his lifeless hand and pressed his index finger against the trigger to leave a print.

The imprint of the rough brick wall on my forehead brings me back to the present. I'm looking left, at the cop, but to my right I can hear the scuffle of the boulder's shoes on the ledge, coming inexorably closer. Who does this guy think he is, a superhero?

People living like Superman, B.B. King sings inside my head, *all day and all night. And I won't say if it's wrong, and I won't say if it's right.*

Time's getting short, I know. Another minute or two at most, and one or the other of them's going to grab me.

I used to be a claims adjuster, I think. How the *hell* did I get from there to here?...

An hour ago, I was sitting at my desk, trying to concentrate on a claim form. Act normal, Millie and I had decided, go to work, live your life, pretend it never happened, there's nothing to tie either one of us to two dead bodies in a Los Angeles alley.

Except then my phone rang, and when I picked it up a terrified Millie was on the line.

"Mr. Taylor," she whispered fiercely, and then she caught herself and said, "Al! He's not dead!"

I thought I must have misunderstood her. "Who?" I demanded. "Terry? He had a hole the size of a—"

"Not Terry, Tony! When the gun went off last night, it kicked him back into the wall and knocked him out. He was bleeding and unconscious, but he wasn't dead!"

"How do you—?"

"He came to the diner! Just now! He grabbed me and pulled me outside and—I'm sorry, Al, I didn't want to, but he hurt me. He made me tell him who you are and where you work! He says you killed his brother, and he's on his way to your office right now! And there's something else—"

Maybe there's something else I can do to protect Millie and me, to keep us both safe, but I can't for the life of me think fast enough to figure out what it is.

I'm pretty fast myself, B.B. King sings inside my head, but I know I'm not fast enough to find a way out of this mess.

The boulder named Tony d'Agosto is closing in on me, only a couple of feet away. He's not shouting any more, just muttering under his breath, and, honestly, I think that's worse.

I sneak a glance to my right. The back of his head is bandaged from where he'd crashed into the brick wall in the alley, and there is murder in his black eyes.

I turn back to my left, clinging to one last shred of hope, but I know the uniformed cop won't do anything to help me, thanks to that "something else" Millie told me on the phone, an hour ago...

"There's something else," Millie said urgently. "Tony's not a gangster, Al—he's a policeman, a homicide detective. He's got

you dead to rights for Terry's murder, he says, and the court will throw the book at you, not just for shooting Terry but for trying to frame Tony for the killing. You've got to get out of there, Al! He's on his way!"

I should have taken off, like Millie said. I should have gone straight to the bank and cleaned out my accounts and run. I don't know why I didn't. Instead, though, I just sat there at my desk and stared blindly at that stupid claims form until I heard the commotion out in the lobby, and then I panicked. My office has just the one door, which opens right out into the lobby, so I couldn't go that way. But the Bradbury—LA's oldest land-marked building—is old enough that it's still got windows that open, so I threw open my fifth-floor window and, like an idiot, climbed out onto the ledge.

Like an idiot, I close my eyes again, hoping against hope that dangers I can't see will somehow, miraculously, disappear.

Idiot, I scold myself, and I open my eyes. I'm facing the Brad-bury's historic brick wall. I look to my left and see the uniformed cop, gun in hand, scowling, all trace of friendliness gone. I look to my right and see Tony d'Agosto inching closer.

Better not look down, B.B. King warns me, but at this point, what do I have to lose?

I look down.

There's a crowd gathered on the sidewalk, peering up at the show, a line of cops holding them back. I'm too high up to know for sure, but I think Millie might be down there in her pink uniform, her soft hands cupped around her red lips, shouting words that don't quite reach up to my perch.

A cop to my left, waiting to arrest me for murder. Detective d'Agosto to my right, coming to arrest me or beat the shit out of me or both. And five stories of nothing but air beneath me, with a cement sidewalk carpeting the bottom.

A fire truck screeches around the corner of South Los Angeles onto East Third. It will pull up in front of the Bradbury within seconds and disgorge men with a big trampoline-like net, ready to catch me if I fall.

Oh, B.B., Riley B. King sings inside my head, *sometimes it's so hard to pull things together. Could you tell me what you think I ought to do?*

Maybe a jury will believe Millie over Tony at my trial, and they'll let me go.

Maybe a good lawyer might get me off on a technicality.

Yeah, sure, I think, or maybe I can fly—up, up, and away, like Superman, faster than a speeding bullet.

Probably not, but what the fuck?

I look at Tony d'Agosto and say, "Sorry about your brother."

I look at the uniformed cop and say, "Sorry to disappoint you, pal."

I look down and mouth the words, "Sorry, Millie. Honest to God."

I raise my hands from the bricks and lean back and fly away, full speed ahead.

FINAL REUNION
Michael Bracken

Gavin Wilcox slowed his rental car as he approached the outskirts of Mertz, Texas, remembering how local cops delighted in ticketing drivers unfamiliar with the abrupt decrease in the posted speed limit where the state highway entered town, and he let the car drift down Main Street.

Mertz had changed little during the years he had been away. Dairy Queen was still the only fast-food franchise, banners supporting the high school's football team still drooped across the main drag, and every Friday the Mertz *Merchandiser* still posted the front page of that week's edition in the newspaper office's front window.

Gavin reached the other end of town before he turned from Main Street and brought his rental car to a halt in front of the ramshackle bungalow where he had spent the entirety of his childhood. He killed the car's engine, grabbed a canvas overnight bag and an aluminum briefcase, walked up to the porch, and leaned into the bell.

A moment later his mother opened the door and stared at him through the screen. Never an attractive woman, the years had not been kind to her. "Why are you here?"

"I came to do a job."

She pushed open the screen door and said, "Might as well come in. I'm heating leftovers."

A few minutes later, over yellow potato salad and reheated brisket from Polumbry's Pit Bar-B-Q, Gavin asked, "Whatever happened to Rose Munson?"

"What'd you expect?" his mother said. "You broke that girl's heart, but she moved on. Eventually."

Before leaving town the morning after high school graduation, he had cut Rose's photograph from his yearbook and had carried it in his wallet ever since. "She still around?"

"Works over to the *Merchandiser.*" His mother raised her eyes to meet his. "You leave that girl alone, Gavin. All you ever give her was disappointment, so she don't need nothing you got now."

"I—"

"And she weren't the only one you disappointed."

With little else to discuss, mother and son exchanged only a few dozen more words before turning in for the night. Stripped of other memories—gone were his books and LPs and everything else acquired while growing up—Gavin's childhood bedroom retained only his lumpy twin mattress. After he settled onto it, he fell into a deep sleep.

Sandwiched between the Methodist Church's clothing resale shop and Polumbry's Cards & Sundries, the newspaper building shared common walls with both. The front page of the previous Friday's Mertz *Merchandiser* posted in the front window featured an article about West Texas Land Management Company's most recent purchase of property south of town. Gavin paused momentarily to read it before he stepped past the honor rack and entered the newspaper's front office.

On the other side of the counter, at a desk littered with back issues, sat a slender woman tapping away at a computer keyboard. Without looking up, she asked, "May I help you?"

Age had etched fine lines into the corners of Rose Munson's hazel eyes, and the color of her auburn tresses was no longer natural. Just as in her senior photo, she wore her shoulder-length hair parted in the middle. She'd made no effort to mask the freckles splashed across the bridge of her nose or the inch-long scar on her chin.

"Rose?"

She stopped typing and looked up. Recognition lit her eyes, but her expression never wavered. "Your mother should have told me you were coming home."

"She didn't know."

"So, you don't talk to her, either."

Gavin shook his head. While talking to Rose, he memorized the layout of the newspaper's front office. The counter that separated them reserved a quarter of the large open space for customers, and a large desk belonging to the publisher occupied the far left corner. Doors at the right rear led to the back half of the building.

"How can I help you, Gavin? Are you here to place an ad? I can take your order. Are you here to provide a news tip? I'll make a note. Are you here to—?"

"I just wanted to see you."

"Well, you've seen me. Now, get out of here. I'm working." Rose glared at him for a moment before returning her attention to the computer.

Gavin hesitated, but when she said nothing more, he turned and let himself out.

He spent the rest of the day reacquainting himself with his hometown—the schools where he had spent much of his time after hours in detention and the police station where he had spent time in a different kind of detention—before returning to his mother's home. He parked his rental car in front of the house and phoned his employer with the burner phone he'd been given before leaving Houston.

"I'm here."

"Took you long enough to check in," Carter Bledsoe said.

"I had some things to do first."

"You aren't the prodigal son. Do your job and leave."

After Bledsoe ended the call, Gavin sat in the car staring at the street before him. He hadn't asked for the contract and had tried to refuse it. He had not been successful.

Gavin climbed out of the car and went inside to find his mother in the kitchen preparing dinner. They spoke little while they ate and less afterward, but he saw the disappointment in her eyes every time she looked at him.

The Mertz *Merchandiser*, like many still-surviving small-town newspapers, had long ago stopped operating its own printing press. Each Thursday evening, *Merchandiser* staff uploaded electronic files to a printing plant in the next county, and the following morning a truck delivered several dozen bundles of tabloid-sized newspapers ready for local delivery.

Gavin stood in the alley behind the newspaper office early Wednesday morning, examining the loading dock, what he could see through the tiny window on the rear door, and the sight lines up and down the alley. When satisfied, he walked around front, helped himself to a copy of the newspaper from the honor rack, and thumbed to the editorial page where publisher Henry Raylin railed against West Texas Land Management Company's efforts to control a wide swath of property south of Mertz.

"West Texas Land Management Company bought out those willing to sell," read the editorial's summary paragraph. "They bullied those who were easily frightened. What's next for the remaining holdouts? More importantly, why does the company want all that scrub land?"

Gavin tucked the stolen *Merchandiser* under his arm, walked across the street and down the block to Polumbry's Diner, and settled into one of the booths. He ordered black coffee, scrambled eggs, and light toast from an auburn-haired woman with a splash of freckles dotting the bridge of her nose and a nametag that read "Lily." She brought his breakfast a few minutes later, and he almost finished eating before a black skirt entered his peripheral vision. Gavin looked up to see his high-school sweetheart looking down at him.

"I went to your mother's house. She said you'd be here." Rose gestured toward the empty side of the booth. "May I?"

"Please."

She slid in opposite him, straightened her skirt, and stared into his eyes. "Why did you come back?"

"I came to do a job."

"I know what you do, Gavin," she said. "We all know what you do, and your presence here makes people nervous."

He pushed the last of his eggs around his plate before changing the subject. "How long have you been at the *Merchandiser*?"

"Near on ten years," Rose said. "I worked at the Dairy Queen and Polumbry's Antique Emporium and took a few night classes at the community college over in Chicken Junction before Henry offered me a job."

"What is it with you and Henry?"

"He's a good man, Gavin," Rose said. "He's always treated me right."

"He had a thing for you in high school."

"I was yours back then, Gavin, and everybody knew it."

"Didn't stop other guys from looking."

"That what this is about?" she asked. "You think you can come home and step back into my life? It doesn't work like that. Whatever we had disappeared when you did."

"I didn't have a choice."

"You always had a choice, Gavin. You just chose wrong."

"The judge said jail time or military service. I thought the military was best."

"You made bad decisions before you ever stood in front of that judge," Rose said. Vandalism, shoplifting, curfew violation,

111

underage drinking, all things the various Polumbry boys did but with much different consequences. "Trying to rob the County Line Liquor Store was just one in a long string of them."

"What about you?" he asked. "You weren't a bad choice, were you?"

Rose leaned forward and stared directly into Gavin's eyes. "You didn't choose me. I chose you the day Mikey Watters knocked me down playing dodgeball and you lit out after him. That was my bad decision, and I won't make it again."

They stared at each other until Gavin finally glanced down at his plate and his remaining eggs. When he looked up again, he changed the subject. "You like your job?"

"I'm good at it," Rose said. "Do you like yours?"

He shrugged. "The Army taught me to do two things before my dishonorable, and there's no money in saluting."

"So, who are you here for? The Ochoas? I hear the West Texas Land Management Company can't offer them enough to move off their property. Their family's owned that land since before Texas was a state."

Gavin shook his head.

"I'll let them know," Rose said, "but I don't think the news will ease their minds."

She slid from the booth and stood. Gavin grabbed her wrist, the first time he had touched Rose since graduation night.

"I can't do this." She glared at him. "Not now. Not ever."

Gavin released his hold on Rose and watched her walk out of Polumbry's Diner. Her hips didn't swing the way they had in high school. They barely swung at all.

Other than a brief respite following the beating Gavin gave Mikey Watters the day he split Rose Munson's chin, the two men were friends throughout childhood. They did everything together—hunting, fishing, and less savory activities that often resulted in detention together—until the last few weeks of high school. When Gavin was caught trying to rob the County Line

Liquor Store six weeks before graduation, the two distanced themselves from each other, and they hadn't spoken since the day Gavin left Mertz to begin military service.

Mikey remained in Mertz, found a job with the city's grounds maintenance department, and worked himself into a supervisor's position. Gavin caught him at the end of his workday.

"I hope you're hungry," Gavin said. He held two Styrofoam containers. "I brought brisket plates from Polumbry's."

They walked to Mikey's pickup truck and Mikey lowered the tailgate, revealing an ice chest. He said, "I got cold beer in the cooler."

"I could do with a drink."

Gavin placed the Styrofoam containers on the tailgate and took an open bottle of Lone Star from Mikey's outstretched hand.

"I heard you talked to Rose."

"I tried."

"You tell her why you did what you did?"

"Too late for that," Gavin took a swig from his Lone Star bottle. "So, what is it with Henry and Rose?"

"You know how people are. There's talk."

"Why?"

"All them late nights she puts in at the *Merchandiser*. People think the newspaper ain't the only thing gettin' laid out."

When Gavin glared at him, Mikey held up his hands, palms forward. "I ain't sayin' those things," he said, "but other people are."

"So, tell me about Henry."

"He went off to A&M, earned a degree in journalism, and married a girl he met there. I heard she looked a lot like Rose. He worked a few years at the newspaper in Waco and came home when his wife died. The *Merchandiser*'s all his now that his daddy's passed on."

Gavin pulled from his back pocket the newspaper he'd stolen that morning and tapped on the lead article. "Takes the job serious, don't he?"

"Henry's been on a bit of a crusade lately. He's got a bug up his butt about some company buyin' up property south of town. I don't know what the big deal is. They want to buy my mobile home and the land it's parked on, I ain't about to put up a fuss."

Gavin waited until most of the stores on Main Street closed for the day and Henry Raylin was alone at the newspaper. He let himself in through the loading dock, walked past the long-idled printing press, and slipped into the front office. He found Henry at his desk, staring at his computer monitor. The front page of the next edition of the *Merchandiser* filled the screen, a blank space where the lead article should be. Gavin stopped less than a foot away from the smaller man. "You alone?"

Startled, Henry spun around. "What do you want?"

"My employer doesn't like the things you write about the West Texas Land Management Company," Gavin said. "He wants you to stop."

"What's he going to do about it?" Henry asked. "I can take care of myself."

Without warning, Gavin twisted Henry's arm behind his back and pushed the newspaper publisher facedown against the computer keyboard. He drew the semi-automatic pistol he'd taken from his aluminum briefcase and jammed the business end into Henry's temple. "I don't think you can."

As Henry mumbled something, Gavin noticed the small, framed photograph next to the publisher's computer monitor. The photograph showed Rose and his waitress from that morning standing in front of Polumbry's Dry Goods. The younger woman wore a sash identifying her as Miss Mertz, an honor Rose likewise had received during her junior year of high school. Gavin released the other man and straightened. "Say again."

Henry also straightened. "If your employer wants me dead, why aren't I?"

"Rose," Gavin said. He didn't elaborate, and a moment later he let himself out the way he'd come in.

Gavin was halfway to his mother's home when his cellphone rang. Only one person had the number, so he knew whose voice to expect when he answered.

Carter Bledsoe said, "And?"

"I changed my mind."

"That's not an option!" Bledsoe shouted. Gavin held the phone away from his ear. "Either he's dead or you both are!"

"So, come and get me."

Bledsoe disconnected the call.

Prepared for a simple hit, not an armed incursion, Gavin needed more than his semi-automatic pistol for what was to come. He drove his rental car to Mikey Watters's singlewide mobile home on the northern edge of town and pounded on the door. When Mikey answered, he asked, "You still got that double-barrel your daddy gave you on your sixteenth?"

"'Course I do." Mikey let Gavin inside, led him through the mobile home to a rear bedroom, and showed him a gun cabinet containing a double-barrel shotgun and two hunting rifles with high-powered scopes. He unlocked the cabinet and handed Gavin the shotgun.

"Shells?"

Mikey handed him a box of ten. "What's goin' on, Gav?"

"I reneged on a job," Gavin said. "Now I need to ensure someone else doesn't finish it."

"Can I help?" Mikey asked. Gavin never told anyone Mikey had been with him the night he'd tried to rob the County Line Liquor Store. "You had my back a long time ago, Gav. Maybe it's time I had yours."

"You ever shot a man, Mikey?"

Mikey shook his head.

"Then you'd best stay out of it," Gavin said. "I already have enough people to watch out for."

When Gavin's mother caught him cleaning the shotgun in her kitchen late that night, she said, "I heard the Ochoas are leaving town. That your doing?"

He shook his head.

She motioned toward the shotgun. "So, why do you have that?"

"I have to clean up someone's mess."

"You ain't never cleaned up nobody's mess," his mother said. "Everybody else always cleaned up yours."

"Maybe it's time that changed."

She snorted. "Not likely."

When he didn't respond, she left Gavin alone in the kitchen. After he finished cleaning Mikey's shotgun, Gavin spent the last night in his childhood bed, knowing Bledsoe would not make the seven-hour trip from Houston until the next day.

Thursday morning, Gavin ate breakfast at Polumbry's Diner, was served by the same waitress as before, and stared hard at her. Tall, slender, and auburn-haired, Lily reminded him of a young Rose Munson.

When he finished and the waitress brought his check, she confronted him. "Why've you been staring at me?"

"You look familiar," Gavin said. "I think I know you from somewhere."

"You were in here yesterday."

"You were Miss Mertz a few years back, weren't you?"

"The highlight of my life," the waitress said. "Were you there?"

"No, but maybe I should have been."

"Why?"

Gavin shook his head and overpaid for his meal. Then he headed down the street to his rental car, drove it into the alley behind the newspaper office, and let himself in through the back.

Henry looked up from his computer when Gavin stepped through the rear doors. He saw the shotgun cradled in Gavin's arm and the pistol tucked into his waistband. "You again."

"Things are different this time," Gavin said. "Where's Rose?"

"She doesn't come in until later."

"I'll just make myself comfortable until then."

"Why are you here?"

Gavin told Henry about his employer's threat. "I don't think he'll do anything until this evening, but I would hate to be wrong."

"You really think he'll come here? Won't he just send someone else like you?"

"He'll come," Gavin said. "He'll want to ensure the job is done properly, and he'll want to make an example of me."

The phone rang and Henry turned to answer it. He said little, but took copious notes. When the call ended, he just stared at his notes.

Gavin cleared his throat, rousing Henry from his thoughts.

"I know why the West Texas Land Management Company wants the property south of town," the newspaper publisher said. "The government is planning to extend the border wall, and the confluence of highways, railroad lines, and high unemployment makes Mertz an ideal location to establish a staging depot for construction supplies. That means additional infrastructure—roads and the like—and a great deal of money pouring in."

"I'm surprised the Polumbrys haven't caught wind of this."

"They're big fish in a small pond, without any connections to the statehouse or federal government," Henry said as he looked up at Gavin. "Apparently, someone at the West Texas Land Management Company has the inside track—your employer, Carter Bledsoe."

Gavin did not react when he heard Bledsoe's name.

"I've spent months following the paper trail to Bledsoe," Henry said, "and I understand he's a man who isn't afraid to get his hands dirty to get what he wants. Several indictments for violent crimes but no convictions because evidence and witnesses disappear before trial."

Rose bustled in as they were talking, saw Gavin and his weapons, and said, "You're not here for the Ochoas, are you? They already agreed to sell out. You're here for Henry."

"I was."

"And now?"

"And now you should leave."

Instead, Rose settled into the chair she had occupied Tuesday morning and turned on her computer.

"You need to go home," Gavin repeated.

"I can't. We're on deadline." Rose glanced at the shotgun. Again. "Why are you doing this?"

"I've killed a few people," Gavin said, "but I never killed anyone who didn't deserve it."

Henry turned to face him. "What makes you so certain?"

"You're still breathing."

The two men stared at each other until Henry returned his attention to the computer monitor on his desk and began typing. Gavin sat with Rose and watched her write a brief article about the Garden Club's weekly meeting. She also wrote an article about the First Baptist Church's bake sale and another about recent vandalism at the high school.

"Nothing much changes," Gavin said as he read the last article over her shoulder.

"Except the names of the vandals."

He didn't respond to her snide comment. Instead, he said, "The girl with you in the photo on Henry's desk, the one who works at the diner—"

"Henry's daughter, Lily?"

"I thought she might be—"

Rose shook her head. "You only had one shot, Gavin, and you missed."

The phone rang, interrupting them. Rose answered, listened a moment, and then thrust the phone toward Gavin. "It's Mikey. He wants to talk to you."

Gavin took the phone from Rose and pressed it to his ear. "Yeah?"

"There're three guys gettin' out of a black SUV over on the next block. Two of them look like defensive linemen and they're armed."

"Where are you?"

"Across the street, on the roof of Polumbry's Antique Emporium."

"I told you to stay out of this."

"Too late," Mikey said. "I'm in."

"Well, keep your head down and—"

"They've spilt up. One's goin' around back where I can't see him."

Gavin swore. He couldn't cover both doors at once.

"I got the front covered," Mikey said.

When he heard the loading dock door crash open, Gavin dropped the phone, grabbed the shotgun, and ran toward the back. Bledsoe brought muscle, not brains, and the beefy guy entering the pressroom from the loading dock seemed surprised to find Gavin standing in front of him. As he raised his AK-47, Gavin unloaded both barrels of the shotgun.

He didn't stop to check the man's pulse, but returned to the front office, where he found Henry under a desk and Rose, the color drained from her face, sitting on the floor holding the phone he had dropped.

"Be careful," she said. "Mikey says he shot the guy out front, but thinks he just nicked him."

"I told Mikey not to get involved. I knew he couldn't handle a kill shot."

"He also told me he was with you the night you tried to rob

the liquor store, and he told me why you did it. He said you were going to buy me an engagement ring with the money. Is that true?"

Gavin pushed past her without answering. He paused at the front counter long enough to reload the shotgun. Behind him, he heard Rose saying, "Mikey? Mikey, can you hear me? What's happening, Mikey?"

He pushed through the front door.

A hail of bullets shattered the window to his left. Gavin dove across the sidewalk and squatted behind a pickup truck. A second hail of bullets peppered the far side of the truck, and several skipped on the pavement, narrowly missing his exposed legs.

As he rose to his feet and rounded the front of the truck, a third hail of bullets greeted him. One tore into his left arm, rendering it almost useless, but he ran across the street. When the man on the far side rose again, Gavin unloaded both barrels of the shotgun in his face.

"That's impressive!"

Gavin turned at the sound of Carter Bledsoe's voice and found him pushing Mikey ahead of him down the center of the street. Gavin dropped the shotgun and drew his semi-automatic pistol.

"I'm sorry, Gav," Mikey said. "He snuck up on me."

Gavin raised his pistol. "What happens now, Bledsoe?"

"First, I kill you," Bledsoe said, "and then I kill this asshole and the rest of your friends."

"I don't think so."

Mikey elbowed Bledsoe and spun out of the way. Bledsoe and Gavin both fired and kept firing until Bledsoe dropped to his knees and fell on his face.

Mikey ran to Gavin, caught him, and helped him inside the newspaper office. Gavin leaned against the front counter long enough to see Henry sitting at his computer, rewriting the lead story for the next morning's edition of the Mertz *Merchandiser*, before he collapsed.

Rose rushed around the counter to Gavin, gathered her high-school sweetheart into her arms despite all the blood, and asked, "Why did you do it?"

"For you. I did it for you." He motioned in the direction of the newspaper publisher. "So you can have him."

"Henry? I never wanted Henry. I've only ever loved you."

As she bent her face toward Gavin's, approaching police sirens almost drowned out his response. "I chose wrong again, didn't I?"

Rose pressed her lips against Gavin's and felt his last breath whisper against her cheek.

RIPTISH REDS

Joseph S. Walker

Connie was eight the first time the switch clicked in her head and a flat empty hum filled the world.

She was sitting on the playground near the jungle gym, poking a stick into an anthill, wanting nothing more than to be left to herself. But Paul Nugent was walking around her, in ever-tightening circles, kicking dirt at her, keeping up a running stream of insults. "You're weird, Connie. Nobody likes you. You're a big uggo loser."

Paul's followers hung on the jungle gym, laughing, cheering him on. Paul kept looking at them, grinning. "Look at this loser," he said. "Playing with bugs." He came up behind Connie and put his hand against the side of her head and tried to push her over.

That's when Connie felt the switch click.

She grabbed Paul's arm and stood up, twisting his wrist in her meaty hand, so much bigger than any other kid's in the class. Paul tried to squirm away. He might have been yelling, but Connie could only hear the flat hum. A noise that wasn't a noise. She wondered what it was as she marched Paul over to the jungle gym, grabbed the hair at the back of his head and drove his face into the metal bar, feeling his nose break, seeing a splash of red spray out across the dirt.

She yanked Paul's head back and did it again.

Ten minutes later, when she'd been pulled away by three teachers who had to pin her to the ground to restrain her, the hum faded. Connie began to hear sounds again, mostly crying and screams. Two other teachers were kneeling by Paul and the first voice she made out was one of them, Mr. Handel, talking about Paul's face. Much later she would realize that the man was saying it had been *ripped to shreds*. With her ears still confused, though, Connie thought he was diagnosing what had happened in her head, what had made the switch flip and the hum start.

She thought Mr. Handel was saying that she had the Riptish Reds. And forever after, that was how Connie thought of the moments when the switch flipped again. The Riptish Reds.

In the following years she learned to control it, a little. She could feel the pressure when the switch was about to go and, if she concentrated, could keep it from happening. Like holding your breath. Like walking toe-to-heel for a cop. Not that she cared about the things that happened when the switch flipped, but it was always so tiresome afterward. Lawyers and counselors and tests and always, at the end, a door with a lock on it.

Twenty-two years after the playground incident she met Cal at the office of their shared parole officer. He was half her size, tattooed and twitchy, wearing a clip-on tie and orange hair pulled back into a man bun. She noticed him because he didn't look at her with the revulsion most men seemed to feel for her flat face, her muscles, the buzz cut she wore because dealing with hair was a pain. Cal looked at her like he was lucky to be doing it.

An hour later they were in bed at his apartment. When she reached into his pants for his dick it came away from his body.

Cal laughed and showed her that it was rubber, with a coiled tube running to a bag taped to his thigh. "Clean piss from the kid downstairs," he said. "Costs me fifty bucks a bag."

Connie tossed the thing on the floor and pushed him back into the mattress. There hadn't been many men, because of the way she looked, but when she was seventeen she'd learned from a janitor trustee in juvie that sex could keep the Riptish Reds away. At least for a while.

One of the conditions of parole was that she avoid socializing with other felons, so they couldn't go anywhere together. He snuck into her place or she snuck into his. They ate frozen pizzas and drank throat-corroding vodka from big plastic bottles and romped around in bed. He was continually amazed by her body, a six-foot slab of blunt hardened flesh. He clung to her, a free climber on a sheer rock wall. He was making a little cash dealing, and he had pills that made her whole world slow down, that made it seem like she'd never feel the switch flip again. It never occurred to Connie to think she was in love, but she didn't get tired of him.

She did get tired of their parole officer, a humorless black man named Day. He put her in a housekeeping job at a cheap, noisy motel near the airport. Nobody stayed there except sullen, stranded travelers being put up begrudgingly by the airlines and couples who rented by the hour. In every room she made the bed and put vacuum tracks in the carpet and sprayed some pine cleaner around. Then she stretched out on the bed, marking time.

Day got jobs for Cal, too, but they never lasted.

Day made a surprise inspection visit to Connie's apartment once and almost caught her and Cal together, but Cal was able to squeeze himself into the cabinet under her kitchen sink. Connie followed Day around the tiny rooms, staring holes into his back. She could feel the switch, but it didn't quite flip.

"I've got five years left on my parole," Cal said after Day left. He paced the space between the bed and the door, turning sharply on his bare heels. The room was so small that he was almost spinning in place. "I can't do another five years with this motherfucker watching my every move. How long you got?"

"Three and a half," Connie said. She was naked on the bed. She could still feel the switch threatening to go. She wanted Cal to come to the bed. She wanted him to give her a pill and then climb on top of her. Most of all she wanted him to stop twirling around.

"Fuck," he said, but he dropped down onto the bed and for the first time in hours she felt the rising tide of the Reds recede ever so slightly. "We have to do something."

"Like what?" Connie said. "Kill Day?"

Cal made a face. "And then what? Kill the guy who gets his job?" He shook his head and began to absently stroke her calf. "No. We just need to blow town. Go someplace where nobody will be looking."

"Okay," Connie said. "Gimme a pill."

He dug into his pocket and flipped her the little plastic envelope. "California," he said. "But we'll need some real money."

California meant almost nothing to Connie. It was a word from television. Palm trees and young people with huge white teeth. She swallowed two pills dry. Beaches. "Okay," she said again.

"Can you handle a gun?" he asked.

For the next week Cal wasn't around as much. He'd show up at Connie's at two or three in the morning, gliding through the darkness to stretch out beside her. He could move almost silently when he wanted to. She never asked him any questions, but he was full of promises and plans and hopes. He vibrated with wild talk, mostly about old friends sure to have a line on a job that would set them up.

"California," he breathed into her neck, waking her again. It was pitch black and she had no idea what time it was. He smelled of beer and smoke and his bun had come loose, his hair fanning out across her face and skin. "You and me, Connie. Walking down the boardwalk holding hands like civilians."

Two nights later he was there when she got home from work, sitting at the kitchen table that was barely bigger than a cafeteria tray. She closed the door. "Day could have been right behind me," she said. "You need to be more careful."

He waved it away and picked up a paper bag from the floor. His grin was lopsided and he hadn't shaved since the last time she'd seen him. "Check it out, babe," he said, holding the bag out to her.

She took it, thinking he'd brought dinner, but the bag was too heavy for that. She unrolled the top. Inside, loose in the bag, were two big guns and some flat black shapes. Clips, she thought. Another word from television.

"Colt forty-fives," Cal said. "Army issue, fell off a truck somewhere years ago. One for each of us."

Connie had never touched a gun. She rolled the top of the bag closed again and set it down on the table. "Day sees those, we're both going back in," she said.

"I know," he said. He picked up the bag and thrust his hand in, coming up with one of the guns. "He's never found my stash, right? He won't find these either. I've got a hiding place in the laundry room in my building." The gun looked huge in his hand. She didn't know how to tell whether it was loaded.

"Have you ever shot anyone?" she said.

He cocked an eyebrow. "What do you think I was in for?"

Connie figured that meant *no*.

She didn't have a car. She'd never been out long enough to take driving lessons or get a license. Cal had a rusty blue Tercel, but they couldn't be seen together so she took the bus back and forth to the hotel, forty-five minutes each way.

One night after her shift, Day was waiting at the bus stop. There were a few other people there, but Day was the only one sitting on the bench, dead in the middle, his thick legs spread wide. He was eating a sandwich from McDonald's, with a drink and the to-go bag on top of the briefcase at his side. Everyone else at the stop was carefully not looking at him.

When he saw Connie, he grunted and scooted a little to his right to make room for her. She didn't want to sit down but he tilted his head decisively to indicate the empty space. She lowered herself, staying as far away from him as she could, staring straight ahead. She felt the other people shifting themselves, getting ready to listen without seeming to.

Day took a long drink of soda. "Hey, Connie," he said. "I was on my way home, thought I'd swing by and see how work is going for you."

She grunted. *Swing by and ride your ass*, is what he meant.

Day swallowed the last bite of his burger. He crumpled the wrapper and dropped it into the bag. "You want a fry?"

"No," she said.

He took a handful, ate them, wiped salt and grease on his thigh. "I hear you're doing good. Clocking in every day. You liking it?"

"Sure," she said. She was starting to get the dangerous feeling in the base of her skull. She closed her eyes.

"That's good," Day said. "Taking pride in an honest day's work. And you're staying out of trouble? No temper tantrums? No associates I wouldn't approve of?"

"No," she said. She could hear him chewing the wads of fries he kept shoving into his mouth.

"Gone to see your family?"

Her hands tightened on the edge of the bench. She shook her head.

He sighed noisily. "I didn't catch that, Connie. I'd hate to have to send you back inside because we're not understanding each other."

The people around them got completely still. "No," she said. "Just work and home. Work and home."

There was the familiar sound of the bus making its way around the corner. She stood up.

"Okay, Connie," Day said. "I'll be around, you hear? I'm always around."

She nodded tightly. The bus eased to a stop and she got on as soon as the doors opened. Nobody tried to get in front of her. Nobody sat near her. She didn't have to look back to know that Day was still on the bench, drinking his soda, watching the bus until it pulled, groaning, back out into the road. She kept her eyes closed and waited for the pressure in her head to ease away.

She was feeling almost normal by the time she opened the door to her apartment. A man she had never seen before was sitting on her couch. He had stringy black hair and a stomach like a basketball shoved under his shirt. He was drinking a beer. When he saw her his eyebrows went up and he whistled a low tone. "Damn, girl," he said. "Cal don't lie. You're a big one, huh?"

She kept her hand on the doorknob. "Cal brought you here?"

Before he could answer they heard the toilet flush. The bathroom door opened and Cal came out, still pulling his pants into place. She could tell he was flying from the way he was bouncing on his feet, turning every step into three or four.

"Hey, baby," he said. "Close the door, come on in." The way he dried his hands on his thighs reminded her.

"Day was at the bus stop," she said.

"This is Snyder," Cal said.

"The bus stop," she repeated. She closed the door and pulled out one of the chairs from the kitchen table and sat down. "He could have followed me. He might be coming up now."

Cal's eyes shot from her to the door to Snyder. He shifted. "Nah," he said. He tried to put more steel in his voice. "If he was coming up he'd want to surprise you. He wouldn't have been at the bus."

"Who we talking about?" Snyder said.

"P.O." said Cal. "Real asshole. Always riding us. He's the main reason we want to blow town."

Snyder grunted. "I lucked out. My guy, as long as I show up once a month, he could give a fuck. If I came to his office covered in blood and hauling a machete, he'd just sign the form and send me on my way."

"Day ain't like that," Cal said. He went to the window and eased the shade away from the corner and looked out at the street. "Prick takes things serious."

"Cal," Connie said. "Who is this?"

"This is Snyder, babe. You've heard me talk about Snyder."

She looked at him blankly.

He sighed. "We were in together, last time. Cellmates for a while." He came and sat at the other kitchen chair, turning it so he could put his arms across the back and see them both. "He got out a couple months before I did."

"Good thing, too," Snyder said. "I was about to lose it. I was a cunt hair away from going after a guard."

Cal grinned and poked at Connie's arm. "Tell Connie what you're doing now."

"I'm a guard," Snyder said. He and Cal laughed explosively.

Connie waited for them to calm down.

"Different kinda place, though," Snyder said. He lifted the edge of his T-shirt and wiped at his eyes.

"Tell her," Cal said. "Listen to this, Connie. This is just what we've been looking for."

Snyder rolled his head back and forth. Connie had a sudden sharp memory of Paul Nugent, always so happy with himself, always wanting to be the center of everyone's attention. She looked at the wall just above Snyder's head so she wouldn't have to look at him.

"Okay," Snyder said. "You know about the Flynns."

Connie shook her head. Snyder and Cal both groaned. "Sure

you do, babe," Cal said. "That Irish family? They run things around here."

"Run things," Connie said.

"For decades," said Snyder, jumping in before Cal could. "Back to their bootlegging days. Then pot and coke, hookers, some loansharking. These days a lot of meth and oxy."

"Five or six generations," Cal said. "They ran off the Italians, then the Russians, then the Vietnamese. The whole river valley from Pittsburgh to the Mississippi is theirs."

"Okay," said Connie. "So what?"

"So I work for them," Snyder said. "Got to know one of the cousins in stir, and he hooked me up after I got out. Done a little driving, some collecting. Right now I'm part of the security at this cabin they've got in the woods, about twenty miles east of town."

"Snyder showed me how to get there," Cal said. "I can find it again easy."

"There's not much to the place," Snyder said. "They stash merchandise and some guns there. A couple of bedrooms upstairs where people can crash. They've got two back rooms set up to cook, but they don't use them much anymore because they mostly do that in trailers out in the deeper woods. Mainly the cabin is a place to meet and keep stuff."

"Tell her about the back," Cal said, his voice tight.

"There's a kind of office in the back," Snyder said. "I've only been in there once. There's a desk and some shelves, but the main thing in there is a safe. One of those big fucking ones people drop on each other in cartoons. About three foot tall and three wide."

Cal turned to her, his eyes bright. "That's it, baby. Think about what people like the Flynns must have out there. Hundreds of thousands. Maybe millions."

She said nothing.

"There're at least two armed men at the cabin all the time," Snyder said. "Usually me up front when I'm there, and some other guy in the back. People come and go. That's it most of the time."

"We go in on a quiet night," Cal said. "Snyder doesn't raise an alarm. We take the other guy down, tie them both up."

"We tie Snyder up," Connie said.

"Fuck yes," Snyder said. "Better give me a black eye too, make it look good. I don't want these crazy Irish motherfuckers coming after me."

"We tie him up," Cal said sharply, "and go to the office. Whoever's there, we put a gun in their face and make them open the safe."

"What if they can't?" Connie asked.

Cal and Snyder looked at each other.

"We kill 'em," Cal said. "Wait for somebody who can."

"I've told your man, I'm telling you," Snyder said. "I get half. How you two split the rest, I don't give a fuck, but I'm putting my ass on the line."

"And then we're free and gone," Cal said. "What do you think, Babe?"

Connie breathed, her arms crossed. Snyder had let the empty beer bottle fall to the floor. Cal looked at her, his leg bouncing.

"Okay," she said.

They were in bed together three hours later when she said, "They will point a gun at him or cut off his finger and he won't be able to say your name fast enough."

"Fuck, I know that," Cal said. He giggled and reached between her legs. He'd been insatiable since Snyder had left. "Soon as we get him tied up I'm gonna shoot him in the back of the head. I can't believe the asshole thinks he's getting half of our money."

For the next week Cal was like a kid waiting for Christmas. He mapped routes to California and stocked the trunk of the car with spare clothes and bottled water. He watched videos online to learn how to clean and oil the guns. He bought ski masks and latex gloves. He drove to and from the cabin multiple times by different routes so he would know the area, though he never saw the structure itself, just the start of the quarter-mile dirt track leading to it. He got prepaid cell phones for both of them and insisted on calling them "burners." Cell phones were another thing Connie had missed out on, like driving. Having one didn't help her understand the women she'd known inside who seemed to itch for them more than men or freedom.

There were more visits from Snyder. He drew Cal a crude floor plan of the cabin and kept track of who came and went. There didn't seem to be any pattern to it. One night twelve men were there for hours, the bosses playing a marathon poker game while younger men in the next room were breaking bricks of cocaine into dime bags. The next night nobody came at all except one man who spent the whole night locked in the office while Snyder and the other guard, a Mexican who spoke almost no English, watched soccer. The night after that two men showed up with three hookers and went straight upstairs. Cal wrote it all down in his slow, slanted writing. Connie sat on the couch, not listening.

"Let's do it Monday," Cal said finally. It was Thursday night. He bit his lip. "We gotta pick something. I figure Monday night they probably have a lot of cash on hand. From the weekend, right?" He looked at Snyder.

Snyder shrugged. "I guess. They don't tell me shit."

"We gotta pick something," Cal said again. "So Monday. Fuck, it's gotta be more than knocking over a liquor store." He looked at Connie, who was half asleep. "Monday?"

"Okay," she said.

Her Friday shift at the hotel was noon to eight. She was in the supply room with the two other maids, stocking their carts, when a man wearing a blue suit came in. He was bald and barrel-chested and had a clipboard that he was slapping against his thigh. "Ladies," he said. "Lemme get your attention for a minute, please."

Connie crossed her arms and leaned against the wall. The other two maids had about twenty words of English between them. They looked at the man, then Connie. She shrugged.

"My name is Tom Merien," the man said. "I'm the new manager here."

"Manager," one of the other maids said. Connie had never learned their names. "Mr. Greenwald."

"No," Merien said. "Mr. Greenwald has been let go."

Connie had seen Greenwald maybe three times since Day had gotten her this job. Every time he had been sitting in his office, watching TV and drinking straight out of a bottle of bourbon. There was no reason to miss him. She started to turn back toward her cart, but Merien wasn't done.

"I'll be getting things in order around here," he said, tapping his finger on his clipboard. "Our online reviews are terrible, and a lot of them mention dirty rooms. So starting today you can expect to see me up there checking on you, and we will not hesitate to let more people go. All right, ladies, have a good shift."

Connie pushed her cart past him, shaking her head. Corporate bullshit. Merien would be holed up in his office just like Greenwald.

Except he wasn't. Two hours later she was lying on the bed in room four-fifteen, half dozing, when she heard the lock click and the door open. She was swinging her feet to the floor as Merien came in. He looked at her and shook his head and went into the bathroom and almost immediately came back out again. "Filthy," he said. "You wearing yourself out? Taking yourself a little break?"

She stood up. "Just getting started here," she said.

"Right," he said. He sat at the desk and pulled a piece of paper from an inner pocket. He peered at her nametag and scanned the page. "Connie. You're on parole, is that correct?"

She tried taking a long breath. "Yes, sir."

"I'm supposed to fill out a form once a week reporting on you," Merien said. "Keep special track of all your shifts. That seems like a lot of work to go through for a maid who doesn't actually clean anything, don't you think?"

She stared at the floor.

"You want to go back in, Connie?"

She shook her head. He stood up and came closer to her. She could feel it. Building.

"I guess that's a no. You seem kind of dim, so I'm going to make this simple for you. Starting this week you're going to be kicking back twenty percent of your pay to me, or else I'll report that I caught you dealing out of the hotel. You got that?"

She didn't move. She could barely hear him now.

"We might need some other arrangements, too," he said. He reached out and undid the top button of her blouse. "Lord knows you're no looker, but a mouth is a mouth."

The switch flipped. The hum filled the world. Connie swatted Merien's arm aside and charged forward into him, driving a fist deep into his stomach and bringing her other forearm viciously up into his throat. She saw his mouth open but heard nothing but the hum, felt nothing but the enormous release of the Riptish Reds taking her. Merien, gasping for breath, collapsed into her and she shoved him away and snatched up the heavy metal lamp from the desk and swung it with all her strength into his face. She distinctly saw a tooth go flying. He fell to his hands and knees, and she straddled him and twisted her left hand in the back of his collar to hold him up as her right arm rose and fell, driving the lamp again and again into his skull.

She came back to the world sometime later. She was sitting on the edge of the bed, with the broken lamp dangling from her right hand, looking down at the pulpy red mass that had been Merien's head. A door slammed somewhere down the hallway and she shook herself at the noise and understood what she was seeing. She let the lamp fall to the floor.

There was no hiding this. Absolutely no hiding this. This meant going back behind the door, back behind the lock, as soon as they found her.

She stumbled to the door and out of the room, down the hall to the stairs. She couldn't stand the thought of the elevator, putting herself in a tiny room, caging herself already. She came out into the lobby and charged past the front desk, ignoring the startled look from the young clerk with whom she'd never exchanged ten words. Out on the sidewalk she automatically started walking toward the bus stop but then remembered Day showing up there. She turned on her heel and started off in the opposite direction, turning corners at random.

Fall was coming on. There was a bite in the air, and she'd left her jacket back at the hotel. She jammed her hands into her pockets and found the unfamiliar flat shape of the cell phone. It was only when she touched it that she thought of Cal.

"Jesus Christ." Cal leaned over and pushed open the passenger door. "Get in the fucking car before somebody sees you."

Connie hustled out of the doorway she'd been waiting in since she'd called him. The Tercel was a tight fit for her but she got in and Cal was away and around the corner almost before she had the door closed. He was shaking his head, drumming his fingers against the wheel. "Four days," he said. "You couldn't put up with some asshole four fucking days?"

She didn't say anything. She always felt numb after the Reds receded, physically worn out. She'd exhausted herself fleeing the hotel. All she could manage was to hang her head.

"Jesus Christ," Cal said again. He turned off the road and parked the car next to a dumpster behind a carpet store that had been closed for months. He got out of the car and walked around to the trunk, where he rummaged through the California supplies. He returned with a pair of Connie's jeans and a sweatshirt big enough for three men his size. "Here," he said, thrusting them at her. "Change. We gotta get rid of those."

Connie looked down and saw the sprays of Meriem's blood traced across the coarse fabric of her uniform. She got out of the car and peeled it off. Cal threw the bundle into the dumpster as she got dressed again. In three minutes they were back on the street and he was driving toward the building where he lived. "I can't go to your place," she said. "Or mine. Day will tell them where to look."

"Day doesn't know about us."

"As far as we know."

He cursed at that but turned left at the next corner. "Four days," he said again.

"Where are we going?" she said.

He looked at her, then out at the sky. The days were getting shorter but it wasn't yet dusk. "We'll just drive around for a while," he said. "We need to wait for dark."

"What happens at dark?"

She already knew.

"We wait a little while longer," he said. "Then we hit the cabin."

He took another corner at random. She stared at her hands in her lap.

"Snyder won't be expecting us," she finally said.

"I know," Cal said. "But, fuck, baby, we're fugitives now."

"I am," Connie said.

"We are," he said firmly. "We need to blow town and we can't do it without money. You got any better ideas, I'm listening."

She kept looking at her hands. The clothes were gone but there were little flecks of Meriem's blood, drying to rusty brown on her skin.

"Okay," she said.

***

Cal drove restlessly around the city, stopping sometimes on the fringes of big parking lots. He kept the radio on a local news station, hearing nothing about a body found at an airport motel. Connie dozed.

When he woke her, it was completely black outside. She could barely see Cal in the driver's seat in the weak glow of a couple of small dashboard lights. He was holding something out to her. She took it and found herself holding one of the guns inside its clip-on holster, resting on top of a ski mask.

"It's time," he said. "You just follow my lead. Let me do all the talking. All you have to do is keep showing them the gun and not be afraid. Okay, baby?"

She nodded. He brought her hand to his lips and kissed it and then got out of the car. She followed and found herself at the edge of a narrow two-lane road winding through the woods, the lane lines faintly visible. They left the car between two trees just off the road, invisible to anyone driving by. Cal pointed to the right. "About a third of a mile," he said.

Connie had never known a night so dark. Her eyes adjusted slowly, making the road seem to glow slightly, but she kept stumbling as she followed Cal, who seemed much more comfortable out here than she was. She wished she had a jacket to go along with the sweatshirt.

It was dark, but it wasn't silent. The lightest of breezes caused a wave of sound to rise up around them as the trees rustled. Other things seemed to be moving in the underbrush. Once they heard a car coming from in front of them. Cal grabbed her hand and pulled her farther off the road just before it hurtled by, a comet made of light and noise, the night closing back instantly around the hole it created.

There was no gate or mailbox or lamp to announce the turn to the cabin. Connie would have walked right past it, but Cal stopped her. It wasn't even a real dirt road, just two parallel tire ruts separated by a few feet of filthy weeds. Cal walked in the left rut and Connie in the right. The track ran up a moderate hill for a while, then dipped and angled right before starting up again. Once past the dip they could see a glow in the woods in front of them. Cal held out his hand to slow her down. They inched forward over a final ridge and there it was.

The cabin was about thirty yards away across a clearing of mostly bare dirt. In the light from a few windows the whole clearing was covered with tire tracks, but right now there were only three cars, parked up close to the building itself.

"The pickup is Snyder's," Cal hissed. "At least we know he's here."

After the dark of the road and the woods, the lights from the cabin windows seemed dazzling. They were facing the front of the cabin, with a porch that stretched its whole length and a front door with a window on either side. Connie waited for Cal to speak again, to give her instructions. After a long minute she looked at him. He was staring at the building, his lips moving slightly, his hand hovering over the gun clipped to his belt.

"Cal," she said.

He started. "Right," he said. "Snyder's there. We're not gonna get a better shot than this. Let's go." He started to walk straight forward, pulling the gun out.

She had to stutter-step to catch up to him. "Just straight up to the door?" she asked.

He nodded. "Fuck it." He pulled the ski mask down over his face.

She pulled hers down. It scratched her skin and narrowed the world into a tunnel in front of her. Somehow her gun was in her hand. Fuck it.

They were almost to the short set of steps leading up to the porch when Snyder stepped out the front door. He was lighting a cigarette, his hands cupped up around his face to shelter the flame, and he didn't see them until his eyes came up from the task as his hands fell. "Jesus Christ."

Cal had the gun pointed at him. "Keep quiet," he said. He came up the stairs, Connie close behind, her gun hand hanging by her side.

Snyder looked over his shoulder. "What the fuck, man? Do you have any goddamned idea what you're doing? Monday night, you stupid shit." He was hissing, his arms outstretched to herd them back off the porch. "Get outta here before they see you."

"Change of plans," Cal said. He was edging around to his left, away from the stairs, making it harder for Snyder to track both of them. "Take us in. Connie, put your gun to his head."

"Like hell," Snyder said.

Before he could say anything else, there was a new shape in the door, a Hispanic man who was just starting to talk when he saw them. His eyes bugged and he was reaching for his hip when Cal started shooting. The world's gears ground into low and Connie could see everything. Cal's first bullet hit the doorframe and she had time to see the way the wood there splintered before the second bullet hit the man just to the right of his nose. She had time to see the way his skull bulged and broke before she had even registered the sharp, stinging reports of the shots. There was much less blood than there had been in the hotel room when she had killed Merien. The Hispanic man was starting to fall as Snyder reached for Cal's gun hand and Connie watched her own arm come up and put the gun against Snyder's skull and pull the trigger.

As soon as she did that, the world snapped back into regular speed. There was the thud of the two bodies hitting the floor. Cal barked out a laugh. She looked at him, and in the window behind him was a redheaded man in a leather jacket holding a shotgun. She opened her mouth, starting to move forward, and the man fired, the sound of the window shattering coming at the same moment as the spray of red from Cal's side.

Connie dove through the door, firing wildly at the place where the man had been standing. She hit the floor hard but held the gun and pulled the trigger until it was just clicking uselessly. Only then did she open her eyes.

The man was sitting against the wall, the shotgun at his feet.

There was a ragged red hole in the middle of his chest but he was breathing, staring at her. She scrambled to her feet. Cal was in the doorway, leaning against the frame, his ear against the chunk his bullet had dug out of the wood. The wound in his side was much larger than the redheaded man's. He had pulled off his mask and pushed it against himself and it was already soaked in blood. The edges of tattoos rising out of his collar stood out starkly against his white skin.

She reached for him but he shook his head and nodded at the redheaded man. "Safe," he said. "We can still do this." She opened her mouth and he shook his head again. "No choice now," he said. "Please."

She walked over to the redheaded man and crouched beside him. His eyes tracked her. She pulled off her own mask and tossed it aside. "You're gonna open the safe," she said.

He made a noise like a skeleton laughing. "Don't think so. Can't even move my legs. Cross me off."

"Fuck you," she said. She grabbed the back of his collar and pulled him off the wall, ignoring his weak noises of protest. He was dead weight, but she dragged him to the front door and put her other arm around Cal, holding him up and helping him walk into the room.

"Back room on the right," Cal rasped.

"I remember," she said. Dragging the redhead, half dragging and half supporting Cal, she went through into the back. There was a desk there, with a big leather chair behind it and other chairs scattered around. There were two gun cabinets with various kinds of long guns. And there was the safe, just as Snyder had described it, a big cube of green metal with a dial and a handle.

She put Cal in the leather chair and dragged the redhead right up to the safe. "The combination," she said, shaking him.

This time there was no doubt. He was laughing. "Don't need one," he said. "It's unlocked."

She dropped him and reached for the handle. It turned easily and the door swung open.

The inside was filled with rolls of toilet paper. She picked up the top roll from the stack closest to the door. It was a normal roll of toilet paper, wrapped in cellophane with the brand name stamped on it. Same brand they used at the hotel.

The redheaded man was lying on his side at the strange angle where she'd dropped him, and his laughter was punctuated by bubbles of blood, but he didn't stop. "Thing came with the cabin," he managed. "Lock never did work. Stupid bitch. You've killed yourself for T.P."

She reached out and took him by the throat. "I'm not the dead one."

"You will be," he rasped. "Meeting here tonight. Couple dozen on their way." Whatever else he was going to say faded out in a long rasping rattle that grew desperate, then faded, as she locked her big hand around his throat and squeezed.

It didn't take long. When it was done, she stood up and looked at Cal. He was slumped over in the chair, his arm dangling to the floor where the ski mask rested, his eyes looking at nothing. She went and put her hand on his head for a minute.

She thought she could hear engines. Getting closer.

She didn't really know anything about guns, but some of the ones in the cabinets looked like the guns people talked about in the news, the ones that you could use to kill a lot of people. She pulled one out and put it against her shoulder and pointed it at the redheaded man and pulled the trigger once. There was a noise much louder than the handguns and the gun kicked against her and the body jumped as a red mist exploded from the chest.

She slung the gun over her shoulder and picked up another one that looked like it and walked back out to the front room. Her ears were ringing too much from the bang to clearly make out the engine noise anymore, but she didn't need to hear it. She could see them, headlights just coming out of the woods into the clearing, some kind of big SUV with at least one more car behind it.

She'd been walking toe-to-heel. She'd been holding her breath. Now Connie flipped the switch that had been there in her head since she'd seen the lights of the cabin appear in the night. The hum filled the world and this time everything she could see actually did turn red and she walked out onto the porch, pulling the trigger as fast as she could and screaming something she couldn't hear.

SNEAKER WAVE

David H. Hendrickson

Whenever you've got tourists, you've got loose dollars. Whenever you've got loose dollars, there's always some guy who's looking to shake them free. In Lincoln City, Oregon, I'm that guy.

Until you peek beneath its bedcovers, crispy white and clean on the outside but rumpled and stained out of sight, what you see is this: a beautiful coastline that's a delight to walk along, tasting the salty tang on your lips, hearing the waves crash down about you, feeling the soft sand squish through your toes, smelling the ocean air that's pure and clean. You feel that if you can stay here, you will live forever. If you're lucky, you're walking with someone you love, holding hands, fingers interlaced. If you're not so lucky, you walk alone.

Or acquire a *companion* to share your good times. On the beach or elsewhere. The combination, I've found, acts like an aphrodisiac. Put a meek businessman in a hotel room overlooking the Pacific ocean, where he can open the sliding doors and hear the waves crashing down below, and it turns him into a bedroom Tarzan. He all but beats his chest and issues a loud jungle cry.

I know these things and I use them.

They say you can't put a price on a good time. I say they're wrong. I do it every day.

Like I said, Lincoln City looks squeaky clean on the outside. Except, of course, for the Chinook Winds Casino. Casinos evoke for many tourists images of Las Vegas. Gorgeous women for sale. High-stakes games.

That ain't the Chinook. Few of the women are gorgeous; even fewer are for sale. And high stakes? The poker room's no-limit Hold 'Em game has a minimum buy-in of forty dollars and a maximum of two hundred.

Two hundred. Chump change for the guys interested in my services. High rollers. Action freaks. Adrenaline junkies. Those guys don't get out of bed for two hundred dollars. Two grand? Maybe you're talking. Ten grand? Now you're starting to get their attention.

That's where I come in.

If you're looking for more action than the Chinook can provide, either with high-stakes poker or high-stakes women, I'm your man. Ready to shake the tourist money tree.

And if you want both, a shake-the-money-tree combo, all the better. People in the right places—I make good use of a few hustling go-getters in valet parking at the casino and most expensive hotels—will direct you to me.

Which is how a man who called himself Ralph Smith joined our poker game with Jillian, a delectable piece I have a special arrangement with, at his side. She was his for the night, a surgically enhanced blonde with a special way of tightening certain muscles at strategically pleasing times. She was wearing a glittering silver miniskirt and blouse that showcased her implants up top and her lithe, tanned legs down low.

Ralph Smith was a chubby nerd, fifty years old or so, with thinning gray hair. A middle-aged version of the Flounder character in *Animal House*. I pegged him as a stockbroker who'd just made a big score and come to Lincoln City to celebrate. If his last name was really Smith, I'd eat all fifty-two cards in the deck, but in my line of work you don't take photo I.D.s and Social Security numbers for tax purposes. I don't send 1099 forms.

We sat around a wide oval poker table, green felt on top and recessed pockets filled with drinks on the sides. Thick cigar smoke hung in the air. ESPN played, the sound muted, on the large, flat-screen TV on one wall. I rent this suite, a stone's throw from the casino, on a monthly basis, shutting the game down only when Dom, one of Lincoln City's finest, lets us know things have gotten hot.

Dom is one of our regulars. He gets an extra cut. The other regulars were all there, too: Action Dave, Crazy Eddie, Tommy Tilt, Sammy the Greek, Joe the Rock, Sal, Wild Willie, and myself. Everyone, Ralph included, bought in for five thousand dollars, two racks of green twenty-five-dollar chips. I sell the chips in the other room—cash from tourists and chits from the regulars—and lock everything in the safe.

"Let's gamble!" our middle-aged Flounder said, rubbing his hands together and glancing over his shoulder at Jillian, who had taken a seat behind him. An unlit, expensive Cuban cigar rested between his grinning lips. I'd bet half my stack that he'd never smoked a cigar before and if he smoked this one he'd get sick within half an hour. But he was showing off for Jillian, which was fine with us.

We all suppressed our grins. This would be like taking candy from a baby.

Except that even morons get lucky. Ralph was a moron, at least at cards. He might be a sharp stockbroker or whatever he was but when it came to poker strategy he couldn't count to twenty-one without taking his shoes and socks off, then dropping his pants.

But he sure was lucky. He called preflop raises with any two suited cards, chased gutshot straights and other improbable draws, cracked Dom's set of queens with a flush (the seven and four of hearts), and pretty much played like a donkey, but a very lucky donkey. We'd roll our eyes every time he scooped up another big pot.

Jillian was all smiles. It can be boring watching someone play poker, but if I knew her she was happier sitting behind Ralph, clapping him on the back after a win, than earning her money lying on her back or on all fours. There'd be that later, of course, but the more poker Ralph played, the fewer fake moans of ecstasy she'd need to coax out later.

We didn't mind him winning that much, either. As long as he stuck around, he'd give it all back and then some. Almost every time, we could hook the fish into giving it all back plus the rest of his stack. He'd walk away empty-handed, cursing his bad luck when he really couldn't play for shit.

Usually, we take on the tourists straight up. No need for funny business. No marked cards, funny dealing or anything. We don't need to. We're good enough. It's bad for business, an unnecessary risk, when you rip people off if you don't need to.

And we sure as shit didn't need to with Ralph. As long as he stuck around.

Which was looking like a problem. Ralph reached back and slid his hand halfway up Jillian's thigh, looking like a tourist ready to call it a night early and lock up his win. He was up almost five grand and thinking about a different kind of all-in, this one with Jillian.

We'd have to get down to business next time the deal moved to Crazy Eddie, the one big-time card mechanic in our group. I gave him the slightest of nods.

"You know guys," Ralph said, "I think it's time I spent some time with this little lady here." He eyed her cleavage. "Although she's no little lady in some places, if you know what I mean." He laughed wildly at his own lame humor.

"You just got here," Joe the Rock said. He spread his arms wide, his cigar dangling from the side of his mouth, his big bushy eyebrows moving up and down. "You one of those hit-and-run pussies?"

Ralph stopped laughing. His Adam's apple bobbed up and down.

"Christ!" Joe the Rock said, looking at his watch. "The food ain't even got here and you're talking about leaving?"

Ralph blinked. "You've got food coming?"

"Sure," Joe the Rock said. "What kinda place do you think this is? It's a first-class operation."

"Well," Ralph said, glancing back at Jillian. "Maybe until the food comes."

I gave Jillian the eye.

She touched Ralph's elbow. "We have all night, sweetie. We've got plenty of time. You're on a roll. Why quit when you're this hot?"

Ralph shrugged. "I was just thinking I ought to quit while I'm ahead."

Joe the Rock slapped his hand on the table. "A hit-and-run pussy! Just like I thought."

"I'm not a hit-and-run pussy," Ralph said, leaning back as if to get away from Joe the Rock. He looked at me. "I can leave whenever I want, right?"

"Sure," I said in my most soothing voice possible. "Of course."

A nervous frown came over Ralph's forehead. "No one's going to rob me?"

I narrowed my eyes. "I'm not even going to dignify that with an answer."

Jillian leaned forward. "You're on a rush, baby. Play it for all it's worth. Then we can leave and have a good time."

Ralph drew in a deep breath. "Okay. For a little while."

"One time," Crazy Eddie said, "I was up ten Gs at the Bellagio, in Vegas, ya know, and I thought the same thing. Quit while I'm ahead. But I was on a heater just like you, Ralph. And I thought, 'Let me give this baby a ride. You can't go on a super fucking nova heater if you don't stay in the game.'" Crazy Eddie paused for effect and puffed on his cigar. "Wanna know how much I walked away with that night?"

Ralph shook his head. We'd all heard this story a million times. It was part of the sales job whenever a mark had been lucky and wanted to leave the game early.

Crazy Eddie puffed again on his cigar. "Almost a hundred grand. Ninety-six thousand, eight hundred and fifty-four smackers. Now that was a super fucking nova heater! And I almost missed it cause I was gonna walk away at ten. Woulda been the worst mistake ever." Crazy Eddie shrugged. "Hey, I hope you do leave. You're kicking my fucking ass. I can't win a hand against you. You wanna leave, I'll open the fucking door for you. I'm tired of you taking my money."

Ralph grinned and leaned back in his seat. He rubbed his hands together. "Get ready to lose some more, Eddie."

"That's *Crazy* Eddie and don't you forget it."

"Crazy Eddie. Sorry." He chomped on his cigar. "Maybe you're right."

Hook, line, and sinker.

I folded the winning hand to him, tossing it into the muck, and let the hook go all the way down Ralph's throat.

We waited almost half an hour before we took him down so it wouldn't look suspicious. He'd swallowed the hook. There was no hurry. He frittered away a few grand on bad draws that this time didn't suck out, dropping him down to just under six Gs.

Just before the deal moved to Crazy Eddie, a card conveniently got damaged and I opened a new deck. Crazy Eddie spent extra time shuffling, the cards rhythmically thwacking against one another as he manipulated the deck.

When finished, he dealt Ralph two kings and Joe the Rock two aces. They made the appropriate raises and reraises preflop, then Crazy Eddie put down the king of hearts, the seven of spades and the deuce of clubs.

Ralph almost came in his pants. He had the rock-solid nuts. There was no flush draw, no straight draw. He bet, Joe the Rock raised, and Ralph pushed all his chips into the center. Joe called, making it a total of almost twelve grand of chips in the middle, and they flipped over their cards.

"*Fuck!*" Joe the Rock said, playing it up. "You gotta be shitting me." He glared all about the table. "This prick is so goddamned lucky!" He stood up. "I'm outta here."

Ralph cackled and rubbed his hands together.

"Two cards to go," Crazy Eddie said. "Joe's gotta spike an Ace." He flipped over the eight of diamonds.

Ralph leaned forward and spread his hands wide to scoop up all the chips.

Crazy Eddie flipped over the Ace of spades.

Ralph's hands touched the chips, then he froze. His eyes widened in disbelief.

"Wow!" Joe the Rock said, acting stunned. "It's a miracle!"

Ralph looked about to cry. "What just..."

Jillian touched his shoulder. "It's okay, baby."

Ralph rocked back in his chair. He shook his head.

"That's a tough one," I said, shaking my head. I got to my feet. "You want to rebuy?"

Numbly, Ralph shook his head. "I don't have anymore. That was all I had."

"Man," Crazy Eddie said. "That's a tough way to go."

"Well," I said. "At least you still have Jillian. For the rest of the evening. You'll check out tomorrow and still go home with a smile on your face."

Ralph shook his head in stunned disbelief all the way out the door.

Jillian took him back to her hotel where she and I rent adjoining suites. Each one has a bedroom with a desk beside a large flat-screen TV, a fully applianced kitchen, and a main room with another TV, desk, coffee table, sofa, and a floor-to-ceiling window with luxurious drapes pulled aside. Jillian always uses her suite regardless of her true intentions, claiming safety concerns. Which, if she's actually going to deliver the goods, as she often does, is a legitimate concern.

Some marks can be in a very nasty mood when they leave and a few have tried to take it out on her. From my adjoining room I view the hidden cameras to make sure she's safe. A few times I've had to trigger the fire alarm to save her from harm.

Each time, I assess the possibility of blackmail. I follow through only if it looks like a sure thing with no chance of backfiring.

Most times, though, I just enjoy the show. Jillian knows where all the hidden cameras are and gets off on knowing I'm watching. You can tell the way her nipples get hard and her chest heaves. Her voice, talking to the pathetic Ralph of the night, grows husky. She's really talking to me, not to them.

And does she follow through, delivering the services promised?

Sometimes yes, sometimes no.

She always dances for them.

But really for me.

What she does next is anyone's guess. I don't pretend to understand Jillian; she doesn't pretend to understand me. Things work best that way.

If she delivers, I don't watch. I can't.

If she doesn't, she slips out of the bedroom, saying she has a surprise for them, then goes quietly through the adjoining door and greets me with a hug. We wait for the befuddled and increasingly angry curses from the next room, watching on the three flat-screen monitors.

Sometimes, though, she gets vicious for reasons she never explains. She turns on the Ralph of the night and gives him what she calls the *around the world, inside out.* "Around the world" in the parlance of her trade is when you get to take her in the mouth, pussy, and ass. "Inside out" in her personal parlance, is when instead of taking it, she dishes it out. Not literally, figuratively. She gives it up to the hilt, hold the lube. She releases whatever anger she's stored up and pity the poor sap who has to take it.

Tonight, the poor sap is Ralph. And I can tell as soon as she winks at the camera that he's going to take it.

Why one and not the other? Is it because one "client" is so

physically repugnant, she can't bear the act? I don't think so. I don't think physical attraction or repugnance means anything to her. Not anymore. Maybe never did.

Tonight, she slips through the adjoining door, naked, closes it and erupts in laughter sure to carry to Ralph's bedroom. He looks up and she laughs louder.

Around the world, inside out.

He waits for a while and then walks out of the bedroom part of the suite, befuddled and looking all around.

That's when I slide into her and she groans louder and louder, climaxing as she watches him fumble at the adjoining door that he'll never open.

Moaning louder and louder, her teeth bared, anger filling that beautiful face.

It excites me, too.

We think we're done with Ralph, but we aren't.

Naked but no longer excited, he buries his head in his hands for a long time. We watch. I'm spent, at least for now. Until perhaps we replay the recording. I may have one more left in me.

I'm ready to pull the fire alarm if he becomes destructive. The suite, after all, is in Jillian's name. She'll be responsible.

But he just sits there sobbing.

"Poor baby," Jillian says. Her nostrils flare.

Ralph slowly gets to his feet, his member shriveled and useless, and walks to the bedroom where he yanks the sheet off the bed.

"What's he doing?" I ask.

And then we both know.

He ties one end of the sheet to the bedroom doorknob, loops the sheet over the top, and fashions a noose.

"Go back in there!" I say. "Make up some excuse. Say you're sorry. Anything."

Jillian just stares at the screen with a look on her face equal parts horror and hunger.

"What's wrong with you?" I move for the front door to hit the fire alarm in the hallway. It might stop him. But Jillian grabs my arm.

"No!" she says.

"We can't—"

"Give it to me."

"What?"

Her breathing is heavy. "*Give it to me.*" She strokes my crotch, her eyes never leaving the monitor, watching Ralph drag a chair into place, climb atop it, and slip the noose over his head. In her huskiest voice, she says, "Give it to me now, dammit."

It's the best sex, the best *anything,* ever.

Along the Lincoln City shoreline, we have sneaker waves that come out of nowhere. Before you know it, one engulfs you, then drags you out, helpless, past the point of rescue.

Sometimes our sneaker waves have nothing to do with the Pacific Ocean.

ROUGH JUSTICE

Steve Rasnic Tem

Davis had been sitting on the bed and talking to Paula for about an hour. She was asleep the whole time, passed out, drunk. Paula was drunk a lot. It made her hard to talk to and it made Davis question why he was with her. For the sex, sure, but sometimes Davis needed to tell her things, and he couldn't while she was awake. She never understood much of anything he said, and her stupid comments always spoiled it and made Davis want to slap her.

He never slapped her, but he pretty much always felt like it, so he was sure someday he would, if they stayed together. "You keep saying you want kids," he said, even though she was snoring, loudly, like she was dying. That happened to drunks sometimes. Sometimes when they were asleep, they just stopped breathing. How could she be a mother if she was going to die like that, leaving him with a kid? "We can't have kids. If you weren't so stupid you would know that." She growled something in her sleep, like she had heard what he was saying and she didn't like it. She turned over onto her side, her hands making a prayer under her head. She looked almost sweet that way, soft, and Davis couldn't remember the last time she'd looked soft.

"Did you hear me?" He slapped her on the butt. Not too hard, but hard enough. She didn't wake up, didn't even make a sound. She was out of it.

It was loud outside, even for a Saturday. All morning the other tenants had been out in front of the building talking about that baby who'd been murdered yesterday over on Sixth Street. Mae Swenson, Old Bob, a bunch of others, walking up and down out front, a smoke or a beer in their hands, yakking. You'd have thought the president had been killed, not some ordinary kid.

He left Paula in bed to sleep it off. He didn't want to be there when she woke up. She'd be sad and sloppy and she'd want to kiss him with a sour mouth, crying the whole time. She cried when she was drunk and she cried when she was just sobering up. Davis didn't need that today.

What Davis needed, Joe Billings would bring in about a half-hour, to that drainpipe on the parking-lot side of the old Hardware. Every week they found a different spot—Davis was careful that way.

All he had to do until then was hang out front with his neighbors, then when Joe showed up, walk casually over to that drainpipe at the end of the street and just say hello while Joe handed him the envelope with one hand and took his cash with his other. The powder in the envelope was speed mostly, but Joe always cut it a little differently each time, so Davis never knew exactly what he was getting on any particular day. He liked it that way—you needed a few surprises in this life. He'd take a benzo later tonight to bring himself down. It was all about the timing.

Mae was bawling over that baby she didn't even know, and her top was inside out and twisted crooked like she didn't know what she was doing. You had to pay attention to those things. This was information Davis might be able to use later—he never knew in advance what might be important. Sometimes Mae had money, and Davis would fool around with her until she gave him some. But she was old and ugly and built funny, so he had to be drunk to mess with her, and sometimes it wasn't worth it if she was in a talking mood.

"That baby got murdered *by its own daddy!*" Mae walked back and forth, smoking cigarettes like she was eating them. "Baby died last night, poor thing. *Poor, poor thing.* Daddy told the cops the baby fell out of its highchair. But I keep hearing he threw that baby *down.* Like it was *trash!*" Her face was ugly with tears and streaked makeup. Davis looked down the street at the drainpipe, thinking Joe had better get here soon. He kept thinking it would have been worse if the kid had been older and talking. He'd never been around babies much. But they didn't seem much like real people. More like stinking, sweaty dolls or little robots. Kind of creeped him out.

"Oh, they'll get him! They got that DNA now!"

Hell. Davis looked around. Old Hector had come out of the building, and now he was jabbering at Mae.

"I heard he beat that child half to death!" Bob hadn't said that much in a month.

"I hear he's a drinker. Some go crazy."

"Oh, they'll get him."

Davis couldn't stand listening to that crap. It made him agitated. If he'd been thinking straight he would have kept his mouth shut. But he heard himself saying, "He'll get away with it, unless they get a confession. Cops got any *balls*, they'll beat it out of him."

That shut them up. Davis had been in jail enough that they probably figured he knew. About that time he saw Joe Billings hanging around that drainpipe so he walked away from the bunch of them, like he was just going for cigarettes.

The business of the day took about five seconds. It went so smooth Davis felt like laughing. He surprised himself when he asked Joe, "You know about that baby over on Sixth Street?"

Joe had been smiling big time, but knew enough to stop. "Heard this morning. It were a shame."

"You know the daddy?" And just like that, Davis tore open

the envelope, bent over and snorted. Seized the day.

"Hey, *easy* son. We're still in public. But yeah, everybody knows Walter Brown."

And just like that the idea floated out of Davis's mouth. "Then you take me there." Joe looked so stupid it made Davis laugh. "You gotta drive," Davis told him. "You're the des-egg-knee."

Joe pointed Walter Brown out on the sidewalk, just before the bad man ducked into the gym. Bright green shirt, looked like a giant lime. Davis pounded the dashboard several times—he wasn't sure if he was disappointed that the guy was in a public place, or scared because the guy was so big, or excited because they'd found him.

"So what do we do now?" Joe sounded whiny.

"You pull over there on the side where we can see the front door and the alley. Didn't you ever watch any cop shows? They call this a 'stakeout.' You're on your first stakeout, my man."

Walter Brown might have been some kind of athlete, but apparently he still needed his smokes. They watched him take his first break in the alley, wearing a T-shirt and gym shorts, leaning against the wall and taking a drag. When Walter went back inside Davis waited a few minutes. "We're going over to that alley."

"What? *Why?*"

"You don't wanna know, okay, Chief?"

When they were almost to the door Davis took off his yellow shirt and tied it across his face, like one of those old west outlaws, except it was way too big and made him feel goofy, which just made him irritated with Walter Brown, which was maybe a good thing. There was a piece of two-by-two near the wall. Fortuitous. Davis leaned over and grabbed it.

"Davis, what are you going to do with that?" Joe's eyes got big.

"You distract him when he comes out, okay? Before he sees me."

"What if he don't come out again?"

Davis considered. "That'd be okay, too. We walk away. You heard of *karma*? If he gets lucky he gets lucky. We did what we could. Justice is rough that way."

Davis didn't know what he'd do if anybody else came out. He hadn't thought that part through. But about fifteen minutes later there was Brown, opening the door, needing a smoke again. He looked right at Joe, who just stared at him.

Davis swung the piece of scrap full into Brown's face just as he turned around. Joe jumped up and down, plainly scared but laughing stupidly. Brown fell like a tree, hands pressed into his face, blood pouring through his fingers and all over his T-shirt. "Help," came out like a gargle, not loud enough to call anyone. Davis was scared Brown was going to get back up, so he hit him across the backs of his hands with the board and kicked him in the side. The hands fell away, fingers twitching like they were electrified, leaving Brown's torn and bloody face for all the world to see.

"Jesus alive!" Joe shouted.

"Don't say my name!" Davis warned, and waved the board like he might use it on Joe if he had to. Then he crouched over Brown, who was wriggling around on the asphalt.

"Did you kill your baby?" Davis asked it softly, trying to be careful.

"What?" Brown had his hands over his face again. "Stop!"

Davis raised his voice angrily. "I said did you kill your baby?"

"No!" Brown struggled like he might be trying to get up, but Davis poked him with the two-by-two. Brown tried to squirm away.

"Lie to me again and I'll just keep hitting you."

"I said no!"

"Did you want to get rid of it—or was it an accident?"

"I told you, no!" Brown managed to sit up. Davis panicked

and hit him across the head with the board as hard as he could. The scrap snapped just above his hands. Joe was jumping around so much it was like he was dancing. Davis felt sick, wondering if he'd just killed Brown.

But Brown was blubbering, his cheek against the greasy pavement. "Acci—dent." He could barely get it out.

Joe leaned over Brown, looked up at Davis. "I don't think he can see us—he's got blood in his eyes." He stared back down at Brown. "Accident?"

Brown spat out the words with his broken-down mouth. "Shouldn't...left me...alone with the baby...kept crying...I jiggled him...tried to make him laugh...just did it...wrong. I just did it *wrong*!"

Davis couldn't think of anything to say to that. But he wasn't going to hit Brown again. "Okay, that's it. We got two witnesses, you...*copy* that? We got two witnesses to your confession. That should be enough for the law." Joe was hopping around, looking like he wanted to say something, but not saying anything, which was really distracting. Davis stared at him. "What?"

Joe ran over to him, pulled him aside, started whispering in his ear until Davis pushed him away. Then Joe whispered at a safer distance, "We can't be witnesses."

"Now, don't you say my name," Davis warned again, raising his fist. "What are you saying?"

"I said we can't be witnesses," Joe whispered. "Then they'll know what we, you, did to him!"

Davis looked down at Brown, who was rubbing his head against the pavement. Was he saying no? What was he saying no to? Davis stepped over to Brown, leaned over, staring into his mess of nose. "Okay then. You tell the police what you told us, then it's done. It'll go easier. You don't tell, we come back, we might kill you. Maybe not. I'm not good at this. There might be another accident, hear?"

Brown did something weird with his head. Davis grabbed Joe and shoved him toward the mouth of the alley. As they were crossing the street Davis mumbled, "I was wrong."

Joe looked like he'd eaten something nasty. "You don't think we shoulda done it?"

"Naw. I just thought we could *tell* people about it. I thought we could tell them about what *heroes* we were. How *stupid* was that?"

It was close to ten when Davis let himself back into the apartment. He'd had a few beers at a place ten blocks over, and he was slowly coming back down. Nobody had known him there, so they'd left him alone like he'd wanted.

Paula was still asleep. The place stank of stale beer and cigarettes, body odor. She wanted a kid. Every couple of weeks or so she'd cry about it. Broken record. He sometimes tried to think he might like a kid someday, a boy he could teach some things.

He went over by the stove, pulled out a drawer, took a steak knife. Sharp enough, he reckoned, but dull enough, too. He walked into the bedroom. She was asleep on her belly. He got up on the bed and straddled the small of her back, grabbed her hair, pulled her head back, put the knife on her throat.

"What the...Davis?"

"Don't move. I got something to tell you." He leaned over to her ear, brushed it with his lips like he was going to kiss it. He pressed the knife against her skin, imagined a red line against the blade. "No kids," he said. "You get pregnant on me, I'll kill you."

Later he sat on the edge of the bed, looking out the window. Paula was behind him, pretending she was asleep. He might have to get himself fixed. He just might. He felt like he'd done good today. He felt like maybe he'd saved some kid's life.

HARD LUCK CASE
James A. Hearn

July 2018. Huntsville, Texas.

There's something about the red brick walls of the Texas State Penitentiary at Huntsville that sucks the brightness from the daylight. In the distance, the prison squats in the middle of its namesake town like a poisonous toad, a drab edifice of guard towers and razor wire. It's the place where the worst of the worst are locked away to wither and die, be it from old age or lethal injection.

As I drive down State Highway 30, I pass a familiar sign: *Warning—Hitchhikers May Be Escaping Inmates*. A dry chuckle escapes my lips. Any hitchhiker caught in this heat would likely be dead in an hour. The sun is blazing in a cloudless sky, as if to punish Texas for its sins.

I turn off my truck's struggling air-conditioning system, remove my Stetson, and roll down the windows. Hot air blows across my skin, and in the rearview mirror my thinning hair sways like sickly gray stalks above a furrowed brow. Red-rimmed brown eyes beneath bushy brows stare back at me from a face I hardly recognize.

Oh, the wrinkles are the same, just deeper, and the bend in my once-too-often broken nose is as pronounced as ever—but

I've never felt my age like I do today. The weight of fifty-eight years of hard-living and reckless choices is pressing down, closing in. One day, sooner than I'd like to admit, the world will shrink down to a pine box, my personal prison for the rest of forever.

God, how I hate visiting Bobby on his birthday. It's not that I don't want to see Bobby; he's not my blood, but he's the closest to a son I'll ever have.

No, the source of my disquiet is The Walls. Inmates have been calling Huntsville that since the time of John Wesley Hardin. The notorious Old West gunslinger, so mean he once shot a man just for snoring, did time here. Satana, a captured Kiowa war chief, was imprisoned here before his "escape" in 1878—by suicide. In his final years, Satana was reported to stare for hours through his prison bars at his people's traditional hunting grounds. The Walls had driven the poor bastard mad.

"There but for the grace of God go I," I say aloud. If the discipline of the U.S. Air Force hadn't kicked the shit out of a rebellious seventeen-year old with chips on both shoulders, I could've ended up in Huntsville. Just like Hardin, Satana, and thousands of thieves, rapists, and killers.

And one innocent young man named Robert Earl Stone.

Bobby was a good kid who had caught a tough break. I'll admit he's a little rough around the edges, with a temper like his dad's, but what kid doesn't get into a few scrapes? Especially when he grows up without a proper father.

My good friend Alex Stone had a temper, too, but Alex had the self-discipline to control the violence within him, to direct it in a socially acceptable way. If you can call war socially acceptable.

Alex, killed while serving in Kuwait, never met his newborn son. When Desert Storm was over, I came back to Austin on the strength of a promise made to a dying man: "Watch over my boy, Trip," Alex had implored me. "Keep him on the straight and narrow."

I had tried my best. It didn't help matters that Alex's widow, a deeply religious woman, hated my guts. The promise I'd made didn't matter one whit to Lydia Stone. Not only was I a heathen—apparently anyone not a Southern Baptist—I was a man of wicked habits, given to strong drink and adultery, as my two ex-wives will attest.

The years passed.

In civilian life, I became a private detective. In between the cheating spouses, bottles of bourbon, and two failed marriages, I kept tabs on Bobby. I watched Alex's little boy from a distance, blending into crowds at tee-ball games and school plays, secretly celebrating every base hit and wincing at every flubbed line in *Peter Pan*.

Then one day, a car accident sent Lydia to her beloved Jesus. Little Bobby was adopted by Alex's mother, Janet Stone, a good-hearted woman who'd always treated me like a surrogate son.

I've never been good with kids, but Bobby took to me immediately. I became "Uncle Trip"—a beloved father figure without the burden of enforcing a father's discipline. With Grandma Janet's blessing, I taught Bobby the essentials: how to throw a football, defend himself in a fight, and shoot a gun.

When Bobby came of age, I found it unnecessary to have "the talk."

"The birds and the bees?" asked Bobby, incredulous. He went on to explain how babies were made, in exacting detail, then added this piece of advice: "If a girl talks too much, just kiss her until she stops."

Bobby grew up strong, in body and spirit. He became restless at school, easily bored with his lessons and quick to anger with other boys. A wrong look, a careless bump in a hallway, would land him in a fight. He took up smoking at sixteen and seemed to have a new girlfriend every few weeks.

What worried me most was his volatility. He had a brooding, James Dean quality that could explode into violence.

"Bobby's just excitable," Janet told me one day. "Alex was the same way. He'll grow out of it."

The day after Bobby graduated high school, Janet and I

threw him a party. I presented Bobby with a deer rifle, a Weatherby Mark V Magnum .30-378 that had belonged to my father. Janet cooked his favorite meal: brisket, baked beans, potato salad, and peach cobbler.

After dinner, Bobby took a long swig of Dr Pepper, belched contentedly, and announced he was taking a job in the oil fields of West Texas. Janet was devastated, but I'd halfway expected something like this. Bobby had been ready to spread his wings since he was twelve.

I hoped hard work on a rig might check Bobby's restless energy and keep him out of trouble. And for two years, I thought it had. Then I received a phone call in the wee hours of the morning.

"It's nothing, Uncle Trip," Bobby told me. "I broke my probation, is all."

"Probation for what?"

"Don't worry, I didn't do it," Bobby said casually. "It was her word against mine, but I couldn't chance a jury trial. So I took the deal."

I listened as Bobby explained the underlying offense he'd taken probation for. My only consolation was that Janet wasn't around to learn about this. Innocent or guilty, just hearing the news would've killed her.

"Tomorrow, I gotta go with my probation officer before the judge. Explain things. It'll be okay, Uncle Trip. You don't need to come," Bobby said before hanging up.

I showed up anyway.

I've never been at ease in a courtroom, especially during a criminal proceeding, and the Pecos County Courthouse was no exception. I guess it's the thought that an all-powerful State can take a person and do whatever it wants. Show mercy; impose a fine; take away their liberty; put them to death.

The next morning, Bobby sat at the defendant's table with his probation officer and a court-appointed public defender in a tattered suit. All three men looked bored, and the attorney was literally nodding off.

Judge Scranton, however, was wide awake. He sat between the Texas and American flags in his billowing robes, black as thunderclouds, his eyes flashing. Scranton, I later learned, was up for re-election and promising to be "tough on crime," as if he could personally keep the people of sleepy Pecos County safe from...what? Coyotes?

To make matters worse, Scranton's opponent was the very prosecutor who'd offered Bobby probation. What better way to discredit a political rival than to make an example of a "criminal" who'd allegedly beaten the system? That's why Scranton put Bobby away for thirty years for keeping the rifle I'd given him.

"Felon in possession," Scranton told Bobby. "You broke the terms of your probation, boy."

I can still hear that reedy voice, still see that wagging finger. I used to dream of cutting off that finger and making Scranton eat it.

"You skated by the last time you were in my courtroom, Robert Earl Stone," continued Scranton. "A cowardly prosecutor took the easy road and offered you probation for touching that little girl."

Little girl? The alleged victim was sixteen going on twenty-five, a high school dropout living with an older sister Bobby was dating. Sister was late getting home from work, and Bobby had arrived early for a date.

According to Bobby, the younger sister, Katelyn, was coked out of her mind when she answered the door. Bobby came inside to wait. Little sister came on to him, hard, saying she wanted a taste of what big sister was getting.

Bobby had refused Katelyn's advances, politely at first, but she hadn't listened. She became wild with anger, sometimes hitting him, sometimes trying to kiss him. So he had had to get physical with her. She had fallen to the floor, crying, and he'd left in disgust. The next morning, the police had come calling.

Soon after Bobby went to prison, Katelyn checked into a

drug rehab clinic in Houston. After she'd dried out, she disappeared off the face of the Earth.

I've tried to find her, to see if she'd recant her story. I went so far as to enlist the aid of the Texas Rangers, calling in a favor to my longtime friend, Captain "Big Jim" Garrison.

Nothing. Katelyn Harper's probably buried in a pauper's grave, or servicing foreigners in a white slavery brothel halfway around the world. You could see in her dark eyes a deadness, like she was a girl destined to die before she turned twenty.

And this cokehead was the angel Judge Scranton was avenging.

"You put your hands on that girl, didn't you, Stone?" Scranton had snarled. "Shoved her to the ground. Straddled her. Felt her breasts. But you got scared when she screamed, and you ran out."

I sat behind Bobby, incredulous, listening as venom spewed from this small man. The stenographer, I noticed, had stopped the meticulous clack-clack of her machine. This screed from the bench was off the record.

"The prosecutor was too scared to go to trial with no physical evidence and no witnesses, other than the word of the sixteen-year-old victim," said Scranton. "You got away, boy. Not this time."

The gavel banged down like the report of a gun. The public defender roused from his nap, blinking owlishly, as Bobby was sentenced to thirty years.

Bobby leaned over the defendants' table and wept while his "attorney" picked up a ratty attaché case and quietly headed for the exit.

That was ten years ago, and Bobby has twenty years left. I'll be dead by then. When they lay me in the ground, my promise to Bobby's father—to watch over his only son—will be my life's worst failure.

Unless I pull off the biggest gamble of my career and spring Bobby out before he turns into an old man, like me. But before I roll those dice, I have to ask him one question.

I pull up beside a sign reading *Texas State Penitentiary at Huntsville—Visitors' Entrance,* cut the engine, and lock my .38 Special in the console.

I grab two Styrofoam coolers and step out into an enveloping ocean of heat. Dusty gravel crunches under my silver-tipped boots as I walk up to a door. The Walls loom before me like a giant red coffin.

A prison guard named Burt looks at my Texas driver's license and scratches the bald patch on his head. Behind me, other visitors are passing through metal detectors. One elderly woman, who says she has a steel plate in her hip, is off to one side for a pat-down. Another guard is taking apart her metal cane. You'd think this was the Ben Gurion Airport.

"Charles Thomas Allison III," says Burt. He squints at me, then at my license. "Name is familiar, but I can't place it. You ever been to Goliad?"

"Not lately," I say. My work as a private investigator has taken me all across the state. I think I stopped in Goliad at a corner beer joint, maybe twenty years ago. Had a cold one, danced with a girl, gave her a memory, then hit the road. Those were carefree, lonely years. Before a lady with a heart of gold, another P.I. named Denise Fletcher, waltzed into my heart.

Denise had wanted to come with me, but I'd said no. Bobby's imprisonment is my personal hell, not hers.

"Who're you here to visit?" asks Burt.

"Robert Earl Stone."

Burt nods and shoves a Krispy Kreme doughnut into his mouth, his fat fingers leaving smears of chocolate on my I.D. "You any relation to the prisoner?"

"No. His father and I served in the Air Force together in Desert Storm. Saved my life and a dozen others, then died of his wounds the next day."

"No shit?" says Burt.

"No shit."

Burt snaps his fingers. "I know you! I saw your picture with the governor a few months ago, at some high-dollar gala. He a friend of yours?"

"Client."

Burt continues to stare like I'm Elvis back from the dead. I ask for my I.D., and Burt hands it back through a slot in the bulletproof window between us.

"What's with the Styrofoam coolers?" asks Burt. Before I can answer, Burt shouts at a guard working the metal detector. "Hey, Armando! This guy has two coolers! What the hell are y'all doing over there?"

Armando shrugs his large shoulders. "I searched them and ran them through the detector. Dr Peppers and barbecue from the Salt Lick down in Dripping Springs."

"I don't care if they're carrying the Ten Commandments, he's not bringing them into my prison," yells Burt.

"Take it up with the warden," says Armando. "One cooler is for him. The other is for the prisoner."

"Quit shittin' me," says Burt. He picks up a corded phone and calls Warden Marrs. The voice on the other end is gruff, threatening hell if his special delivery is delayed. I watch with satisfaction as sweat pops out on Burt's brow.

He hangs up the phone. "Sorry, Trip. I mean, Mr. Allison. Will you step through the gate? Leave one cooler with Armando, please."

Burt pushes a button and a barred gate slides into the wall. I step over the threshold with my cooler. Behind me, the gate closes, a sound of finality that sends a shiver down my spine.

As I follow Burt through concrete corridors, I catch glimpses of prisoners dressed in their all-white—not orange—jumpsuits.

I guess Texas just has to be different.

* * *

In a corner of the Visitation Room, I watch the man seated across from me down an entire Dr Pepper in one go. Bobby sets the bottle down and belches loudly.

From across the room, other prisoners and their families cast envious eyes on our meal. Burt and another guard named Jake stand facing them, arms folded across their chests. It's as private a meal as a prisoner can get inside The Walls.

"Pardon me, Uncle Trip," Bobby says, "but I've been waiting an entire year for that drink."

"Care for another?"

"Hell, yeah." Bobby pops the top on the table's edge and the satisfying hiss of escaping carbonation fills the air.

I slide a Dixie plate piled with brisket, baked beans, and potato salad over to Bobby and make a similar plate for myself. The meat and beans are as cold as the potato salad, but Bobby attacks the food with a will.

I sandwich some brisket between two slices of Mrs Baird's bread. As I set to, I wonder if I'll have the courage to ask my question, and whether Bobby's answer will change my mind.

Between mouthfuls, Bobby asks how I ever got the juice to bring Dr Peppers and Salt Lick barbecue into the toughest prison in Texas.

I tell him that's confidential, which is true. Warden Marrs swore me to secrecy the night I brought his missing teenaged daughter back from Acapulco, safe and sound.

We eat in silence for a few minutes. Except for Bobby's all-white jumpsuit, there's no outward sign he's ten years into a thirty-year sentence. Crow's feet frame either side of his bright brown eyes, but they're devoid of the hopelessness I've seen in other men serving long sentences. Bobby's clean-shaven face is as handsome as ever, and his hair is close-cropped, almost military. The easy smile reminds me so much of his father Alex.

"Happy thirtieth birthday, Bobby," I say, raising my bottle.

The smile suddenly vanishes. Bobby's eyes lose their luster, and he puts down a forkful of brisket. He inhales deeply and lets his breath out in a long sigh.

"It's no use, Uncle Trip."

I lean forward. "What's no use?"

"This charade." Bobby waves a hand at the meal. "I'm going to die behind The Walls, sure as Satana. Maybe I'll hurl myself out of a hospital window, head first, just like he did."

"Don't say that!"

"Truth to tell, I'm not even hungry," Bobby confesses. "I've been forcing it down, trying to smile through it all. And I feel like such an ungrateful bastard."

"Alex, you've done nothing wrong!"

"Yes I have, Uncle Trip." Bobby looks at me meaningfully. "Since I've been here, I've done plenty."

I reach across the table for Bobby's hand, but he shrugs it off. "Tell me if anyone's bothering you. You know I've got pull with Warden Marrs." And I've used it. Not only to have these private little meals, but to secure good cellmates for Bobby and for his cozy position in the prison library.

"Oh, I took care of it myself." Bobby lowers his voice so the guards don't hear. "Just like I always have with anybody who hurts me. Ever since I bit off Lester the Molester's right ear, no one bothers me."

"You...bit off a man's ear?"

Bobby's eyes bore into mine like twin drills. "Tore it clean away from his skull and spat it on the shower floor. But that's not the worst of it."

Bile stings the back of my throat as I listen to Bobby's story. A few years ago, a serial rapist with a taste for young boys arrived in Huntsville on a life sentence. His name was Michael Lester Wilkins, but everyone called him Lester the Molester. But never to his face. Lester was a monster come to life, the kind of man who'd make the Pope doubt God's existence.

For a while, Lester made Bobby his playmate. Then one day, Bobby asked Lester to change things up, make them more interesting.

"Come down here, big fella," Bobby cooed. "Let me whisper sweet nothings in your ear."

"What're sweet nothings?" asked Lester.

"Oh, don't be coy! Sweet nothings are foreplay."

Lester, smiling broadly, lowered his ear to Bobby's mouth. A few seconds later, Lester the Molester was face down on the shower floor, minus one ear. Bobby jumped on Lester's back, his hands pressing the larger man's face into the drain. The water backed up while Lester thrashed on the floor like a giant white worm.

Lester drowned in three inches of water.

"So you see," Bobby finishes, "I really do belong here. Go back to your ranch on the Pedernales River, Uncle Trip. Marry your lady friend. What's her name?"

"Denise," I say.

"Denise," says Bobby dreamily. "I've always liked that name. Why don't you marry her?"

"I've asked her a dozen times. She says why mess up a good thing?"

Bobby laughs, and for a second, I remember the happy boy he used to be. Then the laughter stops, and his face ages twenty years in an instant. He stands up. "Stop coming here. Get on with your life."

I lay a hand on Bobby's arm, but he refuses to sit down. "Bobby," I begin haltingly, "there's a question I need to ask you. I need you to answer me honestly."

"What is it?"

I suck up my nerve. "Did you do it?"

Bobby stares at me a long time before answering.

September 2018. Austin, Texas.

A steady rain drums against my windshield as I drive through downtown Austin. Beside me, Denise quietly clutches three large envelopes against her chest. *For Donald Abrahms,*

Editor, Austin American-Statesman is written on one of them.

"Are you sure Bobby's telling the truth?" Denise asks again. Her blue eyes are large and contemplative in her smooth, cream-colored face. She's ten years my junior, though she seems younger than that today. What she sees in an old codger like me, I'll never know.

"Bobby says he didn't do it," I say.

"That's not what I asked, Trip."

"I'm as sure as I can be, Goddamn it!"

Denise reaches for my hand. The familiar exhilaration races through me, just like when we first met. That day made us both millionaires, but that's a story for another time.

"Trip, I had to ask," Denise says. "Before we risk going to prison ourselves for blackmail."

I let go of her hand and pull the truck over. The driver behind me barely misses my bumper as he whips around us, horn blaring. "If you want out, you say the word."

Denise's blue eyes flash. "Trip, I'm going to forget you said that because sometimes you fly off the handle and say utterly stupid things. You know we're in this together. Now you damn well better apologize."

I pull back into the street. "I'm sorry. You sure we're not married?"

"Why mess up a good thing?" Denise leans over and kisses my cheek, and I catch the scent of Head & Shoulders shampoo in her auburn hair. Nothing smells better to me, not even yellow roses in spring.

I turn into the parking lot for the *Austin American-Statesman* and stop the truck. Denise takes the envelope addressed to the newspaper's editor, running her slender fingers along its edges. She hands me the other two envelopes.

"Now remember," I say, "if you don't hear from me by six, give that envelope to Mr. Abrahms."

Denise nods grimly. She pats the side of her purse, where a 9mm Beretta sits nestled in a secret pouch for quick access. "If I have to come find you, I'm bringing hell with me. No matter who's responsible."

I don't doubt it. "I love you, darling."

Denise answers with a kiss that melts my heart. She opens the door and steps into the rain. I pull onto Congress Avenue and drive toward the governor's mansion.

The man sitting across from me leans back in an over-stuffed leather chair and studies the contents of one of my envelopes. Every once in a while, he purses his lips together and lets out a low whistle.

The Governor of Texas is a handsome man of about fifty, long and lean, with thick, dark hair swept back from a widow's peak. The heavy creases of his face, coupled with a pair of eyeglasses, give him a grandfatherly expression that belies a shrewd ruthlessness.

Off to one side, two black-suited men stand by the door to his office. I notice the bulges of holstered guns under their left armpits.

I lean forward. "Governor, would you tell Heckle and Jeckle we need some privacy?"

The governor puts down the documents. "Benny, Floyd. Wait outside. Tell Jackie to hold my calls."

The two men leave, and I relax a little.

"Whiskey, Trip?" The governor doesn't bother to wait for a reply. He walks to a wet bar and pulls out a bottle of Garrison Brothers Whiskey.

"No ice," I say.

"I agree. Dilutes the taste."

He hands me a glass, but I do not drink. Instead, I walk over to a corner of the governor's massive pecan desk and take a lamp in my hands. I feel the sides of the lamp, under the shade, to find the electronic bug I'd installed the last time I was here. I disconnect it.

"Trip, why're you undoing your handiwork?"

"This conversation's off the record," I tell him. "Have you installed any other devices?"

"No."

I search the office anyway, then sit back down. "Have your people found any other moles in your staff?"

"None, thanks to you. Your surveillance system ferreted them all out. No more transcripts of my private meetings are showing up in the newspapers."

"I'm glad to hear that," I say. "Now, let's talk about Bobby."

The governor picks up a document, frowning. "A gen-u-ine hard-luck case. One witness, no physical evidence, and no trial. He takes probation, then gets caught with a deer rifle. The judge gives him thirty years for breaking his probation. Harsh, but legal. His judicial appeals have been exhausted. Been locked up in Huntsville for ten years. Does that sum it up?"

I slam a fist onto the desk. "There was never a trial on the underlying charge! No chance to confront the witness against him in open court. No jury of his peers to weigh the evidence. Does that sound like due process?"

"He didn't go to jail for that," the governor says. "He broke his probation by owning a weapon."

"Is thirty years a fair punishment?" I say through clenched teeth. "Judge Scranton was up for re-election and looking to make an example of someone. His opponent was the prosecutor who offered Bobby probation. Bobby was railroaded, and you know it."

The governor spreads his hands, palms up. "I know something about elections. Voters don't elect people who grant pardons to men accused of touching little girls, no matter how unfair or circumstantial the evidence may be."

"Katelyn Harper was sixteen, with a birthday coming up two weeks after the alleged assault. The age of consent in Texas is seventeen."

"Moot point, Trip. She didn't consent, and it wouldn't have

mattered if she had."

"She was a cocaine addict. Now nobody knows where she is."

The governor lets out a throaty laugh. "Cokeheads have rights, too."

"So you won't help me? Even after I saved your campaign from ruin?"

"In today's climate, handing out that pardon would be political suicide. My hands are tied, Trip."

"Like hell." I pull out a second brown envelope from under my jacket. The envelope hits the desk and spins once, coming to rest by the governor's whiskey glass.

He eyes the envelope dubiously. "What's that?"

"Open it."

The grandfatherly expression is gone, replaced by a wicked grin beneath glittering dark eyes. "Are you blackmailing me, mister?"

I take a casual sip of my whiskey, hoping my hand doesn't shake. "Open it."

"Very well." He rips the envelope open. As he stares at the photos taken by his own security cameras, incredulity and anger war for preeminence on his face.

I glance at my watch. "It's five minutes to six. At precisely six o'clock, another envelope with the same photos will show up at the *Austin American-Statesman*. They're itching to take you down, and they will, unless I make a phone call."

The governor's brow has a sheen of sweat. "You're bluffing."

I don't answer. The seconds tick by in silence.

The governor stabs a finger in my face. "I could make you, your accomplices, and these photos disappear." He snaps his fingers. "Easy as that."

I couldn't care less what happens to me. But the highball glass nearly cracks in my hand at this threat against Denise. I gulp down the contents to steady my nerves.

"You could," I say flatly. "But if you harm me or anyone I love, there's no place you can hide that my people won't find you. You'll never be safe. Never be able to jog around Lady Bird Lake or ride with the top down in your convertible." I force a smile to my face. "But why all these threats when there's an easy solution to be had?"

The governor glances at his gold Rolex. "There's nothing easy about this, Trip! How can I possibly give a gubernatorial pardon without ironclad evidence of Stone's innocence? I won't sacrifice my career and my reputation without a story people will accept!"

Reputation! A wave of reproach buffets me for helping this odious hypocrite stay in office. For a moment, I think about letting those photos hit the papers, come what may. If the Texas legislature didn't impeach him, he'd for sure be thrown out in the next election.

But the moment passes.

"The only evidence against Bobby," I say, "is the testimony of a missing girl who's probably dead. That's to our advantage."

"How?" The governor's voice is plaintive, his eyes desperate.

I've landed the hook. Now to reel in my fish. "After Bobby went to prison, Katelyn wound up in drug rehab. We'll plant evidence in her medical records that she confessed to her doctor that she lied to the police. We'll give the story to a friendly news outlet. They'll write an editorial about an innocent man languishing in jail."

The governor takes up the thread of my thoughts. "I'll hold a press conference, explaining how I learned of this young man's plight. I'll sign the pardon on live TV."

"You can still be tough on crime, all while demonstrating you care about prisoners' rights."

The governor nods thoughtfully. "Stone will be home for Thanksgiving." He extends his hand, and we shake on it. His cold, almost reptilian skin sends a shudder of revulsion though my body.

***

Christmas Eve 2018. Blanco County, Texas.

"Merry Christmas," Denise says as she walks into my ranch house with a bundle of packages. Her auburn hair is spilling out of a floppy Santa hat, and her curves make her ugly Christmas sweater into a thing of beauty.

"Merry Christmas, darling." I kiss her cheek and shut the door, but not before a gust of wind sends dead leaves swirling inside.

Denise sniffs the air. "That chili smells divine. Who'd have thought such a fine-looking man could cook?"

"Is that why you keep hanging around?" I laugh.

Denise looks me up and down with a measuring gaze. "That's one reason, cowboy. Is Bobby here yet? I've bought him some Christmas presents. Ten years' worth."

"Put them under the tree," I say. "I'll pick up Bobby from the Johnson City bus stop in an hour."

Denise disappears into the living room, while I return to the kitchen to check the chili.

This will be my first Christmas with Bobby since he was a boy. I've spent all day cooking and cleaning, and the ranch house is decorated with enough Christmas lights to make Clark Griswold envious. A fat yule log is crackling in my fireplace, while Bing Crosby croons "White Christmas" from the TV.

Even a month after Bobby's release, I can hardly believe my boy's free. He's living in an apartment in San Antonio. While he gets on his feet, I'm paying the bills. Who knows, maybe he'll go to college one day. It's never too late for a new beginning, right?

I take a sip of homemade eggnog spiked with bourbon and feel the warmth fill my very soul. The world's burdens feel lighter, and I can almost believe in the words of an angel heralding peace and goodwill to all men.

The phone rings.

"Merry Christmas, Big Jim," I answer. I put the phone on speaker, set it on the counter, and keep stirring my chili.

179

"Merry Christmas, Trip."

"The Texas Rangers got you working? What's the point of being a captain if you can't have a holiday?"

"This isn't a courtesy call, Trip."

I turn off the burner beneath my pot. There's an undertone of suspicious accusation in Big Jim's normally gruff but friendly voice.

"Let's have it."

"I finally got a hit for the girl you've been looking for. Katelyn Harper."

My heart sinks into the pit of my stomach. Had she read about Bobby's pardon in the newspapers? Regardless, her lies couldn't hurt him now. Once signed, the pardon was final. But she could still make trouble for the governor.

"What about her?"

"She's dead," says Jim. "Shot in her front yard three days ago in Midland. Went outside to pick up the morning paper, looks like. Dead before she hit the ground."

Katelyn's haunted, dark eyes return to mind, and I remember thinking she was destined for an early grave. She took ten years from an innocent man's life, but she didn't deserve to be murdered in cold blood.

"Any leads?" I ask.

"None."

"Jim, do you know for sure it's her? She's been missing for a long time."

"Positive," says Jim. I listen as he spins out a tale of the missing girl. She'd left the country after drug rehab, a stowaway on a cruise ship to Barbados. Met a rich Brit, a young oil executive for BP. They married on her eighteenth birthday and moved to London. There, Katelyn and Walter Brickman started a family, and life seemed perfect.

"The Brickmans moved to Texas two months ago for Walter's job," finishes Jim. "She came home, a young wife and mother, only to be murdered on her front lawn."

"So why're you calling me, Jim?"

"Why were you looking for her?"

"I've got nothing for you," I say. What good would it do to tell him to arrest the man who signs his checks? I wouldn't put it past Big Jim to send a police cruiser to bring me in for questioning, friend or not. I continue stirring my chili.

"Okay, Trip. I had to ask."

"Sure." I think of the governor's black-suited goons, Heckle and Jeckle. Which of them was the triggerman?

"This is a real head-scratcher," says Jim. "More like an assassination than a typical run-of-the-mill murder. Katelyn was shot at long range, probably 400 yards."

The wooden spoon slips from my fingers and sinks slowly into the chili.

"The bullet was an unusual caliber," continues Jim. "Forensics dug it out of an oak tree, a .30-378 Weatherby Magnum."

Dear God, no.

Big Jim wishes me a final Merry Christmas; I mutter a goodbye and hang up.

"Trip?"

Denise is at my elbow. Her eyes are wet with tears, but her lips are compressed in a hard line.

"You heard?"

She nods. "You think it was Bobby?"

I recall Bobby's words, spoken on his thirtieth birthday: *I took care of it myself. Just like I always have with anybody who hurts me.*

"It was him." I feel a weakness in my knees, like the Earth is spinning away on its axis, leaving me behind. "Katelyn Brickman was killed with a .30-378 Weatherby Magnum. That's the caliber of rifle I gave to Bobby for graduation."

"The one he got busted with," says Denise. "That doesn't mean it was him."

"Katelyn's dead because of me, sure as the world," I say. "Sounded like she'd turned her life around. A wife and a mother

181

to small children. And my boy killed her."

I grab my shoulder holster from a wall peg, strap it on, then check my .38 Special. The familiar clicking of the spinning chamber is a comforting sound.

I turn to Denise. "It's time to go get Bobby."

SECOND CHANCE
Barb Goffman

"Hey, wake up."

Someone nudged my foot. Son of a...I hadn't been sound asleep. No way that'd happen with the washers and dryers constantly swooshing and rattling. But damn, I'd *been* dozing. I'd heard this laundromat was cool for kicking back. Why were they hassling me?

"Ray, wake up."

Ray? Who knew my real name around here? I pushed an eye open. Blinked 'em both a couple of times to make sure they weren't lying to me. "Bro?"

It was like looking in a funhouse mirror at the carnival Ma took us to when we were kids, back before she chose meth over the two of us and disappeared. My twin was standing right in front of me. But he didn't look like me no more, not in those clothes. Clean jeans. A shirt straight from an Abercrombie ad. And his sneakers shined like new. I hadn't owned anything new since we'd been dumped in foster care. But my little bro—by eight whole minutes—seemed to be doing fine.

"You're not an easy person to find, Ray."

"Didn't know you'd been looking."

I hadn't seen Eddie in years. We'd been practically glued

together till we were ten, when that old biddy social worker
snatched us. By then we'd been living alone in that dump of an
apartment in Springfield, Virginia, for a few weeks. It had been
freezing. February. We'd known something bad would happen
sooner or later 'cause the landlord had stuck an eviction notice
on the door. But we'd never thought they'd split us up. It
would've been like Ma making us peanut butter sandwiches
without the jelly, back before she split. Unthinkable. But all of
this had been unthinkable, once upon a time.

Eddie had already been having a hard time dealing with Ma
running off, so when the social worker said she couldn't find
any foster parents to take us together, and Eddie started crying,
I did the best thing I could. I begged her to switch the foster
families they were sending us to. It'd make Eddie feel better, I
said, 'cause the ma in the family I was supposed to go with
looked like ours. Dark brown hair. Big, kind-looking chocolate
eyes, like Ma's before she started using. And a wide smile that
didn't feel fake. So Eddie went with her, and I was handed off
to the family that was supposed to take him.

We saw each other a few times after that, but Eddie's new
ma ended the visits when I got "too wild" and started running
from my foster families. As if I was the problem instead of the
dirtbags they kept sticking me with. I ditched a dozen homes
filled with perverts, rageaholics, or plain old jerks with too many
rules. Finally I turned eighteen and aged out of the system.

Eddie crouched down and wrinkled his nose. I swallowed
hard. I knew I stank. Who wouldn't after living on the streets for
six months? Usually I didn't give a damn, but Eddie had always
looked up to me.

"What do you want?" My voice sounded angrier than I'd
intended.

"I'd like to buy you dinner. Catch up. That okay?"

"Yeah, I guess so." Eddie looked like he could afford it.
"You still with the…" I snapped my fingers twice, trying to
think of the name of that lady with the kind eyes. If I'd been

smart, I would've written down her name and phone number a long time ago, but I'd never been good at planning.

"The Williamses," he said. "Yeah. Same foster family the whole time. They've been real good to me."

I was glad. Mostly.

I sat up and grabbed my backpack. Caught him eyeing it. It was filthy, with a rusting zipper and worn-out strap. But it was mine, one of the few things I took with me when my final douchebag foster family kicked me out on my—*our*—eighteenth birthday. Now it held everything I owned, which wasn't much. Some dirty clothes, a knife for protection, and a garbage bag to wear when it rained.

When I stood, Eddie stared at me.

"I can hardly believe it's you," he said. "Can I give you a hug?"

I hadn't liked being touched since I lived with old man Bass, but this was Eddie, so I said okay. He wrapped his arms around me for a few seconds. It creeped me out at first, but then I relaxed and it felt good.

We walked a few blocks, heading to a dive bar I'd passed before. The summertime heat was baking the D.C. sidewalks, making me feel even ranker than usual. Eddie said he'd been searching for me since he'd finished high school that June. He had some sort of present for me. When he'd finally gotten my last foster family's address so he could deliver it, he'd learned that no one had seen me in months. But word was I'd planned to try my luck here in the city. Eddie had been bothering folks in every D.C. alley and under every highway overpass since then, hoping someone might know me. He'd hit pay dirt this afternoon. He'd run into some old woman—Crazy Sheila, I figured—near the freeway. She told me about the laundromat just yesterday. She told him, too, thinking he was me, cackling about how my memory must be going.

When we reached the front door of the bar, I stopped, worried they'd kick me out 'cause of how I looked and smelled. Even places like this had standards. But Eddie patted my shoulder in a reassuring way, just like I'd done for him the first day of elementary school. We'd been standing on the steps of that huge building, and he'd been scared to go in. I'd never expected the tables would turn.

"It's no sweat," Eddie said now. "Come on. You can clean up in the restroom if you want."

"Okay," I said, though there was no way I'd do it. The crapper in there was probably dirtier than me.

I was widening my eyes as we stepped inside, trying to adjust to the dim light, when the overwhelming stench of stale, cheap beer nearly made me gag. Smelled like the shit my last foster mother started each day with. "Poor woman's Starbucks," she used to call it.

Eddie pointed at an empty table in the back, and we headed that way. A couple of guys eyed Eddie as we passed. Wow. My bro was more out of place in this dump than I was.

"Order whatever you want," he said as we sat on the rickety chairs.

I hadn't had a real meal in months. I mostly scrounged from trash bins, finding bits of cold, half-eaten food that rich people threw away. When we were little, before Grandma died, Ma used to take us to her house and grill burgers in the backyard. I was so hungry now I could practically smell that charcoal warming up.

"Burger," I told the skinny blonde who showed up to take our order. "And fries. And a big Coke."

She glared at me like I was dirt.

"The same for me, please," Eddie said.

The blonde left, and I tilted back on the chair's rear legs, enjoying the cool air wheezing down from the overhead vent. "Seems like you've been doing all right," I told Eddie.

He nodded, smiling. But his eyes looked sad, just like the night they ripped us apart.

"I won a scholarship to George Mason University, over in Fairfax," he said. "A full ride. Room, board, everything. Classes start in three days."

"No shit." Part of me was proud as hell. The other part wondered why he was bragging to me of all people. I leaned forward and fist-bumped him. "Good for you, bro."

His smile faded. "Did you finish school?"

"Nah. The teachers all had it in for me."

My last day of high school had been on our last birthday. I'd come to the house—it was the fosters' house, not mine, they liked to remind me—after school to find my things stuffed in a black plastic garbage bag. The state wouldn't pay for me no more, now that I was eighteen, the old man said, so I was out. At that moment I realized I really should have come up with that transition plan the social worker had been yapping about.

I slept on friends' couches for a couple of weeks, but all their 'rents made it clear I wasn't welcome long-term. So I hit the D.C. streets. Figured I'd find more places to hang in the city than where I'd been living in the Virginia 'burbs.

Eddie set his hands on the scarred wooden table. I couldn't help noticing how clean they were. No dirt under the nails or nothing.

"I feel terrible about how things have turned out," he said. "If only you'd gotten the same breaks I had, you could be heading off to college now, too."

If only I'd gotten the same family you had, you mean. Oh wait, I almost did.

"Nah," I said instead. "I was never smart like you."

"Yes, you are. I bet you didn't apply yourself. You always liked watching TV too much."

I clenched my fist. I didn't need this shit, especially from him.

"I'm going to help you, Ray," Eddie went on. "I promise. Just like you used to help me. I'm going to get a part-time job to save money. I'll give you some every month, assuming I can find you. Eventually I'll get an apartment for both of us. And once you have a permanent address, you'll be able to get a job, too. Everything's going to work out. You'll see."

Now he was treating me like a freaking charity case? A free

dinner was one thing, but no way I'd let my kid brother take care of me.

"You moved into that dorm yet?" I asked to change the subject.

He nodded. "A few days ago. But I've hardly spent any time there. I really wanted to find you while I still had time to look. Classes are going to be a bear."

"Maybe we could go there after we eat. You could show me the place. Let me clean up."

"Yeah, we could do that." He bit his lower lip, like he was thinking hard. "But you can't stay with me," he finally said. "I'm sorry. I'd let you, honest, but I have a roommate, and the place is tiny, and...well, I don't want to get kicked out. There are all these rules attached to my scholarship."

Like I'd been asking.

"Chill. It's cool. I just want to see where my bro's gonna be hanging."

He nodded again, clearly relieved. The blonde dropped off our burgers, sneering my way. My face grew hot. Between Eddie assuming I'd expect to crash with him and this stuck-up bitch acting all better than me, I wanted to punch something. Instead I leered at her and chomped into my burger, letting the juice dribble down my chin. Her eyes narrowed, disgusted. Loving how uncomfortable I was making her, I decided to go all in. I opened my mouth full of food and smiled.

A few hours later, we were cruising in Eddie's car, back in the city, heading to a bad part of town. He wasn't happy about it.

"Are you sure I can't drop you at a shelter?"

"Nah. I hate those places. Make me feel closed in. I like being out in the air."

He'd taken me over to his dorm after we ate. It was a three-story institutional brick building. His room had two beds, wooden desks, and small dressers, with worn gray carpeting and a smudged window. It was the freaking life of luxury. A large bathroom for everyone on the hall had a bunch of showers. I stood under one for a while, letting the grime and bad memories wash away. It was so nice to have soap again. I shaved and cut my hair in there. Short, like Eddie's. When I started getting dressed, Eddie tried to get me to wear some of his clothes—a fresh shirt and clean jeans. He wanted to throw the few clothes I had into a washing machine. For a moment I was tempted. Now that I was clean, even I could tell how rank my clothes smelled. But I said no. I didn't belong there. It was time for me to go.

Now Eddie was driving and talking again about how we'd live together once he saved up enough cash. "Take this." He handed me a cell phone. "It's pre-paid. Has three hundred minutes on it. I programmed my number in it so you can call me."

More charity.

"Thanks." I shoved it into my pocket. "Turn right." We pulled into a deserted alley. The smell of piss and rotting garbage from a dumpster hit me through the open window. "You can let me off here."

He stopped the car beside a burned-out building. "Here? This place looks pretty sketchy."

Who the hell was he to judge? "Nah. Abandoned buildings are good places to squat. Don't worry."

I clasped his hand—the hand I'd held when he'd been scared to go on the kiddie roller coaster. It was clean, with smooth, uncalloused skin. No scars. No cigarette burns. Eddie had been living large all these years while I'd been fighting to stay alive.

I pulled away and got out, slamming the door behind me.

"Wait." Eddie jumped from the car and hurried to me. "My family—my foster family, I mean—had a graduation party for me. All their friends gave me checks. You need the money more than I do." He slipped an envelope from his pocket. "Please take it. This is the present I wanted to give you."

I peeked inside. Sweet Jesus, there must have been several hundred dollars in there. Maybe a thousand.

I nearly opened my mouth to say no. To tell him I couldn't take his money. To thank him for searching for me and wanting to help, but I could make it on my own. But then a voice inside my head whispered, *Screw that.*

Eddie could afford to be nice to me because he'd gotten what should have been mine. The cool foster family. The ones who cared. Who had rich friends who gave out checks. Who helped him get that scholarship with the free room and board, setting him up for the good life. Hell, Eddie had been living the good life for the last eight years because I'd given him my placement. Mine! And now he was telling me I couldn't crash in his pad because of some freaking rules. But I was supposed to take his *charity*?

I stared at him. His face was the same as mine but softer. He hadn't seen the crap I had. Hadn't lived with crack addicts and whores. Hadn't been locked in a closet for days at a time. And he'd never had to stay awake night after night, on guard to stay alive. Eddie had the same look he'd had before Ma left. Young and naïve. I envied him.

And I hated him.

I shoved the envelope in my backpack, my fingers brushing against the cool, smooth metal lying beside it. Before I knew what I was doing, I grabbed the knife and stabbed Eddie hard in the side of his neck. As the knife slid in, the rage from all the blows I'd taken these past eight years poured out of me. Blows I'd taken instead of Eddie.

When the blade couldn't go in any farther, I stopped, stunned. "Eddie!" I cried as he fell to the ground, the knife still wedged in him. He looked so small. So helpless. I crouched beside him, shaking, my arms wrapped around my knees. *What did I do? What did I do?* I rocked back and forth on my heels, listening to Eddie's breathing growing more and more shallow. I swallowed hard a few times, then forced myself to stop. No way I was gonna cry. I had to consider my next move. *Think, Ray, think.*

I could use the phone he'd given me to call an ambulance. Call, then run. But if Eddie lived, he might tell them what I did.

And I'd get locked up. I couldn't live in a cell. Being shut in a closet for nearly a week had taught me that.

Of course I still could get caught. Was anyone watching? Had anyone seen what I did? I glanced around. No. The alley was empty, with the sun fading behind the buildings and night coming on fast. The thick air was so still, you'd think God was holding his breath—except there was no God. Not for me, anyway. I'd known that for a long time. And if God did exist, no way he'd help me now. Couldn't undo what I'd done. My only choice was to get rid of Eddie.

I left the knife in his neck so his blood wouldn't spurt out. Learned that from an old episode of *Law & Order*. A wheezy, gurgling sound oozed out of Eddie as I dragged him behind the dumpster. I hoped he'd die quickly. But he kept watching me, eyes wide, sad, and surprised. I looked away, focusing on my next steps.

After yanking off his sneakers and jeans and carefully removing his shirt without shifting the blade, I tore off my clothes and put his on. Made sure I had his phone and wallet. Then I shoved Eddie's legs into my ratty jeans, jammed his feet into my cruddy sneakers, and tugged my stained shirt over his head, careful not to move the knife.

I couldn't help but stare at him now. His eyes had become glassy. I felt his wrist. No pulse. He was dead. My baby brother, who I'd always promised to protect.

Fighting off tears again, I shook my head. Guilt wouldn't help me now. Besides, Eddie had already had his second chance. Finally it was my turn.

I grabbed the envelope full of cash from my backpack, threw on my garbage-bag raincoat to protect my clothes in case any blood sprayed my way, and slipped the knife out of Eddie. Then I picked him up and dropped him and the backpack into the dumpster. A bunch of flies flew out and dive-bombed back in.

"I'm gonna make you proud, Eddie. I promise."

My goodbyes done, I yanked off the garbage bag, used it to

wipe down the knife, and tossed 'em both on the car's front seat. Then I drove off as the new Eddie. Good thing a friend had let me drive his beater a couple of times before so I knew what I was doing.

A few miles after I crossed into Virginia, I knotted the garbage bag with the knife hidden in it. Then I pitched it in a large trash bin behind a closed store. I figured the knife wouldn't be found. But even if it was, nobody'd trace it to *my* body. I'd be another dead homeless guy in D.C. No one the cops would spend time on. Just another dead nobody.

Meanwhile, for once in my life, I was gonna be somebody. Eddie. The kid who had all the right breaks. Passing for him would be easy. No one at the college knew him. Not really.

Of course deep down, I was still me, the guy things never went right for. It didn't take long for that to sink in. I didn't know any of Eddie's passwords, so I couldn't use his laptop. I couldn't remember to respond when somebody called me Eddie, so people were looking at me funny. And Eddie's course schedule...man, oh man. He'd been accepted into the engineering school. I'd barely passed algebra. No way I'd earn the grades to keep his scholarship. Soon enough, they'd throw me out.

I tried to picture what would happen next. I couldn't live with his foster family. They'd immediately know I wasn't him. Maybe I could find a cheap motel to live in for a while. But the wad of cash Eddie had given me wouldn't last. Before I knew it, my second chance would be gone. I'd be back on the streets.

I'm going to help you, Ray. I promise. Eddie's pledge floated through my mind. Money. An apartment. Eddie had offered to do all the work, and I could've reaped all the benefits, if only I hadn't let my pride and anger get in the way. If only, for once in my life, I'd planned a little and thought things through.

If only I'd protected my little brother one more time—from me.

CLICKBAIT
Mark R. Kehl

The night of the home invasion, Bobby Lyon was busy jabbing a seventy-three-year-old index finger at his smart phone, reading reactions to the day's auction:

> 1970s' Box Office Legend Sells off Assets
> Bobby 'Yes, He's Still Alive'
> Lyon Liquidates Life: Everything Must Go!
> Bankrupt Film Star's Mementoes Disappoint on Auction Block

That last one was garbage. The auction had gone well enough, would take care of his creditors with enough left over to put him up at Halcyon Garden Assisted Living for however long he had left, given his failing liver and everything else the doctors nagged him about. The auction had gone just fine in reality, but reality didn't matter anymore. Only the headlines were real.

> Court Orders Star of 'Badge Boys' Series to Sell Everything
> 'Badge Boys 7': Kicked in the Assets

That's what passed for wit these days. They called it "snark," as if that made it okay, not hurtful, not mean, not an attempt to score a laugh at the expense of someone else's feelings. Yeah, he had probably made more *Badge Boys* pictures than was wise. If he had mixed in some heavier roles, his career probably could have withstood the divorces and the financial woes, maybe wouldn't have nosedived in the '90s the way it did. But those pictures had been *fun*, a great excuse to hang out on set with Tony Trevor and his other buddies, and they had made *so much money*. The first three anyway. It was never the same after Tony O.D.'d.

Former Box Office Champ Sells All to Pay Debts, IRS
Auction Spans Career of Hollywood Legend
Old Stars Don't Fade Away, They Liquidate at Auction

Bobby Lyon was enthroned as usual on his scooter, which he called Doreen after the Camaro he drove in the 1975 hit *Interception*, about a football player turned cop. Everyone said it was his best picture. Some people credited the stunt work and the innovative chase scenes, but it was the one film for which he had been nominated for a Golden Globe Award for best actor.

He used to take Doreen, the real Doreen, one of three silver Camaros with a shark-tooth grin stenciled up the front quarter panels, and drive the twisty Pennsylvania roads into town, back when he still used to drive, back when he could walk more than ten yards without having to take a breather, back when every step in public wasn't a roll of the dice on a broken hip and a viral video. Now the original Doreen was on her way to an auto museum in Myrtle Beach. The current Doreen, the scooter, had the same silver paint job and shark-tooth grin and had cost five times what the Camaro went for in the '70s.

Doreen—the electric scooter Doreen, in which Bobby Lyon hunched over his smart phone, diving down endless rabbit holes of snark and gossip—was parked where she had been parked the last several hours, in Pinehurst's Grand Room.

Bobby Lyon loved this room. When he first had Pinehurst

built, the three-story wall of glass at the back of the Grand Room had looked out on descending rows of pines and firs. He had already owned the vineyard in Napa, the ranch in Montana, the beach estate in Florida, the penthouse, the condos, the villa. Why not a Christmas tree farm five miles outside the tiny Pennsylvania town where he had grown up? When his career and his finances had started to fall apart and he was forced to begin selling off assets to pay the creditors, the IRS, and the ex-wives, Pinehurst was the one property he would not consider giving up, until it was the only one left. Some wag in the tabloids had re-christened it "Dis-Graceland."

He used to be able to look out the back window for miles across the mountains of his home state, but not for years. Bobby Lyon had been forced to sell off most of Pinehurst's acreage to developers. Part of the deal stipulated that they put up the wall around his remaining parcel, so he wouldn't have to see the cookie-cutter houses they tossed up all around him. In a way, it had been a blessing. Before the wall went up, birds used to kamikaze into the house's glass walls two, three, four times a week. The sickening impact resounded throughout the interior, and Bobby Lyon would have to send Conrad out to render any euthanasia that might be necessary. But since the wall went up the bird collisions had dropped to once every month or two.

The Grand Room was empty now, the furnishings all sold at the auction, except for the massive fireplace of stacked stone in the center, where he had once toasted marshmallows with beauty queens and heads of state, and a dozen life-sized statues of himself in various poses of valor and seduction.

The auction company vultures had declined to accept the statues. No market, they'd said. The statues wouldn't bring in enough to justify the shipping, and low sale prices would hurt other bidding. At his urging, Bobby Lyon's reps had looked for other buyers, but not even Planet Hollywood wanted them. Finally they found a theme hotel in Branson willing to take the complete set, but they wouldn't pay, not even the freight charges. Bobby

Lyon agreed to cover the shipping himself out of his share of the auction proceeds. He couldn't abide effigies of himself winding up in landfills or decorated like transvestites in dorm rooms. It's why he had bought them in the first place, the ones that weren't given to him as gifts. They were like an army of full-scale voodoo dolls he had to protect from the stabbing pins of ridicule and humiliation. He probably would have been better off smashing them to rubble, but it was done now.

The phone's low-battery warning chimed. Bobby Lyon scowled at the device and switched from scanning headlines to trying for the tenth time to determine whether the last fan site devoted to his film career—he had been the number-one box-office draw four years running, for Christ's sake!—was experiencing technical difficulties or was, in fact, as defunct as the rest.

It still would not load.

The site was run by Gladys Polley, he knew from years of lurking, and he switched to Gladys's Facebook page and then to her Twitter feed to see what she had to say about him there. He had never met Gladys, had never communicated with her in any way other than her worshipful online attention to his movies and his anonymous monitoring of her internet presence— another spinster locked into an idealized worship of his screen persona. His bread and butter these days. All his male fans had long ago moved on to the next charismatic pretty boy who made holding a gun look cool. But the "women of a certain age"—God, how he despised that phrase—were his for life. Unfortunately, that was turning out to be a lot less infinite than it had seemed in his glory days.

Gladys's Facebook was all craft fairs and other people's grandkids. Her Twitter offered only an unprefaced link to another headline:

Bobby Lyon's Bankruptcy Auction
as Disappointing as 'Legal Aliens'

Always the same punchline. How he loathed that film, cursed everyone involved, including himself, for being desperate enough to agree to it: *A classic Bobby Lyon cop character teams up with an alien detective to chase intergalactic criminals right here on Earth!* Bobby Lyon for the grown-ups, aliens and special effects for the youngsters: can't miss. His big comeback, like Travolta in *Pulp Fiction.* Only he was acting with a computer-generated space alien that wouldn't be added until later and ended up a crappy, rushed train wreck that looked like a bloated, blue Scooby Doo and sounded—because, *of course,* he had learned to speak English by listening to rap lyrics—like a drunken pimp on helium. Bobby Lyon and the alien spawned an unstoppable internet meme in which Jar Jar Binks thanked them for making him look not-so-bad by comparison.

A squeal pierced the silence of Pinehurst, followed by a snap of breaking metal.

Bobby Lyon looked up from the screen, realizing for the first time just how dark it had become in the Grand Room. He had a moment of disorientation, not having engaged with the environment around him since Louise, his housekeeper, had left for the day.

Other than the phone, the only light came from the security lights outside, which came on automatically at dusk. Pinehurst's exterior walls were almost all glass, as were the interior ones. (After the real estate was auctioned the previous week, one headline had read, "People in Glass Houses Shouldn't Dodge Taxes.") If you stood outside the front door and looked in, you could see straight through to the dry fountain in the backyard. Bobby Lyon, after his financial troubles had forced him to actually look at his bills, had been shocked at how high his monthly electricity charges were and had taken to leaving the interior lights off at night. The security lights provided enough illumination, and when he needed it, he had the spotlight that was mounted on his scooter, on a gooseneck over his right shoulder, but he didn't turn it on now.

He eased the scooter forward across the open space of the Grand Room, toward the sound. Now that most of the furniture had been sold, it wasn't like he was apt to run into anything. He only had to navigate around the looming mass of the fireplace and, of course, the statues. It was like maneuvering through a world where time had stood still.

If anyone had tried to break in last year, any previous year, the place would have been awash in flashing lights from police and private security, but the alarm company was one of the many creditors waiting with their hands out for his auction proceeds. They had discontinued service months ago.

Movie Cop Becomes Real-Life Victim

He had his phone in his lap, could dial 9-1-1 any time, but he wanted to make sure he had good reason before he did. If he got the sheriff up here because a raccoon was raiding the trash, tomorrow's headline would be:

Movie Star Loses Fortune, House, Mind

And he had his gun, the little six-shot automatic, a gift from his agent after John Lennon's murder. Bobby Lyon had always carried it in his hip pocket in case some crazy tried to accost him in a men's room somewhere. Pennsylvania did follow the castle doctrine, and he had a right to defend his home from intruders.

He left the Grand Room and rolled into the hallway, the glass walls displaying the darkness in the card room to the left, the pool room to the right. With the billiard table sold and gone, his gaze carried right on through the dirt-filmed exterior wall. He used to have a crew come clean the windows twice a week, but it had been months since that had been done for the photos for the realtor.

The interior walls, however, were clear as crystal, thanks to Louise, bless her. She and Conrad were all that was left of the household staff, Louise cooking and cleaning, Conrad overseeing the maintenance and driving him in the van to the diner. They were no youngsters themselves, and he hoped they would be all right after decades of living the dream with him here on top of the mountain.

He shook his head. Who was he kidding? They were probably better off than he was, selling off his life one piece at a time, moving into assisted living for as long as the proceeds held out, hoping they would last longer than he would.

Or not. Who the hell cared? The despair that had grown familiar since the world had started tearing away his life in increasingly larger and bloodier chunks embraced him like a ravenous ghost.

Another sound, heavy but muffled, like Frankenstein's monster in bunny slippers. Bobby Lyon stopped the scooter. Its electric whine silenced, he listened to the eerie, almost inaudible sound of the glass walls responding to the wind outside. That sound had unnerved him when he first stayed here, so much so that he hadn't spent much time at Pinehurst in the early years. But after two decades he was used to it, found it comforting even.

He would miss it after Friday, when he moved to the retirement home. He had never imagined his life would turn out this way, twenty years ago when he moved back to Pennsylvania "temporarily," back to where he had grown up and played high school football. At the time he had been at the peak of his film career and had triumphantly returned to build the most expensive home in three counties. As the film roles had dried up and ridicule replaced respect, he'd found solace driving around familiar streets, hanging out at the diner with guys who remembered when he used to be called Robert, before his agent convinced him that "Bobby" sounded friendlier. This house, its feel and smell, its routines, this was home, maybe his only real home since his mother had died and he'd left for the big city, a sixteen-year-old with an attitude and little else. This house—God, he loved it here. He was going to miss it like he had never missed anything. Certainly not any of his wives; by the time the divorces had come through he couldn't stand the sight of any of them. The despair enveloped him again, squeezing his chest like an anaconda.

The familiar squeal of hinges as a door opened. The door to the garage, he recognized from all the mornings he had waited for Conrad to come drive him to the diner. Maybe it was Conrad now. He thought about calling out his name, but what if it wasn't Conrad? Then it occurred to him to use the phone to call Conrad. If it was him entering the hallway behind the kitchen, Bobby Lyon would hear the Hank Williams ringtone, followed by the gruff monosyllabic answer, and he would cuss him out for skulking around after hours. If Conrad answered and was home watching *Jeopardy,* Bobby Lyon could tell him to call the state police and get his ass over here.

The phone had gone to sleep, and as Bobby Lyon jabbed and prodded it with fast-eroding patience, he recalled the low-battery warning and tried to remember when it had last been charged.

The phone was dead, and the charger was in the kitchen. *Damn.*

He heard the low murmuring of human speech, though he couldn't make out the words. Two voices, so definitely not Conrad. Bobby Lyon reached up over his shoulder to the little spotlight mounted there and hesitated.

Gun. All the long arms had been sold at auction, but he still had the little automatic, shiny as a prize. He used to set it on the table next to his chips when he played cards, spin it like he was playing spin the bottle. Lately it had been his drinking companion while he thought about the bills, bankruptcy, and spending his declining years—he called them his "spiraling years"—in a noisy, smelly old-folks home. He knew the feel of the blocky barrel between his teeth, the gun-oil taste as his tongue traced the hole of the barrel like the socket of a missing tooth. But the headline:

Faded Star Takes Own Life

He could not abide the pity such an act would inspire, the

holier-than-thou masses shaking their heads: another broken victim of the Hollywood fame machine.

Bobby Lyon was sure the gun was in a pocket of his robe, but he checked them now, and found both empty. The latest abandonment in a parade of betrayals.

The house trembled with the approach of the invaders, booted feet on the tile, the heavy thunk of bundled metal objects casually deposited. The voices increased in volume and sharpened in clarity until he started to make out words and low laughs, both respectful and irreverent at the same time, like atheists in church.

Bobby Lyon waited in the corridor, listening in the darkness. The light came on in the kitchen, reaching him through three or four intervening glass walls. The two figures slid through the light. Bobby Lyon thought it was like watching fish in the shallow water off his grandfather's dock when he was a boy. They looped around the perimeter of the kitchen and exited into the dining room.

In seconds they would be in this corridor, the central artery of Pinehurst. If he moved now, they would hear the whine of Doreen's motor. Where was that damned gun? He patted the pockets of his robe again, then groped in the vertical pouches hanging down the sides off either arm rest.

Son of a bitch.

He lost the figures in the darkness of the dining room, but as the visual faded the audial grew, the scuff of boots on the floor, the thunk of metal in the canvas tool bags they carried. They entered the corridor, twenty feet away. They had to see his silhouette, but all that was left in the house were the statues and sculptures: His silhouette was everywhere.

"Y'ever see a house with glass walls before?" one was saying.

"Never *heard* of a house with glass walls, 'cept for that saying about not throwing rocks at them."

Bobby Lyon waited until they were ten feet away and switched on the little floodlight, aimed in their direction.

"The hell you doing in my house?" Bobby Lyon growled.

One of them shrieked like he'd been stabbed. Both flinched into defensive postures, arms up, ready to fend off attack. One of the canvas tool bags hit the floor hard enough that Bobby Lyon felt the tremor through Doreen.

"Jesus Christ," the one who had shrieked said, and then, apparently dissatisfied with his own effort, said it again more emphatically: "*Je-sus Christ!*"

Both were out of high school but not yet thirty; that was as close as Bobby Lyon could gauge from his vantage point fifty years on. The one who had screamed was all junk-food-fed bulk, with a round head fuzzed with red-blond hair, like a giant peach. He had thick lips and heavy eyelids and looked like if you cut him in cross-section, like a tree, you'd be able to count the rings, each one representing a party with a keg.

"The hell," Bobby Lyon repeated in the same level tone, "you boys doing in my house?"

The other one was beef-jerky lean, with dark eyes and dark hair pulled back in a stubby ponytail. "We thought you was gone," he said. "This place would be empty."

"It's empty all right," Bobby Lyon said, "but I don't leave until Friday."

"Sorry," the first one said, his voice surprisingly gentle for a big guy. "We didn't mean to scare you."

Bobby Lyon snorted. "Scare me? I'm a seventy-three-year-old who's lost everything, all alone in the dark. What do I have to be scared of?"

"Well, I mean, you hear a couple guys walk into your house in the middle of the night—"

The thin one gripped his friend by the shoulder. "He gets it, Jase." To Bobby Lyon he said, "Sorry, Mr. Lyon. We'll leave you alone."

"You scared the crap out of me," Jase told Bobby Lyon. "You know, you totally sound like Colonel Grimm in *Collateral Damnation.*" He hesitated, then, as if he needed to translate his own babbling: "Uh, it's a video game."

202

Bobby Lyon recalled doing the voice-over for it. He had agreed because it was work and they told him it was something he could literally phone in, but that didn't pan out and they ended up sending some twitchy guy to record him shouting bits of dialogue. He had never seen the final product.

"Yeah, that's me," he said. "*Get your head down and your ass moving, soldier!*"

"Oh my god, that's awesome," Jase said, looking to his friend for confirmation of the awesomeness. "Ruben, can you believe it? This is Colonel-fricking-Grimm's house."

Ruben hadn't relaxed much, still had that ready-to-rabbit tension in his stance, but he gave a thin-lipped smile and nodded. "My dad was a big fan. Watched all the *Badge Boy*s movies whenever they was on."

Bobby Lyon sat back in his seat for the first time since hearing the sounds of intrusion and rested his elbows on the arm rests. "That why you're here? Get the old man a souvenir?"

Ruben shook his head. "No, he's dead a while. Iraq." He took a deep breath. "We should go."

He took a step backward and nodded Jase toward the canvas tool bag he had dropped on the floor.

"What did you boys want with an empty house then? Not much left to steal, unless your backyard's crying out for a statue of me."

"Well," Jase said, "that ain't really true. You got your copper pipe, which we can take to this scrapyard we know and get decent money. You got copper pipes?"

Bobby Lyon chuckled. "Hell if I know. Haven't been down in the basement in years."

"And then there's kitchen appliances," Jase continued. "And a nice place like this might have some fancy doorknobs and such—"

"Jase," Ruben said, "we should go."

"And the furnace," Jase said, all eager now, like a kid showing off what he'd learned in school that day. "We know a guy does contractor work. We can sell him a decent used furnace or water heater or air conditioner or such, and he installs it as new, if he can, or refurbished, and everyone makes out. He told us he needs a furnace, a big one, for a converted barn he's working on. We figured the one in this place would do."

Ruben had taken another step back and was just staring at Jase.

"You came to steal my furnace?" Bobby Lyon said. He took a second to mull that over. "That's a big job. In one night? That's downright ambitious."

Ruben shifted his tool bag in front of him so he could hold the straps with both hands. "We didn't really think of it as *your* furnace, Mr. Lyon. News said the place had been sold."

"How do you even do that?" Bobby Lyon asked. "Logistically, I mean." He felt himself slipping into the backwoods-Pennsylvania drawl he had worked so hard to leave behind, but he had always been something of a social chameleon, getting on as well with the teamsters as with the other talent.

"Well," Jase said with a sort of professional pride, "we got a truck parked down on Haskell Road. We figured after we got the lay of the place we'd bring it up to your basement access. We got ropes and a dolly and a hand truck. We'd get it out, right, Ruben?"

"Done it before," Ruben allowed.

Bobby Lyon had his hands tented in front of him, his fingers flexing against one another. "Well, it'd be a shame for you to leave empty-handed."

The two men looked uncertainly at each other, and then back at Bobby Lyon.

"You serious?" Ruben said. He reminded Bobby Lyon of himself at that age. His bad-boy looks probably got him a lot of tail, but around here that would mean reckless high school girls and women who spent more time in bars than at home. Probably living the life Bobby Lyon himself would have had if he hadn't hitched a ride to New York City after his mom died.

But Ruben hadn't left and Bobby Lyon could see his future, hard times and hard luck eating away the bad-boy mystique, leaving hard edges on the outside and emptiness within.

Bobby Lyon shrugged. "It's not my place anymore. The hell do I care? Come morning, I'll tell the cops I heard noises, my phone was dead, so I hid in my room till they went away. Or hell, I'll tell them I slept through the whole thing. Drugs I'm on, I could sleep through a demolition derby. I can say I got up in the morning and it was like Santa Claus stopped by on a repo mission."

Jase and Ruben looked at each other for a moment, Jase eager, until Ruben gave a why-the-hell-not? shrug.

Jase reached into his coat pocket and pulled out a condensation-streaked bottle of Yuengling, which he held out to Bobby Lyon. "Beer?"

Bobby Lyon blinked at the bottle, tempted. He shook his head. "Can't, with my medicine."

"This *is* my medicine," Jase said. He twisted off the cap and took a sip.

"No more till we get some work done," Ruben said. "Then you can have all the damn medicine you want. I'm going to check out the furnace. Which way to the basement?"

"Back to the kitchen," Bobby Lyon told him. "Door kitty-corner to the one you came in through."

Ruben headed off into the darkness. Jase looked around uncertainly, then took another sip of his beer. Bobby Lyon flashed back to some of the parties he'd thrown in this house, millionaires from a dozen countries, celebrities, power players rubbing elbows with some of his friends from high school, who stood around exactly like Jase, wiping the sweat off their beer and looking for a coaster.

"Come on, let's have a look around," Bobby Lyon said. "See what goodies we can find."

He adjusted the spotlight over his shoulder to blaze a path directly in front and guided Doreen toward the billiard room.

Ruben's footsteps shuffled along behind him.

"You boys do this kind of thing a lot?"

"Not *a lot*," Jase said. "Just when something comes along. Ruben's mom's got cancer so they can always use the money."

Bobby Lyon tossed a foxy grin over his shoulder. "Not you though. You've got everything a man could want or need."

Jase returned the grin. "Well, I can always use a donation to the beer fund. Or the video game fund. Or the porn fund. I got lots of funds."

Bobby Lyon laughed along with him. "I just bet you do."

In the billiard room, Bobby Lyon stopped and shone the spotlight on the long light fixture suspended over the area where his favorite table used to be. The little glass panels glittered like jewels. "Tiffany's, custom job. Think you could move that?"

"Think so," Jase said. He set his beer, three-quarters gone, on the floor and approached the fixture with an appraising look. Out came a multitool and with a few snips he had cut the power cord and the brass chains suspending one end. He lowered it until it rested on the floor. Snip, snip, and the other end came free. He hefted the fixture under his arm and said, "I'll just put this by the door. Be right back."

Bobby Lyon looked at the brass chains still swaying, the severed links winking in the spotlight. He glanced around the rest of the room, ghosts of good times hovering just beyond the reach of the light.

Hollywood Legend Sleeps Through Dismantling of Home

Not too flattering, but at least his last headline wouldn't be about a bankruptcy auction. He exhaled and headed across the space to the door of the powder room. As it required a little more privacy than the rest of the house, the powder room had walls of stacked stone and felt like the inside of a chimney with a sink and a toilet.

There was a wide, squat window, maybe a foot tall and a

yard wide, set in the wall above eye level, admitting a modicum of natural light while preserving privacy. Many's the time Bobby Lyon had sat on the pot conducting his business with one end while the other gazed up at the rectangle of sky framed by that window, feeling like a man trapped at the bottom of a well. Just the other day…

The memory clicked and he turned the spotlight on the little nook in the stone where the toilet paper was ensconced. And there at the bottom of the nook shone the gleam of nickel-plating. On the eve of the auction, Bobby Lyon had looked up through that window with the gun in his hand.

Movie Star Flushes Away Fortune, Ends Life on Toilet
Former Number-One Box Office Draw Shoots Self
While Doing Number Two

The can had been good enough for Elvis; it should have been good enough for him, but he couldn't do it. It just hadn't felt like the right time, even though it had. It just hadn't felt *enough* like the right time. Like maybe a better one would come along.

"Anything good in here?" Jase asked, poking his head in around the doorjamb.

Bobby Lyon jerked the spotlight away, sweeping it across the mirror over the sink. The reflected beam slashed across the far wall and Jase's big round face. He flinched and raised a shielding forearm.

"How 'bout that?" Bobby Lyon said, nodding at the mirror, gilt-edged and shaped liked a knight's shield.

Jase was still blinking non-stop but said, "Looks good to me." He squeezed in with Bobby Lyon and Doreen and lifted the mirror off its hook.

After Jase withdrew with his latest treasure, Bobby Lyon stretched across the toilet to retrieve the gun. He slipped it into the pocket of his robe and then maneuvered Doreen back out of the powder room.

The brilliance of the spotlight splintered through the glass walls, gave the illusion of a hall of mirrors. At the main corridor, Bobby Lyon saw the bathroom mirror on the floor, against the wall, and heard sounds from the Grand Room at the back of the place. He headed in that direction and made out two silhouettes moving among the still ones, the beam of a penlight scribbling through the shadows.

They had their backs to him, but Doreen spotlighted them like two prisoners trying to escape in an old black-and-white movie. Ruben was trying to disconnect one of the speakers mounted ten feet up on the fireplace. He had one foot balanced on the narrow ledge of a protruding stone about four feet up and the other on the shoulder of a bronze statue of Bobby Lyon. His boot was grinding against Bobby Lyon's bronze face as he worked.

"Hey," Jase said, glancing over his shoulder. He hefted one of the speaker's mates, already disconnected. "These ought to fetch a few bucks."

Bobby Lyon positioned Doreen with a statue of himself, arms akimbo, on his right. He pulled the gun out of his robe pocket and braced his outstretched arms against the marble buttocks of the statue.

"Hey, Jase," Bobby Lyon growled.

"Hold on a second," Jase said, reaching up, ready to accept the next speaker from his friend.

"*Now, soldier!*"

Jase turned and blinked back at Bobby Lyon, raising a hand to shield his face from the light. "What for?"

"'Cause it won't look as good if I shoot you in the back."

He squeezed off a double tap, just like the retired FBI trainer who had served as technical consultant on *Deadly Witness* had taught him. The first shot hit center mass, which was good, because the second only chipped stone off the fireplace. Jase collapsed backward into the hearth, his legs sticking out.

Ruben tumbled to the floor and didn't waste time with

surprise or words, already bolting toward the front of the house. Bobby Lyon twisted, firing in the dark, cussing. One, two, three—the first two shots disappeared into the darkness. Number three shattered the raised hand of one of the statues. Bobby Lyon looped Doreen around and pursued at top speed. *One round left.* The ammo box was in his nightstand. No time to get to it. If Ruben got out of the house, it would be his word against Bobby Lyon's. Bobby Lyon would claim he surprised the two intruders and fired only after they threatened him, taunted him, didn't think the old man had the grit to do what his movie characters did on a regular basis, and after he had shot Jase coming at him, Ruben had run. Bobby Lyon chased him out, protected what was his.

> Intruders Get 80s-style Justice from Bobby Lyon
> Old Action Heroes Never Die, They Just Blaze Away

Bobby Lyon steered Doreen with one hand, the other holding the gun ready in case he managed to catch Ruben. The spotlight blazed the trail before him. When he got to the kitchen he would lock the door to the garage, plug in his phone and get the state cops on the line. If they had someone in the area, they could probably pick Ruben up before he got to the truck on Haskell Road. By that time, Bobby Lyon would have told his story, and any bullshit Ruben told them about Bobby Lyon encouraging them to loot the place and then ambushing them would sound like just another lowlife trying to spin the facts.

A shadow shifted to Bobby Lyon's left, separated from the base of one of the statues, and rammed Doreen broadside.

"You old bastard." Ruben grunted and Doreen lurched to the side, tilting, toppling, as Ruben flailed for the gun. "You killed my best friend."

Bobby Lyon leaned against the tilt. If Doreen went over he would be helpless. He lashed the tiny gun wildly at Ruben's shifting shadow and connected to little effect, but Ruben danced back anyway, understandably wary of taking a point-blank bullet. Doreen dropped back level with an abruptness that hammered Bobby Lyon's spine and jarred his upper denture loose.

Frantic footsteps danced away in the darkness. Bobby Lyon kept the gun ready but didn't fire, stingy with his last shot. His other hand groped over his shoulder for the spotlight, jerked it wildly across the room trying to find Ruben before he could blindside him again.

A house-shaking thud resounded throughout Pinehurst, reminiscent of the kamikaze birds. The spotlight revealed on one glass wall at eye level a Rorschach smear of grease, sweat, blood, and saliva, a phantom mask floating there that seemed sheepishly surprised. Bobby Lyon tilted the light down to where Ruben lay stretched out on the floor, disoriented from his collision. Ruben shifted to his side in a fetal curl, his hands moving slowly, touching blindly around his mashed nose before moving to his chest.

Dumb bastard probably thought he'd been shot.

Bobby Lyon stopped Doreen a half dozen feet away and braced his arms across the steering yoke.

Ruben made it to his knees, blinking through blood and tears against the spotlight.

"Why?" he said, a great gulping expression of grief and despair more than a question.

If this were a movie, Bobby Lyon would say something like, "Ask the devil when you see him," but this was real life and no one but him would remember what was said here tonight, and he just wanted it over. Besides, if he spoke, he was afraid his upper plate would fall out, so he fired the last bullet into Ruben's chest and let himself collapse back in his seat.

Bobby Lyon sat still for a moment, letting Pinehurst's familiar sub-audible hum seep back in, envelop him like a favorite blanket. Then the gagging odor of feces cut through the gun smoke and Bobby Lyon realized the body on the floor had released its bowels. Not the way it happened in the movies.

He put the gun back into the pocket of his robe, resettled his upper plate, and then headed Doreen toward the kitchen and his phone charger. Should he call the police first or call Conrad and have him do it? Which, he wondered, would look better? Then he remembered that sometimes they leak 9-1-1 calls to the internet, and they go viral.

Bobby Lyon started rehearsing out loud as he rolled through the darkness.

Septuagenarian Action Hero Still Blowing Away Bad Guys
'Badge Boys 7: Geriatric Justice'
Faded Star Receives Hero's Welcome at Retirement Home

KICKS

Steve Liskow

Mick was having a smoke on his break and heard Jonesy tell the guy they didn't allow alcohol on the fully nude side.

"What's the point of that?" The guy wore a corduroy jacket, black slacks, and leather shoes. Most of the regulars wore jeans and flannels with work boots. This guy shaved his head, too, funkier than most of the regulars.

"Our ladies are really hot," Jonesy said. "We don't want anyone to lose control."

"What if a guy wants to do more than look?"

Jonesy caught Mick's eye. "That's the lady's call."

Mick balanced his cigarette on the butt can and eased back into the light. The guy saw him and shrugged.

"Make it a Jack Daniels. I'll see what you got this side." He pulled out a crisp fifty and flicked it at Jonesy. "Give me the change in fives."

Mick couldn't remember seeing General Grant in the two years he'd been working here.

The guy walked over to the platform where Daria was going into the last verse of "Bad to the Bone," clumps of bills surrounding her heels, which was normal. She dropped her halter just as the sax solo started and turned her rear toward the new guy. He

213

pulled out a stool and tossed a bill between her stilettos.

When the music stopped, Daria squatted to pick up the money and the new guy said something to her. Mick met her en route to the dressing room.

"What did that guy want?"

"He asked me when Baby Blue comes on. And how much she takes off."

Baby had walked in three months earlier and in mere weeks had worked her way up from the crummy nights to great slots. Mick and Baby—he didn't even know her real name—flirted with each other but that was as far as it went. She was that in-between age, too old to be earning tuition but young enough so the lights still treated her kindly.

"What'd you say?"

"I told him later...and everything."

"You ever seen this guy before?" Mick asked. The guy slouched on his stool and pretty much ignored Jasmine. She looked like she wanted to make friends, and Mick knew her car payment was due. Everybody owes somebody.

"Uh-uh. But I don't like him already."

Daria disappeared backstage before Mick could tell her to warn Baby. He figured she would anyway.

He eased through the flannel shirts and baseball caps, not many on a Tuesday night, especially this early, and peered into the "No Alcohol" side, where the girls' accessories were tats and piercings. Maybe some of them wore contacts, too. Samantha seemed to have everything well in hand. Mick returned to the main lounge.

Half an hour later, the other guy walked in, shoulders from a Clydesdale and a blond buzz cut so his scalp looked like sandpaper. He wore a blue blazer with a fancy patch on the lapel and ordered Jim Beam. Jonesy gave the no-alcohol spiel again.

"Whatever." The guy laid another fifty on the bar. "Baby Blue on tonight?"

"Yeh." Jonesy glanced at the clock. "Three more times."

"Here or next door?" The guy's voice made Mick think of surf rolling over a beach at high tide.

Jonesy nodded to his right and the guy said, "Make it a double."

He took his change in fives and turned to scan the room. His eyes stopped on Mick's chest long enough to register the logo, which got a reaction the first time you saw it. The place was Clint's, all block capitals, the "L" and "I" not quite touching. Pink on black. Yeah, a low-end strip joint, but they vacuumed the carpet and disinfected everything else regularly. After the fall that messed up his middle ear—and his balance—Mick couldn't do construction anymore.

The blond guy's eyes stopped at Jack Daniels, the guy in corduroy, and he eased over to join him and watch the Asian chick remove another lei. They didn't say anything to each other, but Mick could tell they didn't have to.

He tapped on the dressing room door and asked for Baby Blue.

"You know two guys, one a giant with a blond buzz cut, the other with a shaved head, a little shorter than me?"

Baby Blue's baby blues turned into turquoise nickels. "Where are they now?"

"Watching Holly getting de-lei'd."

"They travel in threes," she said.

"The blond guy just came in," Mick told her. "The other guy showed up, I don't know, maybe forty-five minutes ago. But they both asked about you."

"Daria told me about the first one."

"Look, you want, we can kick them out."

Baby shook her head. "They'll just wait for me outside."

"Who are they?" Mick wanted to touch her. Even in the crummy light and a makeup-stained shirt, she was gorgeous. He wanted to ask her real name, too.

"I…had kind of a misunderstanding up north. I didn't think they'd care enough to…"

"Baby, you got friends here. Like I said."

She ran a hand through her long dark curls. "Mick, will you do something for me?"

"You kidding? Name it."

"Take a run outside, will you? See if there's a black Caddie out there with Ohio plates."

"Sure, no problem."

"Wait a second, hon." Her fingers closed on his biceps and he realized she'd never touched him before. "There might be a third guy. Smaller, but mean as a snake. He's got a caterpillar moustache and he packs heat."

"Okay. When are you on?"

"About twenty minutes." She looked like she was going to say something else but changed her mind.

Mick ambled outside. Clint's was the only surviving joint in a block with cracked sidewalks and four working streetlights along the curb. Those lights showed him a bunch of pickups and beat-to-hell sedans, but no Caddie. He turned the corner. The vacant buildings formed three sides of a square, and the girls parked their cars in the center, where two pole lights lit the cinders to the stage entrance. The stage door didn't have a handle on the outside, but someone usually stuck a magazine in the crack to keep it open while the girls went outside to smoke.

When Mick reached that central parking area, he saw a hard orange line in the wall and realized it was the back door, open a crack, as usual. Then it occurred to him that it was so bright because both pole lights were out.

He slid along the wall and let his eyes adjust. A fingernail moon dropped enough light for him to see a strange car among the regulars. When he squinted, he recognized an old Cadillac, big as a tank. He couldn't make out the license plate without getting closer, but someone was sitting behind the wheel.

Back inside, he tapped on the backstage door again and Baby Blue opened it just enough to peer out at him.

"Caddie's out there," he said. "Guy sitting in it."

"Swell." She wore her blue latex outfit, which meant she was going for broke this time out. Well, bigger tips.

"Jim Beam and Jack Daniels are still drinking hard stuff," he said. "They can't join you."

"I've got two more sets after this one."

"Baby, I can help you." The music changed and he couldn't make out the words. Since his fall, he had been tone-deaf, too. "Tell Clint you're sick, I can drive you home."

"I don't like people knowing where I live, Mick."

"So come to my place, spend the night there. These guys don't find you, they'll be gone tomorrow."

"Nice try, Tiger." She almost smiled and he felt like a little kid again.

She closed the door and he drifted over to the arch by the no-alcohol side. He worked five nights a week—weekends included—and had the social life of a mummy. He wanted Baby Blue so much he felt stupid around her. She was smart, funny, he'd even seen her with a book backstage.

Kinsey finished up her set, six guys slobbering on the platform, bills thick as crabgrass. She wore her waist-length hair in red, green, blue, and purple stripes. When she got off the platform, she looked like M&Ms with great legs.

"And now, gentlemen, let's have a big welcome for Baby Blue."

Baby appeared through the curtain and glanced over his shoulder. Jack Daniels and Jim Beam had drained their glasses and approached the arch.

Mick blocked their path. "Sorry guys, you just had liquor. Gotta wait half an hour before you can come over here."

"This a joke?" The blond stepped close and Mick smelled his breath. The guy was so big he could probably drink a fifth without blowing a point one.

"House rules." Mick signaled Larry and Turbo, but before they got there, Jack Daniels shrugged.

"Whatever." He slouched back over to Jonesy and ordered two Diet Cokes. He and his sidekick moved to the far platform and sulked at the new girl.

Mick knew Baby would be on again in about fifty minutes. What could he do about these guys by then? Who chased a dancer all the way from Ohio? And why? Jim Beam and Jack Daniels seemed to fill up the whole space around the far platform. One touched the other's arm and pointed to the right.

The VIP room. Anything went in there, and the bouncers stayed out unless they heard trouble. A gig there meant major money, so none of the girls turned it down. If they wanted to try for Baby Blue in there...

More regulars drifted into the place. The girls danced fast and the clock moved faster.

Jim Beam bought two more Diet Cokes and paid with another fifty before the pair eased their way through the flannels toward the no-alcohol side. The bartenders called it the "no hard stuff" side, just to tick the girls off. Mick knew he couldn't keep them out this time, and Baby'd be back on in fifteen minutes.

The drums drove everything else out of his head. He caught Turbo's eye and pointed at the clock—break time—and stepped out the front door. He trotted down the block and around the corner, slowing down when he was only steps away from the central parking lot. He crouched and looked around the corner.

The Cadillac squatted near the stage entrance and the driver still sat behind the wheel. Smoke drifted out of the car window and an orange bud bloomed when he inhaled. Mick eased along the wall and opened the stage entrance wide so the guy would think he'd come out that way. He pulled out his cigarettes and pretended to fuss with his lighter before looking toward the car.

"Hey, buddy." He got closer and the light from the stage door fell on the license plate. Yeah, Ohio. "My lighter just died. You got fire?"

"No problemo." The guy opened the door and stepped out. He was shorter than the shaved guy, but Mick could see a bulge under his arm. He pulled a Bic from his pocket and the flame jumped up.

"Thanks, buddy." Mick leaned forward and drew on the cigarette until the tip glowed bright as Baby Blue's eyes. He stood and dragged again while the guy stuck his lighter back in his pocket.

When the guy's hand was trapped, Mick jammed the burning cigarette into his eye. The guy screamed and his other hand jerked up toward his face. Mick let go of the cigarette and pushed the hand away, then punched him hard on the bridge of the nose. He heard the crunch and let the guy collapse into the shadows. He reached into the car and found the trunk release.

The man had stopped twitching by the time Mick dropped him next to the spare tire. He took the guy's cash and credit cards before he closed the trunk again. He debated a minute, then left the keys in the ignition before he returned to the stage door.

"Baby Blue here?"

Holly shook her head. "Some of us work, you know."

"I gotta talk to her."

"She'll be back in a few minutes. Go around front, I'll tell her."

"But—"

"The show's out front, Mick." That was Vanessa the leather girl. She ran things backstage.

He hustled around to the front and slipped inside. The space seemed more of everything than when he'd left, more crowd, more heat, louder music. He could smell the sex and the danger and zigzagged toward the arch where he hoped Baby was still okay.

She was down to no concealed weapons and both Jack Daniels and Jim Beam were closer to the ramp than they should have been. Mick felt the drumbeat in his gut and stepped forward in time to see Jack Daniels pull a wad of bills out of his pocket.

"Wanna go next door, honey? Just for kicks?"

Baby's eyes didn't move off the bills, but Mick could feel the vibe—like she'd rather swallow a cobra.

"Someone's in there right now," she said. "And I got another set coming up."

"A thou right here. More if you work for it."

Mick wanted to kill them both. Baby Blue looked over the blond's shoulder.

"The space'll be free in fifteen minutes. Let me change. Um, you guys got protection?"

"Don't worry, honey."

"I always worry."

"Not three months ago you didn't."

Baby looked at Mick and shrugged.

"Fifteen minutes. Why don't you buy a girl a drink while you're waiting."

The so-called champagne had less kick than flat ginger ale, but Jack Daniels returned to the bar. Mick watched him pay before he met Baby at the stage door. She held a pair of thigh-high boots that gleamed like an oil slick.

"Whoa," Mick said. "Nice kicks. Never seen those before."

"I don't wear them much, just for special occasions. You like them?"

They looked like they'd reach clear up to her neck, heels thin as knitting needles and not much shorter.

"Uh, yeah." He remembered why he was there.

"You can go out the back," he said. "The third guy won't stop you, you can be miles away before these guys figure out you've split."

"They'll find me again." She hefted one of the boots. "It's got to end here."

"What do you need from me?"

"Don't do anything stupid, Mick."

"I want to help."

"You are. Promise me, okay?"

He felt like a little kid again. Baby slid a fingernail over his chest and cold zapped down his spine.

"When they go into the VIP, chill outside. I've got my iPod,

I'll program the third song for 'Baby Blue,' and that'll be your signal to come in, okay?"

"You want me to bring other guys, too?"

"No friggin' way." She closed the door before he could tell her he didn't know the song.

He drifted over to Turbo. "You know a song called 'Baby Blue?'"

Turbo chewed his gum. "Oldie. Some '70s band, Badfinger maybe?"

"How's it go?"

"Uh, wait a sec." Turbo pulled out his phone and punched a few icons. "Here."

He held it out and Mick shook his head. "I'm tone deaf. Show me the words."

Turbo's fingers flew across the screen and Mick saw Jack Daniels meander toward the VIP room with a bottle the size of a bowling pin. His scalp gleamed red, blue, and green under the stage lights before Jim Beam followed him through the arch and pulled the curtain shut behind them.

"Shit. Hurry up, will you?"

"I'm looking, I'm looking. Okay, here." Turbo held up his phone and Mick stared at the screen. He swiped his thumb across the letters to make them bigger. He mouthed the words and turned back to Turbo.

"What's the rhythm like?"

Turbo flipped back to the video and snapped his fingers. "Dum, dum-dum, dum dum dum DUM...It stops and starts, lots of guitar stuff in between."

"Okay. Thanks."

Mick wondered what those guys would want Baby to do for that thousand...and what they wanted to do to her. He wished there was a fire door out of the VIP that he could go through to get to Baby faster...or that she could use to get away. But the door to backstage was the only way. The Fire Marshall hadn't been thrilled about that, but Clint had had the girls work it out with him.

He heard voices beyond the curtain, but the music outside was so loud he couldn't hear words. He couldn't hear Baby's music, either. He pushed his ear against the fabric.

"Drink up." That was the bald guy. "Come on, quit screwing around."

"I thought that was what you were paying for."

Mick heard the music start up, Baby's iPod. He knew Clint had iPod speakers in there so the girls could program their own music without messing up the dancers outside, but he couldn't recognize the song. He closed his eyes and whispered to Baby to kick up the volume. A minute later, she did, but it didn't help. He might as well have been listening to a cement mixer. He looked back. Nobody was watching, so he slid inside the curtain and held his breath.

Beyond the curtain, the passage turned left so nobody could see the action in the room. What happened in the VIP stayed in the VIP. Mick saw the reddish glow of the dim lights. Voices drifted underneath the song, still not sounding like the one he was waiting for. He wondered how long the songs were. A girl could be in the room with a guy until his money ran out. Well, that was the whole point, they weren't selling Girl Scout cookies.

The song changed, Mick screwing up his eyes to make out the words, but it didn't work. Was this the second song? The beat didn't sound like what Turbo had showed him, and he couldn't make out the words. He eased up to the corner but didn't look around it. If the men were facing his way, they'd spot him.

The song changed again, and the beat was even further off. Mick strained and this time he could hear words, something about having a brand new love. Not even close…

A clank, then a grunt.

"You bitch…"

Mick surged around the corner, his eyes straining to make out shapes in the dark,

Baby Blue in those boots, the bottle in her hand, one of the men sprawled back over a love seat. The big blond guy towered over Baby and blocked her next swing. He twisted the bottle out of her hand and slammed it against the table. Liquid splashed everywhere and he came up with a jagged club.

"Enough games, you little…"

"Hey!" Mick said it loud enough so the guy heard him and turned. He had four inches on Mick, and probably sixty pounds. And that shiny broken bottle.

Mick rushed the guy, gave him a head fake. The bottle missed his face so close he felt liquid splash onto his cheek. He feinted again but the guy didn't go for it. When he got close, the guy jammed the bottle into his ribs and his right side burned. A fist caught him above his ear and his knees turned to mush.

"Asshole." The guy rolled him over and Mick saw that jagged bottle inches above his face. He tried to roll away, but his whole body felt heavy. The guy smiled for a second, then he straightened up suddenly and the smile turned into a grimace. Baby Blue high-kicked like a Ninja and one stiletto sank into the guy's chest. His eyes opened wide and his mouth even wider before he sank to his knees. Baby Blue stepped back and kicked again. This time the toe of one boot smacked off the guy's temple and he sagged to the carpet.

Mick tried to get up but his guts exploded in pain when he moved. Baby came over and he saw those incredible boots.

"Mick," she whispered. "Get up, baby, come on."

He struggled to his knees and felt blood soaking his T-shirt. Baby grabbed his arm.

"You gotta get out of here." He could barely hear his own voice. "I didn't hear the song."

"Baby Blue," she said. "By Gene Vincent. Old Rockabilly, I thought everyone knew it."

"Shit," he whispered. "Wrong song."

"Can you walk, now you're up?"

"Yeah. I'm fine." Mick clenched his teeth and told himself

the fall off the ladder'd been a lot worse. At least he was still conscious.

"Go find me a screwdriver, okay?" Baby said. They looked at the two men and Mick wasn't sure they were breathing. "Hustle."

"You gonna be okay with these guys?"

"Fine. Go now and clean yourself up."

His side felt hot, then cold, but he signaled Turbo and stumbled behind the bar where Jonesy frowned.

"What the hell?"

"You got a toolbox back here? I need a screwdriver."

"What for?"

"Just do it."

By the time he returned to the VIP, Turbo had taken the men out through the backstage door to the central parking lot. Wearing hot pants and a halter above those boots, Baby followed and told them to dump the guys in the trunk of the Caddie. Then she unscrewed the license plates and tossed them into her own car.

"Those guys are gonna wake up," Mick said. "They'll raise holy hell in there."

"Don't think so." Baby Blue kicked the fender with one of her boots and Mick saw a dent form around her toe.

"Jesus," he said.

"Steel toes," she said. "And the heels." She brushed her lips against his cheek. "Thank you, Mick. You need to get yourself fixed up. And I've got another set."

Turbo helped Mick around to the front and cleaned him up in the staff room.

"Damn lucky Clint doesn't come in Tuesdays," Turbo said. "He'd have a major cow."

"Yeah." Mick wondered if he'd need stitches the next morning, maybe even a tetanus shot.

An hour later, he met Baby Blue outside after her last set.

"I'll dump the Caddie," he told her. "If you follow me, you can drive me back and then take off."

He headed toward the river. There was an embankment a

mile south of town; he could open the windows and let the car roll down the slope. Nobody would find it for weeks.

Half an hour later, Baby Blue pulled her car back into the parking lot with Mick in the passenger seat. His car was the only one left and the pole lights were still out. He looked at her behind the wheel, the fire in his side gnawing deeper with every breath. He wanted to kiss her, but knew it was all gone now.

"What's your real name?" he asked.

She squeezed his hand.

"Polly."

He watched her car disappear around the corner before he unlocked his own car and drove back to his crummy apartment. He felt older than dirt, but his side felt a little better. He eased from behind the wheel and walked across the parking lot. Before unlocking his front door, he looked back at his car.

Something was missing. He walked back and stared at his trunk. Then he went around and stared at his grille.

Yeah, she'd taken his license plates, too.

KILLER SUSHI

Stacy Woodson

The salmon's lifeless eye stared at me through the glass display. Behind the carcass, filleted chunks of fish were arranged in a perfect peach row. I gripped my menu, eager to read the selections. But I couldn't look away—the salmon's expression unsettling. It was like the fish knew it was the end but didn't know what to do—sort of like me with my marriage.

"Any specials this evening, Tomohiro?" I finally asked the sushi chef behind the counter.

Tomohiro had been in the midst of cleaning his workstation, and he tossed his rag aside. Smells of fish and bleach wafted into the air. He pointed to a dry-erase board on an easel on top of the granite bar. Scrawled in red marker, *Chef's Special Roll: Screaming O.*

An interesting name. I wondered if Tomohiro understood the connotation. I started to ask about the special when Ray slid into the seat next to me. He wore a paratrooper T-shirt that was too tight, and his biceps strained against the sleeves.

"Strip-mall sushi?" He shook his head. "Seriously, Adam, you spend your Thursdays here?"

"Fayetteville isn't exactly a foodie's paradise." Except for my stint in Okinawa, it seemed I was always assigned to army installations in backwater towns. At least Fayetteville, North Carolina, had a mall and a Discount Tire, which was better than my last duty station.

I pushed my menu over to him. "Trust me. A little sake, a little sushi, you'll feel better."

Ray shook his head. "I need a little something, but fish ain't it." He sighed. "Can't we go to a pub? Get drunk. Chase tail. You know, like real men do after a breakup."

"You need perspective, not a one-night stand."

"Says you." Ray glanced up. His eyes hovered on the ceramic Japanese bobtails on the shelf above the bar. A battery-powered paw moved slowly back and forth like it was waving. "This isn't the kind of tail I had in mind."

"*Maneki-neko.*"

"*Maneki*-who?"

"It means beckoning cat. They're supposed to bring the owner good luck."

"Look at that litter up there," Ray said. "Owner must be one lucky bastard."

I wondered why I bothered.

Koji, Tomohiro's sous chef, emerged from the kitchen and adjusted his kimono-style chef's coat. He joined Tomohiro behind the bar and gave me another menu.

I raked my hand through my thinning hair, something else my wife found unacceptable. I blinked and tried to focus on the menu, but my mind drifted to Trish and her fresh serving of infidelity excuses:

You didn't love me enough.

You didn't need me enough.

You weren't there for me.

Now, I was here with Ray while Trish did god-knows-what with Mr. Perfect.

I finally gave up on the menu. "Surprise me, Koji."

He nodded and turned to Ray.

Ray twisted the bezel on his Suunto watch while his eyes

glided over the menu. He glanced up at an order Tomohiro had plated. "Glad I drank that protein shake before I got here. Damn stuff looks kid-sized." He pushed his menu aside. "Sapporo. And a California roll to start."

Koji's jaw flickered. Ordering a California roll from a well-trained sushi chef insulted the art of sushi making. Of course, Ray didn't know that. His version of culture was NASCAR. I suggested different Maki rolls—something more traditional—but Ray waved them away.

Koji returned to his station. He pulled out a bamboo mat covered with plastic wrap and placed seaweed on top. Then he picked up a bamboo paddle, scooped rice from a wooden tub, and dropped the mound onto the seaweed.

Ray slipped his wooden chopsticks from their paper sheath and rolled them against each other like he wanted to start a fire. "Seen Oscar?"

"Not since we were here last week. When I left, he was in sake heaven."

"Think he finally did it?"

"Broke up with Nina?"

Ray nodded.

"Oscar said he'd sort it out when he got back from Airborne school."

"Three weeks from now?"

"More or less."

Ray's eyes narrowed. "So, Oscar went the conflict-avoidance route with Nina."

I shrugged. "It's a technique." I took a similar approach with Trish.

"Things won't be different when he returns." Ray shook his head. "Trust me. This I know."

"Look at us—you, me, Oscar—we're pathetic."

Ray sniffed. "Like some Lifetime television movie."

A waitress brought us bottles of Sapporo and damp cloths perched on bamboo stands. Ray's eyes followed her back to the kitchen.

If Trish were here, she would have smacked Ray on principle. *Trish.*

My heart sank again just thinking about my wife. I wondered how we got to this place, if there'd ever be a time I wouldn't associate everything with her.

I picked up the white towel. It was warm against my fingers. I wiped my hands. Tried to focus on something other than her but came up with nothing. So, I poured my beer into a glass and stared at the yellow-edged posters—a picture parade of perfect sushi pieces—thumbtacked to the wall behind the bar. It reminded me of a place I'd taken Trish when I was stationed in Okinawa.

Ray grabbed his beer, took a long pull from the bottle, wiped his mouth with the back of his hand and looked at me. "She left this morning," Ray said. "Took everything but the master suite."

"Everything?"

"Even the light bulbs."

"Wow."

Ray nodded, bottle poised for another swig. "Yup. Went into the bedroom, flipped the switch, and *nothing*. Bulbs gone from the ceiling fan."

"What's up with the scorn?"

"She blames me," Ray said. His voice rose, the tone mocking. "I made her cheat. All the deployments, what's a lonely girl to do? Blah. Blah. Blah." He waved his beer bottle back and forth in time with his rant.

Koji placed a California roll in front of Ray and a roll in front of me—pink meat nestled around layers of rice, seaweed, and avocado.

"Screaming O," Koji explained.

I nodded. "*Domo.*"

Ray picked up the soy sauce, filled a small ceramic saucer, flicked a dollop of wasabi into the liquid. He swirled the mixture with his chopsticks until it turned tan. Then he pulled them out and licked the stained tips. "Looks like that time you spent in

Okinawa paid off."

"What do you mean?"

"The Japanese and the cat thing."

"*Maneki-neko.*"

Ray rolled his eyes at my correction. He clamped onto a piece of California roll, choked it out with his chopsticks, and dunked it into his tan concoction. Seconds passed before he finally rescued the roll, soy sauce running down the sides. He angled the roll above the saucer until the dripping stopped. Then, he lifted it to his lips and shoved it into his mouth.

"Can you even taste the fish through that sodium-laden mess?"

"What's the difference?" Ray mumbled, mouth still full.

I sighed.

Ray clicked his chopsticks together and attacked his second piece of sushi.

I picked up a piece of Screaming O with my fingers and slid it into my mouth. The rice separated, unloading layers of sweet and salty flavors. I rolled it around in my mouth—the fish chewier than I'd expected. But overall, I was pleased with Koji's selection. I reached for my beer and noticed Ray's plate was nearly empty.

Ray beckoned to Koji. "Spicy tuna roll and another one of these." He lifted his empty beer bottle.

Koji signaled to the server for the Sapporo and then reached into the refrigerated display case. He picked up a bright red section of fish. Tomohiro smacked Koji's hand and grunted something in Japanese that I didn't understand. Koji released the tuna and walked to a bank of low-profile refrigerators. He opened one, pulled out a container of leftover fish, and returned to his station.

I laughed to myself. I couldn't blame Tomohiro. It wasn't like Ray was going to taste the difference between fresh and day-old fish.

"Heard about that prank we played on Smitty?" Ray grinned.

Smitty, another guy in our unit, was notorious for being late. And as a consequence, he was always stuck with additional duties—polishing floors, mowing the grass, picking up cigarette butts. Any crappy job the platoon sergeant had on his list, he gave to Smitty.

"Prank?" I asked, encouraging Ray to continue, grateful to talk about something other than women.

"You know how Smitty drives to physical training at the crack of dawn? Sets the alarm on his phone. Sleeps in his car until it's time for formation."

I nodded.

"Yesterday, we plastic-wrapped his car."

"With Saran Wrap?" I asked, not sure if I'd understood.

Ray nodded.

"While he was inside?" I still stared at him in disbelief.

"Over the hood, under the car, around the doors." Ray snickered. "Then we called Smitty's phone, pretended to be the platoon sergeant. Gave him the riot act. Where the hell are you? Why aren't you in formation? That kinda thing. Smitty bolts up in his seat—all flustered, tries to open the car door, but can't. The look on his face…classic."

"What are you, twelve?"

"Come on, dude. You know that's funny."

I laughed. We both did, over and over again.

More beer.

More sushi.

More stories.

And I realized, as long as I had people like Ray in my life, no matter what happened with Trish, things would be okay.

Hours passed, and the place began to empty.

Ray leaned heavily against the bar, now. He slid his wedding band back and forth on his finger, his eyes distant. "I loved her, you know," he said, to no one in particular. He drained Sapporo number six, pushed up from the bar, and weaved toward the bathroom.

Tomohiro's eyes lingered on Ray's empty plate. The chopsticks were crossed on top—an ominous reminder of a ritual performed at Japanese funerals. I realized the etiquette mistake and placed Ray's chopsticks on the paper sheath still on the table and then signaled for the check.

A few minutes later, Ray ping-ponged back into his seat.

"You okay?" I asked.

"Never better," Ray mumbled.

"Maybe you should take some time off. Let things settle a bit. Local leave may not be a bad idea."

"Good call, man." Ray pointed his finger like he wanted to punctuate his statement, but it just weaved like the rest of his body.

Instead of the check, Tomohiro appeared with a porcelain flask and a small ceramic cup. He slid them in front of Ray. "Wake from death and return to life."

Ray gave me a puzzled look.

"It means turn a desperate situation into a success," I explained.

"On the house." Tomohiro turned toward the kitchen before Ray could respond.

He stared at the flask. "What is it?"

"Sake."

Ray frowned.

"Seriously. You haven't had sake before?"

Ray shrugged.

"Sake is alcohol from fermented rice. It's Tomohiro's way of empathizing with your relationship situation."

"He heard what I said?"

"He hears everything behind that bar."

My phone vibrated. I pulled it from my pocket and looked at the screen. A text from Trish. My body tensed. I looked up.

Ray's eyes were on me. "Trish?"

I nodded.

He waved his hand. "Go man. One of us needs to figure out

this whole relationship thing. Maybe you'll be the guy."

"How are you getting home?"

Ray lifted his phone. "Uber."

I squeezed his shoulder. "Thanks, man." I reached into my pocket and tossed money onto the bar. "Try the sake. It won't disappoint."

Sushi happy hour this week was anything but happy. I found the divorce papers after Trish left for her shift at the hospital. I opened a desk drawer and there they were, staring at me just like that god-awful mackerel stared at me now.

I pulled out my phone and sent a text to Ray: *At Tomohiro's if you want to wallow in it. First round on me.*

Koji glanced up from his station.

I tried to force a smile. "Evening, Koji."

"Mr. Adam."

I was surprised he knew my name.

He signaled for the server. She walked over, and Koji whispered in her ear. A minute later, she placed a Sapporo in front of me. I gripped the bottle, not bothering with the glass, and took a long drink. It tasted bitter, just like me.

I looked at the whiteboard that listed the Chef's Special: *Ray of Sunshine*. Nothing like I felt, and I laughed at the irony. Tomohiro emerged from the kitchen. I pointed to the special. He nodded.

I checked my phone. No texts. No calls. Not even an alert from my newsfeed.

Where was Ray?

He was supposed to be on local leave. Maybe he had decided to get away? I couldn't blame him. Maybe I should take a vacation, too. I considered New York City. I'd always wanted to see the Metropolitan Museum of Art. Washington, D.C., could be an option. So many wonderful pieces of history. Or maybe I should take a page from Ray's playbook and go to

South Carolina's South of the Border. Their campy, faux-Mexican style and kitsch décor might be just what I needed to lift my mood. Trish used to laugh at the two-hundred-foot sombrero-shaped tower when we drove past the exit on Interstate 95.

Trish.

And here I was, thinking about her again.

I shook my head, took another sip of beer. Checked my phone. Still, no Ray. I sent another text and then picked up my paper menu. I folded the edges—one crease, two crease, three crease, four—until a red and white crane took shape. I worked on the origami, but my mind was still stuck on Trish.

What about the counseling we'd discussed?

Didn't commitment mean anything to her?

One more fold and the crane was finished.

Finished like my marriage.

My muscles tensed. I ripped the head off the crane and tossed the decapitated bird. It flopped onto the plate of sushi Tomohiro just placed in front of me. He fished out the paper.

My face flushed. *"Domo."*

I considered the sushi, but instead took another sip of beer. And then another. "Trish and I were married in Vegas," I said, aloud. To Koji, to Tomohiro, or maybe just to myself. "What did I expect? It wasn't exactly a foundation for matrimonial bliss. But I was a private back then, we had no money, and it made sense at the time."

Tomohiro and Koji exchanged a glance and kept working.

"I loved her, you know."

God, I sounded like Ray. I glanced at my phone. No message. *Where the hell was he?* I sent another text. I could use one of his ridiculous plastic-wrap stories now.

I finally turned to my food, slipped the roll into my mouth and waited for the symphony of flavors. But Trish continued to haunt me. And all I tasted was heartache.

I finished the roll, drank more beer, scrolled through pictures on my phone. Trish on our wedding day. Trish on the Vegas

Strip. Trish in our house off the Yadkin.

Trish. Trish. Trish.

Each reminder, a stab in the heart. My shoulders sagged. I downed another beer, headed to the bathroom, the place almost empty. I glanced at my watch. Nearly closing time. I guess Ray wasn't coming. I gave up on him and sent a text to Oscar. Airborne school should be over for the day. Maybe he'd be up. I needed at least one person to feel sorry for me.

But nothing from Oscar.

I was alone.

When I returned, Tomohiro arrived with a tray of sake.

I held up the ceramic cup.

He poured. "Wake from death and return to life," he said, before he nodded and returned to the kitchen.

Tomohiro and his broken-hearts club.

I wondered how many other pathetic patrons he served sake to each night. I lifted the glass and sipped.

More sushi.

More sake.

The room began to blur.

More nothing.

Schlink.

Schlink.

Schlink.

The sound pulled me awake. The light was bright and harsh.

I blinked.

I breathed.

I blinked.

Fluorescent bulbs and stained ceiling tiles blurred into focus.

Schlink.

Schlink.

Schlink.

Where the hell am I?

I tried to sit up, but I couldn't move. My body was smashed against something hard, the resistance too much. I curled my fingers—the tips against something cold and smooth. I pressed my chin to my chest and peered down. And that's when I saw it. *Plastic wrap.* It cocooned my body. My stomach tightened. *Oh god.* I thrashed right. I thrashed left. The plastic bowed and flexed but didn't give. I arched my head, saw a commercial stove—a *Maneki-neko* perched on the shelf above. And then I got it. I was in the kitchen at the sushi place, wrapped against a stainless steel table.

My mind went to Ray and how he'd plastic-wrapped Smitty inside his car. He must have arrived after my sake stupor. Typical Ray to think a practical joke would cheer me up.

"Ray," I yelled. "You got me. You bastard. Now get over here and cut me out."

Footsteps.

A face peered down at me.

Not Ray's.

Instead, it was Koji—knife in one hand, sharpening stone in the other.

Schlink.

Schlink.

Schlink.

"Very funny, guys." I laughed.

Koji stopped sharpening and called over his shoulder. "What do we call this one?"

Tomohiro came into view. He stared at me.

"Prank of the year," I supplied.

Tomohiro's face brightened. "Adam Bomb," he said, decidedly.

Adam bomb? "Odd name for a prank, but hey, whatever. Now cut me out. I got to hit the bathroom." I shivered, suddenly realizing I'm buck naked under the plastic. A little over the top, but Ray was known for his flair.

Tomohiro nodded at Koji.

I waited to feel the tug of the plastic and hear the smooth slip of the blade. But instead of cutting me free, Koji sharpened his knife again.

Schlink.

Schlink.

Schlink.

With each flick of the wrist, his Suunto watch caught the light. The time piece familiar—*Ray's watch.*

That can't be right.

"Okay guys. You've had your fun." My voice trailed off, the bravado gone. "Ray, come-on, man. Enough is enough."

But no Ray—just Tomohiro and Koji standing over me with serene expressions.

"Mr. Adam," Koji whispered. "Wake from death and return to life."

"I'm saran-wrapped to a table and you're quoting Japanese idioms to me?" But my mind cycled the phrase again—over and over. It reminded me of hope and rebirth and Tomohiro's sake—sake Oscar, Ray, and I drank as we mourned our broken relationships. The sake a gesture from Tomohiro, a way of sympathizing with us. Or was it something more? I scrambled to connect the pieces.

Screaming O-*scar. Ray* of sunshine. The sushi specials. Were they Tomohiro and Koji's twisted form of rebirth?

The idea nearly too outrageous to comprehend.

And yet...

No Ray. No Oscar. I'd heard nothing from them in days, nothing since I'd left them at Tomohiro's with his sake. And now, after my own sake stupor, I was strapped to a table in Tomohiro's kitchen.

Screaming O. Ray of sunshine. *Adam* bomb...

I was their next weekly special.

Oh god.

Koji leaned forward, knife in hand.

"You don't need to do this," I pleaded.

But Koji wasn't listening to me, his eyes on Tomohiro. Koji looked at him, questioningly.

Tomohiro nodded. "Just like filleting a fish."

A tug and the plastic whispered. Koji's knife pushed through.

I tilted my head back and screamed.

While the cat, above the stove, waved.

BLOOD BROTHERS
Mikal Trimm

I like Dr. Kerchoff. She reminds me of somebody's mother.

Not *my* mother, of course. She just seems like one of those old TV moms, always ready to help. Even when she asks the questions, she seems really concerned.

"What are you afraid of, Douglas?"

Nothing. Everything. "Just...I dunno."

"You don't seem to want to get involved with the others, though. According to Mr. Halfey, you won't speak up in group."

"There are—" *Crazy people there,* I'd like to say, but that would be wrong. I know. "The other people are different than me."

Dr. Kerchoff frowns and makes a note. Not like she's mad at me or anything. Just concerned. "Do they frighten you, Douglas?"

"Sometimes. Some of them, I guess."

"What about Mrs. Olaff?" Mrs. Olaff is a little prune-faced woman who sits in her wheelchair and drools. Sometimes she makes pictures on the walls with her spit, but usually she just stares into her lap.

"No, not Mrs. Olaff, I guess." I have to smile at the thought of being afraid of Mrs. Olaff.

Dr. Kerchoff smiles back at me. "Good. That's a *good* thing,

Douglas." She crosses her legs and keeps smiling. "So, are we ready to talk about Tammy now?"

Tammy smiles and her mouth opens and she says whoomph, *and the flames take away her face and hair before I even feel the heat—*

"No. I can't—I don't wanna—"

Dr. Kerchoff nods silently and lets me return to my room.

Shane is here to visit again. He's the only one allowed, now, after that incident the last time Mom and Dad came.

"So, how's it hanging, *kemo sabe?*" Shane has a lighter in his hand. He absently flicks the lid open, shut, open, shut.

He wonders why I don't answer, notices what I'm staring at. "Oh, hey! Sorry." He hastily shoves the Zippo into his pants pocket, embarrassed. "Just habit, man. They won't let me smoke in here."

"Sure. This place makes me nervous, too."

Shane smiles, shrugs his shoulders. "Yeah, this ain't exactly the Ritz, right? How're you holding out in the Land of the Loonies?"

"Not loonies. 'Mentally challenged.'" I already feel better, talking to Shane. He's my best friend. He *gets* me.

Shane gives me the "hard eye," as he calls it. He just looks at me without blinking, very serious in expression, and asks, "Okay, pard. Who's messing with you?"

I want to tell him. I look at him, six-two, blond college-linebacker material, pure muscle. He doesn't *play* football, he doesn't go for sports at all, but he *could,* you can tell. And you know he can fight, just by seeing that gleam in his eye when he asks the question.

"No one, Shane." I lie, badly, but he doesn't catch me at it. "It's all just dandy here in Loonyville."

Shane smiles again, but he's still serious. "You let me know, man. You just let me know." He stands up, already reaching for the lighter in his pocket, visualizing his next smoke, probably.

"Ah don't take kindly to nobody messin' with my friends," he says with a wink. Pure western movie-talk, just like the old days.

Shane walks away with a cowboy's swagger, while I sit here and mind the corral.

Why didn't I tell him?

Night shift.

The lock clicks, and Geoff comes in. He doesn't talk. I hear the flick of his switchblade and the jangle of his keys. Then he's on me, turning me on my stomach and probing my throat with his knife.

"Shhh…" Then the pain starts.

Geoff leaves, finally, tugging up the pants of his hospital issues. I curl up, fighting the urge to scream. No more screaming, I promise myself. Ever.

Shane, where are you…

"Is the chair uncomfortable?" Dr. Kerchoff, ever-caring.

"No. I just, um, I guess maybe I have hemorrhoids or something." Or something.

"I'll have the pharmacy prescribe you some ointment for that. Anything else going on I should know about?"

Does she know something? Can she just look at me and tell when I'm lying? Tammy could do that. It was spooky, sometimes.

"No, ma'am. I just wonder how much longer I need to stay here, is all."

"Well, Douglas, you can answer that question better than I can. Do you *want* to stay here?"

"No. I mean, you've been really nice and all, but…"

She crosses her legs, and I suddenly realize that she's got some pretty nice legs for an older lady. I hope I'm not blushing. I tear my eyes away quickly, praying she didn't read my mind or something. She's looking at her notes, though. I'm safe.

"Douglas." She stares at me again, deep into me, eyes unblinking. "Tell me about Tammy."

Don't. "She's dead." Don't make me think of it. "I mean, she's really, really dead! There's nothing to talk about!" I'm yelling. I can't believe I'm yelling at Dr. Kerchoff.

And here she comes, Tammy laughing and smiling, even though some asshole just doused her with his drink. She walks toward me, her hair dripping, her thin T-shirt clinging to her nipples, and she's too high to care—she thinks it's funny. Hell, it's a rave, right? We're all happy and stoned or zoned or whatever, and the beat is pounding in our ears like the heartbeat of God. She smiles at me, she pushes her way through the crowd, her mouth opens, and...

Whoomph.

Tammy goes up like fireworks.

I don't want to talk about it. Screw you, Doc.

When we were in junior high, I stayed over at Shane's house for the first time. He made me watch old westerns all night long. He told me that his Dad had even named him after a character in a movie. I thought that was pretty cool—I'd been named after my grandfather, and he died when I was two. I don't remember him.

"Watch," Shane said, and I watched those old movies, revived on some streaming service, trying to see what *he* saw. One after another, different strangers riding into different towns. After a while, they all blended into one guy, one Old West superhero, I guess. He rides into town, and people need him, even though they don't know who he is. He helps the weak, even though he isn't a part of the fight. The women love him, even if they're married. The children idolize him, even if he ignores them completely. Then he leaves before anyone can thank him. He just rides off into the sunset, alone.

"That's me." Shane wasn't crying, but I could see the TV screen reflected wetly in his eyes. "I just want to be that guy."

I watched the kid at the end of the movie *Shane,* crying out my friend's name, and I knew what everything meant, at least for a moment. I just wanted my own Shane to say it.

Shane didn't blink, didn't turn his head from the last images of the video.

"I want to be the guy that just comes in and—" He looked at me with his shining eyes. "Saves everything."

That's Shane. That's my pardner.

"You got to get out of here, man." Shane fidgets in his chair; he looks more disturbed by this place than I am. "I mean, this can't be healthy, you know?"

"Healthier than trying to kill myself, I guess." I can say anything to Shane—it's not like my little adventure with the noose is any big secret, anyway.

"Hey!" Shane stands up, grabs my wrist, squeezes hard. "You made a mistake. You were messed up, man. I mean, you watched—you know, you saw something *really bad.* But it's not like you're crazy or something, right? It's not like you'd try it again."

Shane is really hurting me. I twist my wrist, and he lessens up on the pressure, but still he holds on. I'm not sure I've ever seen him this angry before. It's like he just found out I killed his folks or something.

"No." He stares at me. "I wouldn't try it again, Shane. C'mon, I've got a really good friend, right? Why would I want to mess up a perfectly good friendship?"

Shane sits back down, finally releases my arm. "Yeah. That's what I wanted to hear, pard."

"Basically, I have to stay here for fifteen days, minimum. It's the law. After that, it's all up to Dr. Kerchoff, and I think she likes me, so..."

"Kerchoff?" Shane spits out her name like a bullet. "She's a shrink! You think she likes you? You think you're *friends?*" He slaps the table between us. "Every time I visit you, she's there waiting at the desk. Did you know that? And when I leave, she's there waiting, too. You know what she asks me?" There's a challenge in Shane's voice, something ugly and vicious.

"I didn't know she talked to you."

"She wants to know how close we really are, Doug. She wants to know about all the time we spent together before you wound up here, she wants to know about the things we do when we're alone. Doug, she thinks we're *gay*."

"What?" I look at Shane, thinking he's making a bad joke, but he's dead serious. "We're just best friends! How can she think that?"

"Nobody believes in sidekicks anymore, Dougie. Nowadays, when two men ride into the sunset..."

I feel sick, suddenly. Shane keeps staring at me, and I can't think straight. "I had a *girlfriend*."

Tammy smiles and says whoomph...

Shane nods, slowly. "Hey, kemo. Guess what? Doc Kerchoff thinks you might have killed her."

I can't breathe. I'm full of hate and violence, and there's not a damned thing I can do about it. Except...

"Shane?"

He leans closer, motioning for me to keep it down, but he's ready. I can feel the tension in him, just like I can feel my anger.

"There's a guy here that's giving me trouble."

When Shane leaves, he's relaxed. He whistles softly to himself. He's going out to save somebody.

I don't want to talk to Dr. Kerchoff.

I can't believe I ever liked her. I can't believe I found anything about her attractive. She's a cold, manipulative bitch, and I hate her.

"I'm just not seeing any progress, Douglas." I stare at the wall, silent. She waits for me to say something, then finally realizes I'm ignoring her. "This is *serious,* Douglas. In order for you to be released, I'm required to give the state a clear recommendation. I need to be able to tell them that you're not a threat to yourself or others. If you don't cooperate, though, if you don't convince *me*..."

Now she's threatening me. What a great *friend* the doctor turned out to be. Shane was right. "Are we done yet?"

Dr. Kerchoff wants to say something else. I watch her mouth open and close, fish-like. Then her lips tighten into a thin cold slash across her face. She puts her notebook down. "Yes, Douglas." She buzzes angrily for an orderly. "We're finished."

"Did you hear about Geoff?"

It's almost lights out, and two of the orderlies are talking to each other in the hall. My door is open a crack, and they're not whispering. No one whispers here.

"Somebody beat the crap out of him outside his apartment. Cracked his skull, smacked him up bad. Don't look like he'll be coming back for a long time, the way I heard it."

"Guess one of his boyfriends got jealous."

"Man, that's rough!" They both laugh and walk off. I close my door and go back to bed, smiling.

When we were both thirteen or fourteen, Shane borrowed his dad's pocketknife and we did the whole blood brothers thing, cutting our thumbs and holding them together to let the blood mix. "Brothers forever," Shane had said, looking painfully earnest as the blood ran down our wrists. "Forever," I echoed, feeling my pulse and his, the beats meeting there at the wounds.

Shane still believes in forever. He knows what it means.

"They're not letting me leave." I'm sitting here across from Shane, shaking with anger. Shane looks worse than I feel; his face is pale, and I can almost hear his teeth grinding as he takes in the news. "Kerchoff says I have some 'unresolved issues' to deal with."

"*No!*" Shane slaps the table hard with his palm, then begins beating on it with a fist, over and over. "No, no, *no!* They can't just lock you up in here like some kind of criminal! It's not right!"

I lower my voice, give him a look. "Shane, stop shouting or they'll throw you out of here. What if they say you can't visit me anymore, where would we be then?" Shane makes a visible effort to calm down; his muscles shudder with tension.

"Look, don't worry. I'll play their game, okay? I'll speak up in group, I'll be nice and helpful, I'll even talk about—" *and there she is, burning in my memory,* "I'll tell Kerchoff about Tammy. Whatever I can remember. I'll get out of here."

Shane doesn't seem to be listening. "It's not right," he whispers, and then he's gone, out of his chair and past the front desk before I can even call his name.

I sit here alone, feeling like that little kid at the end of the movie. *Shaaaaane...*he'd shouted, and I hear the name echo through my head, but Shane doesn't turn around, he just recedes into the distance.

Tammy is smiling and burning, and she's saying something as she walks toward me. People are screaming all around us, their clothing catching fire as Tammy brushes by them, and all I can think of is the smell of smoke and something else; Tammy reeks of it, an oily, acrid scent stronger than any perfume...

I wake up shouting, only to realize that others are screaming as well, as if we'd all shared the same nightmare. I can still smell smoke, and I realize the odor isn't going away.

I run to my door in my hospital pajamas. It's locked, and I pound on it, screaming for someone to let me out. The lock disengages with a loud click and the door swings open. I run into the hall in time to see the new night-shift guy going from room to room, unlocking the doors and urging the other patients out into the hall, not always gently. Smoke billows from the direction of the staff offices. I can make out individual voices over the din of screaming inmates now, echoing back and forth through the corridor.

"Where'd it start?"

"Records office, looks like!"

"Why aren't the damned fire alarms going off? And where's Carl?" Carl is the night janitor; he'd be cleaning the offices about now. He would have noticed a fire before it got this bad.

I'm so caught up in the exchange that I don't notice Shane until he's right beside me. "Time to hit the trail, Doug," he whispers, tugging at my sleeve to get me to follow him.

"Shane, what are you *doing* here?"

Shane smiles and winks. "Jail break, pard. We gotta get the hell out of Dodge."

"You did this?" My eyes are starting to burn; the smoke is getting thicker. I follow Shane through the clutch of screaming people, and it all reminds me of that other night, the fire, the confusion.

Shane pulls at my arm, snapping me back to the present. "I had to cover your trail. We wouldn't want to leave all those files lying around for anyone to see, right?"

"But Dr. Kerchoff knows—"

"Don't worry about her. Everything's been taken care of." He looks at me, his eyes gleaming through the smoke. "I've had a busy evening." Shane pats his side; when he turns away, I see something hanging there, and it takes me a minute to recognize it. It's a bota, one Shane's had for years. When we were teenagers, we used to fill it with cheap wine and sneak it into the theater under Shane's jacket, then get totally ripped at the midnight movies. I can't imagine why he's carrying it now.

"Hey!" One of the orderlies spots Shane, and he comes charging toward us in full mad-bull mode. Shane moves with the speed of a gunslinger, flicking the top off the bota and aiming a short burst of liquid at the orderly. With his other hand he snaps his Zippo open on his pants leg and lights it in one fluid motion.

The orderly bursts into flame, screaming as he hits the floor rolling, trying to put himself out. Shane grabs my arm and runs, and I stumble along blindly, unable to resist. I smell a familiar, oily scent, and recognition hits me hard enough to make me dizzy. *Kerosene.*

Then we're outside, running through the night, and I'm finally able to breathe again, to think. I stop, and Shane motions me to come on, hurry up, but I'm rooted. "Where are we going, Shane?" My voice is a monotone rasp from the smoke. "They're going to find us. We can't get away."

Shane gapes at me for a moment. "Go? Hell, Mexico, maybe, or Central America, you know, like Butch and Sundance! What does it matter where? We're together again, *compadres!*"

Butch and Sundance were shot down, but I don't mention that, not now. Instead, I picture Tammy, soaked from someone's drink, I thought, running to me in the club, not smiling, no, bad memory—*screaming.* And the smell that wafted off her like cheap perfume, and the flash, the spark, before she did her Roman Candle act. I have only one question left, and then everything I know is wrong, wrong, utterly wrong.

"Why'd you kill Tammy, Shane?"

Shane sighs. The lighter is still in his hand, and he flicks it, open, shut, as I've seen him do a thousand times before. "Christ." He takes a long breath, his other hand resting near the top of the bota. "I was hoping you wouldn't ask me that."

"How could I not ask?" I want to scream, but Tammy's death took that ability away from me. I've screamed enough for one life.

Shane bows his head; his voice is shaking; he's on the verge of tears. "She was cheating on you, buddy. I didn't want to tell you, 'cause I knew how much it'd hurt you, but—"

"No way." He's lying to me, I know it. "Tammy loved me, man, she *loved* me! It was just me and her!"

Shane's head snaps up, his eyes blazing with anger. "Just you and her? Aren't you forgetting someone?"

"You know what I mean!"

"But you don't know what *I* mean!" Shane is screaming now, all of his anger channeled into a wounded roar. "What about us, Doug! Butch and Sundance, all the way! She didn't love you, she just liked getting high, having sex, being the party girl forever-and-ever amen—just a twisted, sick little slut, Doug! I couldn't let her hurt you like that! Not my best friend. Not my *brother.*"

I stand here, not knowing what to believe. I hear the sirens in the distance, the shouts and screams from the institution, and I can't move. My stomach is a cold hard ball, and the rest of me is filled with smoke and ash.

Shane looks at me, tears streaking the grime on his face. "I did all this for you, pard. *All* of it. I wanted to save you."

Shane hands me his lighter, pushing it into my hand when I refuse to respond, closing my fingers around it. Then he takes the bota, uncorks it, and squirts the remaining kerosene all over himself. He drops it to the ground, holds out his arms, and smiles sadly, blinking in pain as the fluid drips into his eyes. "So, what's it going to be, Doug? Do we ride into the sunset, or do we end it all here?"

I stand here and flick the lid of the lighter, open-closed, staring at my friend and thinking about Mexico...

RENT DUE
Alan Orloff

It had taken me thirty-seven years to accept my lot in life, and when I finally did, it felt good to stop tilting at the world and just bob along on life's currents. But a man can't stay adrift forever, so four months ago I washed ashore in this piss-pot of a town and took a room in a shithole of a boarding house with the preposterous name of Hope Hall.

Everything about Hope Hall stank. Tiny rooms crowded together. Cockroach central. Nonstop racket. Broken-down plumbing and disgusting communal kitchen. With no prospects for employment in the offing, I was destined to remain there for many more months.

It was an all-male old-style tenement with high turnover, and it attracted two kinds of men: those who'd seen the inside of a cell and those who hadn't yet been caught. I was one of the former. None of the residents spoke to one another for fear of finding out who they were living among, and I was no exception. I kept to myself, content to wallow in my own misery.

The dive did have one redeeming factor: The price was right. In fact, I hadn't been asked to pay a red cent in rent. The landlady, Lana, a handsome woman despite the hard angles and sharp edges, let me live there in exchange for periodic odd jobs, but so far, she hadn't asked anything of me. She owned a number of run-down apartments and boarding houses in the neighborhood; maybe she felt obliged somehow to throw me a bone. Or maybe it was my charming smile.

Didn't know. Didn't care. I just lived each day as it came, figuring I'd worry about tomorrow tomorrow.

I was a little surprised—although not totally shocked—when she rapped on my door in the middle of the afternoon, in the middle of the week. I invited her in, but since I only had one chair, we stood by the entrance. I towered over her by ten inches.

"Mr. Woodley, it's nice to see you." Lana had squeezed into a sleek black dress, tight in the right places. She was about ten years older than me, but you wouldn't know it by looking. I'd heard her husband died a few years back. I'd also heard she moaned in bed. "I hope things are going well with you."

"I'm fine, but please, call me Arno. To what do I owe this pleasure?"

She sized me up. "You know, I don't think I realized what a big man you are. Muscular. That should work out nicely, all around." She smiled, teeth only, and I was reminded of a crocodile at feeding time. "I've come with a request per our little arrangement. About the rent."

I hoped her request had something to do with me scratching an itch she might have. If that's what it took to square things up for the rent, I was game. There were more unpleasant ways to pay one's debts, I knew from experience.

"I have an odd job for you."

My bubble burst. "Go on."

"I've dug into your background a bit, as I do with all of my tenants. It's my business to know things that might affect me, after all." She fixed her dark eyes on mine. "I'm sure you understand."

"Of course." Always nice to know who you're dealing with.

"I expect that while you may find my request somewhat distasteful, it's nothing you haven't done before, and I trust you'll still uphold your end of the bargain." She ran her tongue across her lower lip, and I tried to imagine what she thought could be distasteful.

I knew I'd have to pay up sooner or later, and now was as good a time as any. I didn't have anything better to do, except pound the pavement, humping for a job, like I'd been doing every day since I alighted in this dreary town. "Let's hear it."

"Very well. You know the pawn shop on Parcher Street? Next to the bakery?"

"Sure." I'd bought a loaf of bread at the bakery once. Never set foot in the pawn shop. Didn't own anything of value, and a guy as broke as me didn't have buying stuff on his mind.

"I want you to rob it."

"Excuse me?"

She laughed. "Well, not exactly *rob* it. The owner owes me money and he refuses to pay me back. So I want you to, ah, retrieve what's rightfully mine."

"By robbing him?"

"Just don't get caught." Her expression hardened. "And if you have to rough him up a bit, then so be it. No one takes advantage of Lana Coreen."

She'd been right about me. I'd done much worse for much less than four months' rent. A deal was a deal. "Give me the details."

Lana laid it all out for me, told me the owner locked up at nine o'clock every night and left out the back door. She wanted me to pull the job the next day, and she only wanted me to take the amount she was owed. She wasn't a thief, after all. "Oh, and one more thing," she added. "Keep my name out of it, will you please?"

"Got it."

Her tone and manner as she outlined her plan told me one thing: Nobody should ever cross her.

She cocked her head at me. "I don't want to make you do anything you don't want to, but this was our deal, right? If you want to break your promise, pack your bags and get out now. Otherwise…" She smiled, and this time it held more warmth. "I expect to see you Friday morning with my money."

The thought of setting out again for parts unknown soured my stomach. I was tired of drifting, and besides, even though this was a shitbag of a town, I was just learning the best places to get drunk. "I'll see you Friday morning, then."

I started to open the door to let Lana out, but she stepped in front of me, fingering a strand of pearls around her neck. "Now that we've got business out of the way, how about a little fun?"

The rumor was true. Lana was a moaner.

On Thursday night, I waited in the alley behind the pawn shop, leaning against a brick wall in the shadows, sucking the last few drags off a cigarette butt I'd found on the ground. It was just after nine o'clock, and I was waiting for the owner to emerge. A nylon stocking perched on the top of my head, like a little sailor's cap, ready to be rolled down. A normal man might have been fighting nerves, but I'd done this so many times I was fighting boredom instead.

Finally, the back door creaked open. I rolled the stocking over my face and crossed the alley in three long strides. The man glanced up just in time to see my fist meet his face. He stumbled backward into the wall, and I grabbed him before his knees hit the concrete. "Let's go, buddy. Back inside. Cooperate and all you'll have is a busted nose. Act up, and you'll have many more scars to remember this evening by."

I clamped my hand around the nape of his neck and shoved him inside, closing the door behind us. He was a spindly, older guy, no physical match for me whatsoever. I spun him around. "Where's the cash?"

He stared at me, still dazed. I slapped him across the cheek.

"Take me to the money."

I grabbed him again and propelled him along, through the

cluttered back storage room into the showroom proper. The small store featured three long glass display cases, with a single cash register. The overhead store lights were off, but the fixtures in the front-window displays gave off enough light to see everything inside clearly.

I hauled the owner over to the cash register. "Let's go, let's go. Open it up."

He fumbled with it for a few seconds, then the drawer slid open with a *ding*.

I pulled a sack out of my pocket, unfolded it, and handed it to the owner. "Hold this." Then I carefully counted Lana's dough from the register and stuffed it into the sack, all with one hand still encircling the owner's pencil neck.

When I finished, I slammed the drawer closed with my elbow and grabbed the sack of money. "See? Painless."

His nostrils flared. "Sinners like you are doomed to suffer for eternity."

Mr. Meek had discovered a spot of courage, it seemed. I was more amused than insulted. "Oh yeah? Well, you know what sinners like me want? A watch. A fucking nice one. You happen to have any of those around?"

His gaze flitted to one side, and I tracked it to one of the display cases.

"Let's look over there, shall we?" I manhandled him over to the case where dozens of watches twinkled under the glass. I gave them a quick once-over. "How about that one? The Omega? My father had one of those, and I'd like to continue the family tradition. Open up the case, will ya?"

"I don't think that would be—"

I mashed his face down onto the glass. "Just open it up. I don't need to hear your opinion on the matter."

"Key's in my pocket." He managed to squeeze out the words as I held his face pressed against the top of the case. I eased up and allowed him to unlock it.

"The Omega there."

He reached for the closest watch, but I jerked him back. "Not that one. Gimme the top-of-the-line model."

The owner reached farther into the case and pulled out a very shiny—and very expensive—Omega. I released my hold on him and snatched it out of his hand. Pushed him back against the wall, but still within arm's reach. "Try anything and you'll be very sorry."

With one eye on him, I set the sack of money down on top of the counter and fastened the watch around my wrist. Nice. Very nice. Just like dear old Dad's.

I glanced at the owner, and he was sneering at me.

"You won't get away with this. I have a strong feeling you're one of Lana's misfits. Just another member of her goon squad. The cops'll find you. Don't think you can hide underneath that stocking."

I laughed. "Do you think I'm afraid of you?"

He spit at me. "Burn in hell. You and the rest of her army of degenerates."

Mr. Meek had transformed completely. Into Mr. Stupid. I stepped forward and unleashed a one-two combination to the gut, then a right uppercut to the chin. His legs buckled and he crumpled to the floor in a heap.

Mr. Meek was a moaner, too.

Lana rolled over in bed onto her side, facing me, covering herself with the sheets. Five minutes ago, she hadn't been the least bit modest when she'd wished me a very good Friday morning. "Thanks again for holding up your end of our agreement. Consider the last four months paid in full." She nodded at my new watch on the cardboard box that served as my nightstand. "Nice piece. I'm glad you found something for yourself. I'm curious, though. Why didn't you take more?"

I'd asked myself the same question when I got home. Didn't have a great answer beyond deciding to go with my gut. "Last time I stole something that needed a fence, things didn't turn out so well. Did five years upstate, in fact."

"Did you at least grab some cash for yourself?" She reached out and tapped me on the nose, playful-like. "I mean, you went to all the trouble to rob the place."

"I just took what you asked me to take. I don't do too well if I have a surplus of money." Somehow money always led to fights, booze, gambling. I'd learned over the years that me and money never mixed with good results.

"Well, the watch is nice. I'm glad you took *something* for yourself. You deserve it."

"Just a souvenir." And guys like me didn't *deserve* anything nice. Guys like me deserved to live in hovels and scrap for our meals.

Something had been bothering me. "Did that guy really owe you money?"

"Would I lie to you?" Lana shifted in bed and the sheets slipped down and I got an eyeful. Two eyefuls. Nothing I hadn't seen before, but it was still nice scenery. She caught me staring and smiled as she slowly pulled the sheets back up. "You're an interesting man, Arno. A real dynamo, too."

"Thanks." I propped myself up on an elbow. "You're pretty interesting yourself. A lady landlord. You like that line of business?"

"Keeps me busy, but it's not very exciting, I must say."

"So, I'm your excitement?"

She laughed softly, to herself, as if she was the only one in on the joke. "More and more, it seems."

"You know, some guys wouldn't like that you're so independent."

She raised an eyebrow, and I wasn't sure she took it as a compliment. "What about you? Do you like that?"

"I don't discriminate. I like all types of women." I coughed to clear my throat. "You rent to a lot of guys like me, right?"

"Like you?"

"Down on their luck. Ex-cons. Drifters. The less fortunate."

"I try to help those I can."

A real saint. "Do you have arrangements with them, too? Like ours? You know, odd jobs in exchange for the rent? Things like I did last night?" I wondered if the owner had been telling the truth about Lana and her army of thugs. I also wondered if Lana screwed all her tenants.

"All of a sudden, you got a lot of questions." Her tone had taken a turn southward.

"Heard some talk, is all."

"Don't believe everything you hear."

I didn't respond and she closed her eyes and I thought for a minute she'd nodded off. Then she opened her baby blues. "You like living here?"

It definitely had its benefits. "More and more."

"Want to pay off your rent for the rest of the year?"

"Sure."

"You haven't even heard what I want you to do yet."

I shrugged. There wasn't much I wouldn't do. "Tell me."

"Another guy owes me money. A *bad* guy. I want you to—"

I interrupted. "Does this guy really owe you money? Or is he like the pawn shop owner? Just some patsy."

Lana glared at me for a couple of beats. Then, "It's hard for a guy without a job to pay the rent. And I'd hate to see someone get evicted who could easily avoid it by doing a favor or two."

I stared back, but she'd made her point.

"As I was saying, I need you to teach him an unforgettable lesson."

"And you think I speak his language?"

"Am I wrong? You did pretty good with the pawn shop owner last night."

I did possess certain talents. I nodded, *go on.*

Lana told me where and when to meet this guy. "I'll arrange for him to be there, but know that this is important, Arno. I need you to take care of him. Be sure to bring a knife. Gunshots attract unwanted attention."

"What exactly does *take care of him* mean?"

She stared at me, gaze steady. "Whatever the situation dictates."

"Kill him?"

She didn't answer, but I could read it in her eyes.

I nodded. I'd killed guys before, when the situation dictated. Besides, I had rent to pay.

On the morning of the meeting, I hoofed it from the boarding house to the rendezvous location in a downtrodden neighborhood on the west side of town. When I found the pre-arranged spot, I paused for a moment to get my bearings. I was standing at the open mouth of an alley, and the opposite end was blocked by a U-Haul truck. There was no sign of the man I was supposed to meet, or anyone else for that matter. I consulted the new Omega on my wrist. Still a few minutes early.

Cautiously, I made my way down the block-long alley, hand in my pocket, gripping the knife. I'd once been ambushed when I was in my twenties, so I always paid attention to my surroundings, especially in situations like this. When I'd gotten about halfway down the alley, I heard a vehicle grinding gears behind me, and I turned in time to watch a white panel van pull across the mouth of the alley, effectively sealing it off on both ends.

I also became aware of a clot of people gathered on a fire escape about fifteen feet off the ground a little farther ahead, on my left.

There were ten or twelve people up there, a few sitting on chairs, the rest standing behind. I couldn't make out any faces, save one. Lana leaned over the side rail with that crocodile smile on her face and a big yellow hat on her head, as if she were in the owner's box at the Kentucky Derby.

The bottom of my stomach dropped three floors. I didn't know what was going on, but I had the feeling I was part of the main event.

To my right, a door swung open on creaky hinges, and a mountain of a man leaped into the alley. I recognized the goon as Rickshaw Flanagan, a dirty SOB who never missed the chance to tout his self-proclaimed title, the Meanest Mixed-Breed in the city. If I wasn't mistaken, he lived in a flophouse over on Bushnell Avenue, owned by none other than Lana the Landlady.

Rickshaw passed a knife from hand to hand as he approached, weight on the balls of his feet, body slightly crouched. He'd done this before, too, I knew, but he didn't have nearly as much compassion for people as I did.

I whipped my knife out, mirrored his stance, and both of us began circling, each looking for a weakness or momentary lapse in concentration to exploit. A few tentative lunges, none successful, and our little dance continued.

Up on the fire escape, people cheered and jeered with each parry. Rickshaw and I were the gladiators in this macabre battle, and I tried to channel my fury at being duped by Lana into a devastating attack on Rickshaw.

I was sure this wouldn't end well for at least one of us.

I was a big man, but Rickshaw outweighed me by forty pounds. He was stronger, I'd give him that, but I was faster. And smarter.

I considered reasoning with him, but what could I possibly say? Our situation was clear. No place to run. No place to hide. Last man standing was the victor. The prize: life.

We kept circling. I kept one eye on the knife, the other on his face, searching for a tell. When he clenched his jaw, I knew he was about to make his big move. I feinted to my left, waited for him to react, then surged directly at him, grabbed his knife arm and twisted, twisted, twisted, using my hip to gain leverage. He grunted and dropped his blade, then started scrabbling to grab my knife hand. I managed to avoid his grasp and stamped my heel down onto his foot, then wheeled and elbowed him in the breadbasket.

I spun around and found myself face-to-face with the big oaf, so I threw a roundhouse with my left. He pulled his head back at the last moment and I didn't connect solidly, but my watch caught him on his rock-hard cheekbone, opening up a nice cut.

He started to counter with a jab. I stepped forward, smashed him in the nose with a hard left, and was rewarded with the sweet sound of his nose breaking. He rocked back from the impact, eyes watery.

I had no choice but to drive my knife into his stomach and rip it upward.

Blood spurted across my face as Rickshaw slumped to the ground.

I loomed over him for a few seconds, making sure he was dead, ready to finish things off and end his suffering if he wasn't quite there. The Christian thing to do.

When I was sure he was gone, I turned my attention to the fire escape where Lana was still at the rail. Her smile had disappeared, leaving an expression cold enough to make ice cubes. The faces of the others were hidden in the shadow of the grillwork landing above, but I'm pretty sure I saw folding money exchanging hands as the observers babbled excitedly.

I turned away from the audience, took inventory. Nothing broken. Nothing bleeding. Just a sore left hand. I glanced down at my left wrist and saw that the crystal of my new Omega had shattered during the fight, probably when it had collided with Rickshaw's Neanderthal cheekbone.

A sudden hush fell over the onlookers, and I felt a presence behind me. I whirled around to face another guy, larger even than Rickshaw, lumbering toward me. I'd seen him before, too. Lived in my building. He'd moved into the unit above mine a few weeks ago.

The new guy had also obeyed Lana and brought a knife. He halted just out of reach and brandished his weapon. The light glinted off the sharp blade.

"Nothing personal, Mack," he called out, baring his teeth. "Just gotta pay the rent."

LAST EXIT BEFORE TOLL
Hugh Lessig

The beggar stands at the end of the exit ramp. His sign proclaims that he fought in Vietnam, that he's homeless and needs money, that God blesses us all.

"But does he forgive?" I whisper.

I have Mr. Berry on the line. He wanted to know when I was approaching the safe house and now he's jabbering away with directions like I'm going on vacation. Still, I'd rather hear that damn nasal twang. A silent Mr. Berry is to be feared.

"Did you just say something, Joe? Something about forgiveness?"

"I'm just talking to myself."

That gets a laugh. "My grandmother said people who talk to themselves have money in the bank. Which reminds me, I need to wire you cash. Once you get off the interstate, turn left into Phoebus. It's a nice little bungalow."

I'm thinking one of two things. Either someone waits for me there, or I'll get settled and comfortable before a tentative knock comes at the door, a killer's hand tapping lightly, like a child wondering if you can come out and play.

The red light catches me and the beggar steps closer. A rhythmic ticking reverberates in the cab of my pickup, Mr. Berry's manicured nails drumming against his desk. Christ, I can see him doing it. Tick-Tick-Tick. Wait a beat. Tick-Tick-Tick. You catalog a person's nervous habits after twenty years of guarding their mistresses, putting out their fires, breaking the thumbs of their enemies and worse, so much goddamn worse that all you hear are the screams that twist your conscience like a pair of needle-nose pliers. Yet that damn ticking sounds like he's sitting next to me, smelling of Grand Marnier and Cuban cigars.

"Hampton Roads, Virginia," Mr. Berry says. "Big military area. Lots of transients. People come and go all the time. You'll blend in and people won't notice you. You sound hoarse. Catching a cold?"

This fucking light won't change. The beggar makes eye contact as I reach for the gun in the side pocket of the door. During the drive from Pennsylvania, I'd steered with one hand and held the gun with the other. I drove down the Eastern Shore, through crossroads towns and stretches of countryside where you wonder what people did for fun. That gun never left my hand. Sometimes I screamed at the windshield. Now my throat is all raspy.

"I got this cold, Mr. Berry. Making me hoarse."

"You'll like Hampton Roads. I got friends there. You can watch aircraft carriers leave Norfolk. Once I saw a submarine, I shit you not. Go for walks on the beach once you're settled in. Enjoy some personal time. When you screw up this bad, it's important to get your head back on straight."

"You want me to go for walks alone? Unprotected?"

"Nothing to fear except the jellyfish. Am I right? Now don't worry about anything. I have to take this call."

He laughs easily, which terrifies me. I rest my head on the steering wheel as the beggar taps on the window. A black ball cap proclaims his veteran status. His T-shirt had once been white. His bony hips barely hold up a pair of blue jeans, shined with dirt and torn at the knees. I think there's a skeleton under those clothes. I lower the window.

"Appreciate some change," the beggar says.

A small pile of coins has accumulated in the middle console

since going into cash-only mode. It takes me back. Mom used to keep coins in a coffee can above the stove. When I was ten years old, I took two fistfuls of change to school, stopping along the way to buy tube socks at the drug store. When recess came, I put the change in one sock and went looking for the eighth-grader who'd been terrorizing us. I swung that damn thing like a berserker and the bastard suffered what they call a blowout fracture, something about a ruptured eye socket. To this day, it remains in my top ten. The playground was stilled to silence. Even Ms. Noel, our crew-cutted, gender-fluid gym coach, looked like she wanted to shit her pants.

"The Vietnam War was a lie," I say. "We had no business being there. How many babies did you kill?"

He takes half a step backward, but only half. His watery eyes wander. "What are you holding down there?"

I laugh and bring up the gun. "It's a hammerless Smith and Wesson, old timer."

He nods. "Hammerless is a misnomer. The hammer is merely enclosed. It's a long, hard trigger pull, but men have another trigger inside their head. The ability to pull that one makes all the difference."

The light had turned green, and now it returns to red. The old man and I exchange looks.

"I'm not starving, and I don't have a sob story," he said. "I'd just like to stop by the McDonald's for some coffee."

He holds out a gnarled hand. I scoop the change from the console and hand it over. A few coins fall onto the shoulder of the road. His smile turns to a grimace as he bends to pick them up. I'm about to drive off when he looks up and squints into the sun. "Why are you so sad?"

"Do I sound sad, old man?"

"There're two tear tracks on your face. I can see the salt trails. Seen it before in some men."

I gun the engine, leaving this man behind.

* * *

Over the next three days, I figure out the roads and tolls, planning escape routes should it come to that, reading the news from Pennsylvania as people wonder who would do such a terrible thing. A psychologist says the poor man who survived will never be the same.

Join the club.

On the fourth day, I find the nearest beach at an old Army base named Fort Monroe that is now home to civilians. I stand in the hot sand, facing the headwaters of the Chesapeake Bay as a giant container ship crawls toward the open sea. I imagine swimming out there, hitching a ride to the four corners of the world. Then the ship recedes, and my tears follow old trails, as if the captain gave up because I waited too long. Something tells me to swim out there anyway and get lost in the current. Just hold my breath and go under. Maybe I'd see a submarine on the way down. Then a couple of kids scamper into the water near me and their mother, or maybe their grandmother, plants an umbrella not twenty feet from where I stand. I doubt Mr. Berry sent her. Her smile washes over me and tells me today is not the day.

On the morning of the fifth day, the beggar appears on my porch. I'm walking past the front window and there he is, like he beamed down from a fucking spaceship. I keep the chain on the door and speak through the narrow opening.

"You the Welcome Wagon?"

He shuffles his feet. The loose sole of one boot flaps against the wood. His cracked face reminds me of driftwood art, those glittering eyes like found stones. He points with his chin to my pickup parked on the street.

"I noticed your vehicle. You were the man who gave me change a while back." He raises one arm and winces. "Is that your land also?"

Knee-high grass covers the vacant lot next door. On the far

side, a tall security fence dog-legs toward a metal-fabricating shop. "That's not my land. I'm renting. Don't know who owns the business, either."

The beggar nods toward the short extension of the L-shaped lot. "I'd like to sleep over there. Maybe build a little fire. I got a couple of blankets and I won't make trouble."

"Why there?"

"The guy who owns that business saves me food. You gave me some change. And people won't see me from the street. I figure that's the trifecta."

"It was just change."

His broken-keyboard grin favors me. "It's still money."

As he shuffles off the porch, I grab his belt loop. "Hold on a second. Tell me about Vietnam. Where'd you fight? You know something about guns."

He gently pries away my finger. "I was there in sixty-six and went back in seventy-two. Most places I fought in didn't have a name, at least none that I remember. Please don't ask if I killed anyone. It's rude. I don't mind the baby-killing insult. Some people need to lash out and it doesn't really mean anything."

I let that pass. "How did you do it? In Vietnam, I mean. You get up every day and go out there, knowing you could die in the next second and never have a chance to think about it."

His eyes shine at me. "You put one foot in front of the other. It's no deep secret. Look, I just want to make a fire and not be bothered."

I call Mr. Berry. He sounds annoyed and promises to call back in fifteen minutes. Half an hour later, my phone buzzes. I'm reading news stories about myself: the mystery man who left a family in tears.

"I need a bigger place," I say. "Maybe you can move me down to Norfolk or Virginia Beach."

Mr. Berry yawns. "I understand your point, Joe, but no can

do. Unless you think someone's made you, which I have a hard time believing. You need to stay quiet and ride this thing out. You're a little radioactive because of that kid."

He wasn't a kid, but whatever.

"Are you taking your blood pressure pills?" he asks.

"Yes, sir."

"You're not a young man. Maybe I'll move you into a senior living high rise. You hook up with some GILF and fuck her brains out, squeeze her saggy tits, take her money, am I right?"

"You say the word, Mr. Berry. I'm all over those saggy tits."

We share a laugh, louder on his end than mine. "Is there some specific concern, Joe? Something I can address with a quick call?"

I tell him about the beggar. He lets loose a long, theatrical sigh. It tells me he's about to lay down the law. "This is your Vietnam thing all over again. The guilt coming back. Combined with what happened in Pennsylvania, I see why it bothers you. Listen to me. Dr. Fucking Phil."

"Did you send the beggar after me?"

"Christ, Joe. A beggar? What makes you think that? You're sixty-eight years old. I owe you my life five times over. I only wish peace for you, my friend."

"What sort of peace, sir?"

He hangs up.

The next morning, tendrils of gray smoke curl skyward from the dog-legged portion of the vacant lot. I can't see the beggar. Maybe he's already reported for work at the exit ramp. I make some toast and coffee and watch from the kitchen table. Fifteen minutes later, he appears and carefully picks his way through the tall grass, ghosting through the fog toward the interstate.

When I'm sure he's gone, I go out and check his campsite. A circle of stones encloses the embers of a once-pitiful fire. His backpack is covered with road grime and it rattles when I pick it up. I unzip one pocket and fish out three amber bottles.

Prescription meds. The names mean nothing. The second pocket has a pint of Wild Turkey, almost empty, and under that is a pristine plastic case. It pops open to reveal a yellow pentagram hanging from a red ribbon. Attached to the red ribbon is the letter V.

I take a picture with my phone and try to put everything back like I found it. Back inside, an online search tells me that the beggar owns a Bronze star with a V for valor. I imagine him as a young man, spraying bullets from an M-16 while carrying wounded buddies to safety.

I read more news out of Pennsylvania. Security footage shows a man in a black stocking mask, black pants and black boots. He looks relatively young and thin, which pleases me. The presence of cameras is an unwelcome surprise, but I'm walking away from the shot. The story recycles the same quote from a local police chief. "This man is a coward through and through. He'll face judgment one day, but in the meantime, we'll catch him."

I fall asleep looking at the phone. In my dream, an Army doctor twists a needle in my arm and says, "This is what you get, you redneck retard." I'm jolted awake, unable to breathe for a few terrifying moments. I return to the kitchen and check the time. It's afternoon now, and more gray smoke rises from the unseen corner of the vacant lot. Is this my new life? Checking the news and gazing out the window?

I tuck the revolver in the waistband of my jeans and walk out there. The beggar sits cross-legged near the fire and rummages through that shitty backpack. "Someone has been through my stuff," he says. "Did you see anyone come over here?"

"It was me. I didn't take anything."

His blue eyes blaze with new-found strength. "Damn, buddy. Maybe I should come inside and rummage through your drawers."

"You won a medal."

"Yeah, for killing all those babies." He stands up and winces in pain. I figure he's just stiff, but then he doubles over and falls to the ground. His shirt rides up to reveal a series of bruises, black and blue and tinged sickly green. I study the pattern with a practiced eye.

"Someone has been beating you over time," I say.

"What about it?"

"Tell me where they are."

He waves a hand. "These guys are going around beating up homeless people. That's why I wanted to hide here. They can't see me from the street, and you look like someone who wouldn't put up with a gang of would-be toughs. There's a VA hospital on the other side of the interstate. They kicked me out of the dom because I snuck in booze."

"Dom?"

"Domiciliary," he said. "The homeless can go there. But the VA got rules. I don't like rules. Hell, I don't like four walls around me."

Once again, we find ourselves in agreement. After years of opening doors ahead of Mr. Berry and checking closets and bathroom stalls, I learned to hate closed spaces.

The sympathy must be written on my face, because the beggar smiles. "What's your problem with the war anyway? You weren't some long-haired protester, burning the flag or skedaddling up to Canada. You look like someone who listened to Merle Haggard and beat up kids who tried to sneak past you with fake IDs."

"I didn't go to Vietnam because I had no desire to get killed by someone hiding in the jungle," I say. "I prefer a straight-up fight."

Listen to me.

"You were scared," the beggar said. "We all were. I came home and couldn't eat in a restaurant without my back to the wall. I got a job as a welder at the Newport News shipyard, but I couldn't deal with tight spaces. Then I drank. You don't show up drunk for work at a nuclear shipyard, let me tell you."

"You got family?"

He pokes at the circle of rocks. "I got an ex-wife and a

daughter. She's going after her doctorate in philosophy, the daughter, I mean. The wife moved on long ago, but my daughter keeps in touch."

He sniffs back a sob and blows his nose out the side. I place two fingers on my jugular as static fills my ears. I take the hammerless revolver and place it on the ground next to him.

"In case those men come back," I say.

That night, I wake up from the same dream with the Army doctor twisting the needle. I'm apologizing for what happened at the physical. I smoked pot for a week and drank bourbon the night before. Then I threw up on the doctor's shoes. But he's still calling me a redneck retard and twisting that goddamn needle. Then I'm up and awake, staring into the dark of this damn bungalow and listening to the phantom echoes of all the screams I've caused. I grab the phone and find news from Pennsylvania.

They're looking at human-interest angles now.

A.D. Cordell ran a small moving company in eastern Pennsylvania, an easy drive to New York along Interstate 80. His real name was Annunziato Cordelli, and he employed men to steal consumer electronics from trucks. He transported stolen TVs, laptops, and phones to Mr. Berry's stores in the Bronx and Brooklyn while operating a legitimate moving business. He mixed in stolen stuff with the family furniture and made side trips to New York.

Everyone liked A.D. Cordell. He made funny commercials about how he could move your stuff without breaking the fine China. He coached Little League and was active in the Chamber of Commerce.

But he had been skimming for months and ignored several chances to square things. Then he said something to Mr. Berry, an insult of some sort, and I got the call. I drove down there, watched his place for a few days and discovered he worked late

Thursday night at his warehouse. It would be a routine job.

That night, the warehouse was cool and dark. I could hear Cordell in the far corner, talking to someone. I moved closer behind pallets and stacked boxes, pulling down my ski mask and checking the thirty-eight. Cordell was asking this guy if the Philadelphia Eagles could win the Super Bowl again. The other guy laughed and said something I didn't understand. The other guy sounded harmless, not that I cared. Graveyards are full of people who end up in the wrong place at the wrong time. I've put some there.

But when I turned the corner, the other man had this saggy-eyed, vacant look, and he saw me and screamed. Cordell reached for something and I shot him in the head.

The other guy howled with grief. It turned into a keening wail as he dropped to his knees, spattered with Cordell's blood and brains. The guy didn't even care that I had a gun. He sat there, shaking a dead man whose head flopped back and forth.

It turns out that Cordell was taking care of this man, who was what they call developmentally disabled. We called it something else back in the day. Cordell paid for this guy's apartment and gave him food and a small paycheck for cleaning up around the warehouse. Somehow, Cordell squeezed that in between Little League and making funny commercials. Maybe that's why he was skimming from Mr. Berry, because he needed extra cash.

So yeah, the human-interest angle is big with this one. The news media are having a field day, speculating about the monster who could do this and leave this poor kid with nightmares for the rest of his life.

I push up from the couch and look toward the beggar's camp. Something moves awkwardly through the tall grass. At first I think a dog has been hit by a car, but then I see the beggar dragging himself toward me. His face appears blackened in the moonlight, but I'm sure it's blood. He stops crawling when I run out.

"Don't touch me," he whispers.

I pull at his arm and his scream cuts through me like a hot knife. It's a scream that comes with glowing cigarette tips and ball-peen hammers and electrodes. I've heard that scream a thousand times, and it continues after I release him, those eyes clenched shut.

"Get hold of yourself," I say.

He curls up into a ball. That pitiful wail brings back the warehouse, that innocent face that will never be the same. It brings back all the years and all the wrongs. Now I'm sixty-eight years old and take blood-pressure pills.

"What's your name?" I demand.

"Charles. Charlie."

"Now you listen. I'm picking you up and getting you off this grass. I won't touch your arm." I put both hands under his hips and lift. A couple of sheets of paper couldn't have weighed more. I lay him on the front porch and go inside for some water and aspirin.

"You got pills in that backpack," I say. "You need something from there?"

Charlie shakes his head. "They won't help with the pain. Anti-depressants, but I don't take 'em. Don't mix with the alcohol. Lord, I can't see."

Blood seeps into his eyes from a forehead cut. It bleeds like hell, but it isn't serious. I go to the bathroom and get my tactical medical pack. It's got clotting bandages and iodine swabs and a small surgical kit to remove bullets. I fill up a couple of plastic bags with ice from the fridge. When I come back on the porch, Charlie is sitting up and moving his shoulder.

"I popped it back into place," he said.

Tough guy, this Charlie.

"Those men do this?" I ask.

"Yes."

"Describe them."

He points across the street. "Right there."

Five young men cluster near a streetlight, white dudes with

shaved heads, hands in pockets. They slouch with pretend courage.

"They took your gun, too," Charlie says. "I'm sorry about that."

The dark street now seems very quiet and I can see more clearly, as if a fog has lifted. I look toward the exit where Charlie and I first met. "They're hopped up on something, more than booze, I think," Charlie says. He looks up with those hound-dog eyes. "I could use a drink of water. I feel awful."

I go inside and pour a glass of water from the faucet. I find my bottle of Maker's Mark, which should do just as well as Wild Turkey. I can't open the front door because Charlie is leaning against it.

"Charlie. Move your skinny ass."

I push against the door and he slumps sideways, his head hitting the porch. Both hands clutch at his chest, his mouth frozen into a grimace, heavy-lidded eyes staring at nothing. I try to close those eyes, but it won't take. Maybe when you've seen so much, your eyes never close. Maybe he wants to watch what I'll do next, to see if I'll redeem myself before it all ends.

The men laugh among themselves, sharing some private joke.

"You killed him," I call out. "You killed poor Charlie here."

One man spread his hands in a gesture of helplessness, as if he doesn't know what I'm talking about.

I put one foot in front of the other, just like Charlie did in the jungle. Now the streetscape is crystal clear, as if I'm seeing things through a young man's eyes, a man with his whole life ahead of him. The punk holds my gun sideways, like some half-assed gangbanger. I don't stop until the gun is inches away.

"You have my gun," I say. "I want it back."

"Sure, old man. Just take it."

He's expecting me to grab the gun or twist his wrist. Instead, I step forward and let the barrel touch my chest. I bend at the knees and put all my strength into an uppercut that sinks into his breadbasket. He falls like a stone and I pick up the gun. He scrambles to his knees, looks at me with wild and confused eyes and vomits near my feet.

I stare at the vile, brown batter and remember how I threw up in front of that Army doctor, screwing up my physical on purpose because I was so damned scared of going over there.

"You killed poor Charlie," I said. "He was a hero."

Another man steps forward, fists clenched. I let him swing and miss, then break his nose with the heel of my hand. A bullet bites into my shoulder and throws me off stride. Another man takes it in the teeth. The trigger pull on a hammerless is long and hard but I've always liked it that way. Two men fall. Then comes a pop-pop and bullets hit me like playground punches. These guys can't shoot straight and now they retreat, laughing in the manner of frightened men. I just put one foot in front of the other, moving forward.

WE LIVE HERE

Jarrett Kaufman

1.

The barefoot girl is tossing rocks into the shallow creek when she hears a car approach on the dirt road. She looks up at the beam bridge. She sees the janky gold car pass by and she catches a glimpse of an old man with a nest of silver hair hunched behind the steering wheel. The car kicks up dust that hovers like a brown cloud over the creek. The girl lingers at the bank and looks down at the meaty stubs of her mangled foot. She'd stopped wearing shoes after the operation because they hurt her bad foot. She knows her parents hate that foot. The girl is certain the gray scars remind them of the accident. She can see that shame in their eyes.

It happened a year ago at a Motel 6 near St. Louis during a snowstorm. The girl's mother woke her. She was shaking her. The girl could hear her father yelling. She saw him and a masked man by the door, grappling over a gun. The mother took the girl from her bed and pushed her out of the window. There wasn't time for her to grab a coat or her boots. The mother told the girl to run. "Run," she yelled and the girl sprinted barefoot in the icy snow. She scurried through the frigid night air and the whirling wet snow, and she went to a Dairy Queen across the street. It was closed and the girl panicked. She banged on the windows. Then the girl heard the gunshot. So she ran. She ran down the street weeping, found a dumpster in an alley behind an abandoned K-Mart and hid in it. She buried herself in the soggy trash and brown snow.

They found her two hours later. "Here," the police officer yelled. "Over here."

EMTs pulled the girl out of the dumpster. They carried her to the ambulance.

"I want to go home," the girl stuttered. Her face was blue. "Can I go home?"

The old man parks. He sits in his Chevrolet Caprice and he watches the girl as she walks up from the creek. The hot August wind gusts across the dirt road and the girl's brown hair flies over her shoulders like ocean breakers. "That's it," the old man says. "This way."

He coughs. The old man fumbles a bottle of methadone out of his shirt pocket and chews down a tablet. He grabs the 7-Up from the center cup holder and takes a gulp to wash down the chalky medication. Then he flips down the visor mirror. He wipes the sweat off his yellow skin; the jaundice has gotten worse. The old man gazes at the dark scar on his face. Parker had done that. Parker had marked him after he'd gone ten thousand dollars in the hole in one night of bad blackjack.

The old man rolls down the car window. He takes out his wallet and sits there and he waits for the girl. He breathes in the humid air and exhales with a moan. He is tired. He is sick. He'd told Parker that, but there was no use. He owed Parker. This was all that mattered.

The old man wags a dollar bill at the girl. "Do you want it?" he asks. "Little girl."

She shrugs. The girl considers the old man. She ponders his

scar. "Yes."

"Here," the old man says. He holds out the dollar. He holds it there.

When the old man opens the car door, the girl springs off the dirt road and bolts into the cow pasture. The tang of wet dung clings to the dank country air as she cuts across the meadow. The girl keeps moving. She crosses a gully that's teeming with blackberry cane. She looks back toward the creek and the gold car is gone. So the girl runs into the woods, walks toward the rail fence and the ramshackle farmhouse where she and her parents have lived for two months.

The girl rushes to the back door but hesitates when she hears her mother yelling at her father through the half-open kitchen window. The girl steps back. Her gut coils. Her father shouldn't be home. He should be at work. The girl punches her fists into the front pockets of her khaki shorts and strolls gloomily to the magnolia tree. She sits down in the grass and leans back against the trunk. She stretches out her legs over the leaf- and twig-cluttered ground and listens to her parents argue.

2.

The father paces the kitchen floor. His hair is tussled. "Just listen to me," he says.

"I could hit you," the mother howls. She clutches a skillet in her hand.

"They're here. I saw a man in town. Why can't you believe that?"

"No," she pleads. "Parker doesn't know we're here. Why can't *you* believe that?"

The mother wanders to the sink. Dirty dishes and a pile of grimy pots are stacked on the countertop. She tosses the skillet in the sink before drifting to the breakfast table. She sits in the chair. Her hair is frizzled from the wet Midwestern heat. There's a rusted box fan positioned in the corner next to the living room. It pushes hot air over the linoleum floor. "No," she frets. It's impossible. She believes that. They had stayed on the move for ten months. "No," she says. "We disappeared." The mother pulls a Marlboro from her purse and lights it. She takes a drag. "You're wrong," she says. She blows smoke. She says, "You're always wrong."

The father looks for the daughter. He glances into the living room. "Sweetheart?" he calls.

"I let her go to the creek. I let her go," the mother says. "She's fine."

The father smirks. He sits in a chair next to the mother at the breakfast table. He gawks at the mess—the shriveled orange peels and the dirty plates and the soiled napkins. He fingers his head where the bullet had grazed his scalp that night at the Motel 6. He looks at the mother. He knows he hadn't really seen anyone in town. He knows she's right. He knows it's his fear and paranoia.

"You said it would be different here," the mother reminds him.

The father says, "I know what I said."

"Do you?" She draws on her Marlboro.

"We can't pretend like nothing happened," he says.

"You're the only one pretending."

They say nothing for some time while the father fiddles with a dry orange peel.

"We can't go back," the mother says. She scratches her neck. "I won't go back."

He had worked as a clerk for three years at Ten Pin Bowl in St. Louis. It was the hub of Parker's racket in Midtown where the gambling profits were laundered. The father had learned that the dirty cash was stored in a chest freezer in the basement office. He and the mother had planned for months and the father had heisted the cash on a Tuesday night after Parker had left to visit his ill mother in Miami. The father broke into the freezer with bolt cutters. He grabbed the cash in an excited frenzy. He would never again have to feed his family Ramen noodles for dinner or buy his daughter a birthday gift at Goodwill. The father filled a duffel bag with sixty bricks of cash that totaled three hundred thousand dollars. Then he sped home. Everything was in order. The mother had packed their bags. She'd destroyed their credit cards and checks and cell phones. They'd driven to a Motel 6 across the Mississippi River where the mother and the father celebrated. They sipped on box wine and played with the cash on the floor, and their daughter lay on the pull-out bed and watched *The Three Stooges* on TV until she fell asleep.

The father drops the orange peel. He says, "If you think frostbite is the worst—"

"Parker," the mother yells. "Parker Parker Parker." She screams, yells, "Stop."

The mother stares at the father in a pitiful gaze as she recalls with a miserable clarity all the cities they've lived in this last year—Indianapolis, Chicago, Milwaukee. After that, there was Louisville and Kansas City and now there's Eldora in Iowa. She watches the father yank on the collar of his uniform. He's worked at the Suzuki factory in town for three weeks now. She knows the game. She understands his need to run. It's what he does. He'll rush home. He'll say he saw someone. He'll say they've been found and he'll demand they leave. But all that was supposed to have ended when they arrived here. He'd vowed that it would stop. He'd even gotten on his knees at a Denny's parking lot in Kentucky and swore it. He'd kissed the mother and hugged the daughter. "I swear," he'd said.

The father watches the mother smoke. He says, "I hate that you smoke. It's—"

"It's what?" she asks. She sparks the lighter twice.

"It's—" the father hesitates. "It's damned filthy, that's what it is."

The mother takes a wicked drag. "Fuck you."

3.

The old man drives the Chevy into the woods and parks the car near a clearing in a knot of pine trees. He turns off the engine. He opens the glovebox. The old man grabs the .38 Special and checks the safety lock. He tucks the revolver into his belt. He opens the car door and walks through the woods to the rickety rail fence. The old man stares at the girl. She reminds him of his daughter Tina. The girl looks just like her, sitting crossed-legged like that underneath the magnolia tree in the glimmering sunlight. The old man rubs his eyes. He looks at the girl again.

"Hey," the old man says. He shades his eyes from the sun. "Little girl."

The girl eyes him. She remembers now. She had seen the old man at the hospital.

It was morning. The father and the mother took the girl from the hospital bed. They sat her in a cold wheelchair. The father said, "Ready?" and kissed her before he pushed her into the hallway. The girl knew that they'd have to leave because a police officer had questioned them the night before about the incident at the Motel 6. He'd sat on a chair and scratched at a red mole on his chin while scribbling on a notepad. Then a woman from Child Services took over.

The father and the mother rushed the girl to the exit near the cafeteria. They pushed the girl through the exit but an orderly followed them outside. "Go," the father said, and the mother rolled the girl to the Windstar. When the orderly reached for the father's arm, the father lunged at him. He struck the man in the neck and the man buckled and writhed on the icy concrete. The father bolted. He dove into the van, started the engine and skidded out of the parking lot. The girl peered out the back window and saw the old man. He stood in front of a red brick building. He was talking on a cell phone underneath an awning that said: *Pickle's Deli.*

The father passed the Arch on I-70. He said, "I had to do it. He was bad."

"How do you know that?" the girl asked.

"Sweetheart," the mother said. She grabbed the girl's nose. "They're all bad."

The old man dawdles in the quack grass. He stares at the girl. He says, "Hey."

The girl peels a chunk of bark off the tree trunk. She smells it.

"Hey," he says again. He grips the rail fence with both hands. "Little girl."

The old man steps into a thicket of orange tiger lilies that sprout near the rail fence. His wife used to garden lilies at their house in Cleveland. "Tina," he says, recalling a day in 1979 when his own daughter was nine years old. He and his wife were lounging on the patio. She drank Lipton's iced tea and thumbed a *Redbook*; he smoked a cigar and watched his daughter chase grasshoppers in the backyard. He called to her. "Tina," he said. She ran to him and he tried to hold her in his arms, but she twisted free. So he yanked her arm. He yelled, "Tina," but she raced to her mother.

"Let her be," the mother said and took the girl into the kitchen for a Popsicle.

"Fine," he said. He grabbed his cigar. "Jesus Pete," he said. He hollered, "Fine."

That night, he left when his wife and daughter were asleep. There was a three-day seventy-five-thousand-dollar poker game in St. Louis. He packed his bag in the dark next to the window. He swiped the emergency cash that was stashed in the sock drawer. He walked four miles to the Greyhound station, boarded the bus and sat in the back row. He sat alone and the bus departed and he didn't know at that moment that he'd never return to Cleveland or that he'd never see his daughter again. He gazed out the window and watched the city buildings fade to a glow on the horizon. The glow shrank to a speck and the speck turned to nothing but the black of night, and he felt joy.

The old man coughs again. The searing pain in his chest blots out the memory of Tina and he is grateful for that. He hacks and this time there's blood in his spit. The doctor said this would happen. He'd said, "Hemoptysis," at the last appointment in July. The old man wipes his mouth clean and chews another methadone tablet. Then he waves at the girl but she turns her head and looks away and the old man flares with rage. He looks at the farmhouse. He hears the mother's shouts echo out of the kitchen window. He hears the father holler, too. The old man touches the handle of his .38 Special and says the girl's name: "Valerie."

4.

The father reaches for the mother and touches her arm in a delicate way, as if she is a fragile doll, but the mother pitches her cigarette at him. Fiery ash explodes in the air. She huffs and lights another Marlboro. "It will be a risk if we stay here," the father says as he struts to the refrigerator. He grabs a carton of milk. The mother huffs again so the father slams the door closed and returns to the table. "What?" he says, then takes a loud nasty slurp of the milk.

The mother sags in her chair. She punches out her cigarette in a piece of old burnt toast that lay on a frayed napkin. She looks at the husband searchingly. The mother has a basic need: She wants the father to feel safe so that he can make her feel safe. "It will be a risk if we *don't* stay here," she says bitterly. She grabs the bottom of her shirt, knots the fabric and twists it in her hands. "I'm tired," the mother says. "I'm so tired."

She pulls at her collar and digs her fingernails into the hives that dot her neck. Her own mother had suffered from hives, as well. She can remember how her mother's neck swelled like a turkey wattle when her father grabbed the Scotch. He was a mean drunk who spent much of her childhood hungover in the city jails. Her mother liked to say he was cursed with Cherokee blood.

The mother scratches the welts and the father grabs her wrist and pulls her clawed fingers off her neck. She gazes up at him. He'd suffered, too. She knows that. She can see the flicker of an old agony in his eyes. It's the same dark pain that she had seen in his eyes when she used to study the St. Joseph's Foster Home Polaroids from his childhood.

"We can live a decent life. We just need to give ourselves that chance," she says.

"Please," the father says. A blue vein forks over his forehead.

The father unbuttons his work uniform then doffs the nametag. The image of the cash they stole from Parker, piled in a heap underneath their bed, crosses his mind once again. Every day at work he stands in a daze at the conveyor belt, riddled with dread as he bolts support brackets to metal bumpers. He's considered taking the money that's left back to Parker. He could drive back to St. Louis, dump the cash—all one hundred and ninety-seven thousand, five hundred forty-one dollars—onto Parker's desk. Then he could drop to his knees and beg for mercy. He could tell Parker he'd do whatever it took to fix it. "Tell me," he'd say, kneeling on the cold floor, "just tell me."

The father takes a swig of milk. He says, "Do we deserve this chance?"

"Our daughter does," the mother says. "She's eleven years old. She's only eleven years old."

"Yes," he says. "I know that."

"You're a good father," she says.

"I'm many things, but that sure as hell isn't one of them."

"Don't say that. I mean it," the mother says.

"It's the truth," the father tells her.

She rubs her hand through his hair. She plays with his curls.

"You're a good man," the mother says.

He sips the milk. He sets the carton down and says, "Yeah?"

"We're good people," she says.

"We're good people?" he says.

5.

"Little girl," the old man bellows. He coughs. He winces. He coughs again.

"What?" the girl says. She spots a leaf in the grass. She nabs it and breaks off the stem.

"Come here," the old man says, "just come here."

The girl lowers her head and fondles her brown hair. She stuffs a wad of it into her mouth and sucks on the strands. The girl's parents had said it would be special at the farmhouse. That they wouldn't move again. They wouldn't sleep in hotels anymore. They promised that. She only had to listen. Her father had warned her to never leave the backyard and now she'd ruined it. He'd just yelled at her a week ago when she had wandered off to the meadow after breakfast. She'd seen a doe and wanted to watch it eat the wet alfalfa near the bean fields. The father had chased her down, grabbed her arm. "You can't do that," he yelled. He shook her. "There are bad people out there who want to hurt you." He'd hugged her. He'd said it again. "Bad people."

The old man mulls in the thistle. He says, "Come here," and the girl stands. She drags her feet through the dry grass. She rubs her bad foot into the ground. The patches of scar tissue that sock her foot feel nice buried in the warm grass like that. When she finishes, she lopes across the backyard. Her heart pounds—like it did that night in St. Louis—as she moves toward the old man. The girl stops at the rail fence. She looks back at the kitchen window and over at the back door. Then she climbs the fence.

She crawls down the other side. She leaps into the tall and bushy chickweed that hums with the chirps and chatters of crickets and of katydids.

"My name's Valerie," the girl says. She moves closer. "My daddy calls me Pretty Girl."

"Well," the old man says. He says, "You are pretty. Yes, you are."

The old man tromps across the wild grass and urges the girl to follow him. He says, "Over here," as he enters the woods. "This way," he says. Sweat beads over his shaggy eyebrows. Gnats swarm his head in a blade of yellow sunlight that splinters through the branches of the tall oak trees. He turns to face the girl. She lulls at the edge of the woods. Her hands touch at the red wildflowers. The old man lowers himself to a knee. He coughs and spits in the weeds. "Come here," he says. When the girl backs away, the old man yelps. "No. Please."

The girl stops. She warily plods into the woods. She walks toward him.

"Sit," the old man says and points at his knee. "It's alright."

She sits on his lap. She doesn't say anything. The girl just stares at his dark scar.

"You can touch it. I can tell you want to touch it," the old man says.

He takes the girl's hand. He places her finger onto his face. The girl touches the scar and the old man shuts his eyes. She traces the scar tissue down the side of his face. The old man pretends that the girl's finger is Tina's finger and his face and his skin begin to tingle. A blissful warmth fills him but when the girl takes her hand back, the old man is rattled. He opens his eyes. He is burdened by a heavy sadness that aches in the marrow of his bones. The girl lifts her bad foot out of the tall grass and the old man takes her foot into his hands. He is gentle with her.

"I got frostbite," the girl says. She presses on his dark scar again.

"I'm—I'm sorry," the old man mutters.

The girl looks at his wrinkled hands. She likes how they cradle her dead foot.

6.

The sun cuts into the kitchen window. It shines a red luster over the messy table.

"I know you hate your job, but you can't quit," she says.

The father frowns. He says, "Yeah?"

"I could cut hair again," the mother says.

"That would be nice," he says.

"I can work at that salon in town."

"You were good at it."

"I saw a sign the other day," she says. "They're hiring."

The father trots to the cabinet. He finds the Jim Beam and two cups.

"I need you to promise me something," the mother says.

"All right," the father answers.

"You can't talk about Parker anymore."

"Fine," he says and fills the cups.

She says, "You can't *ever* say his name."

"I won't," he says, then grumbles.

"You have to promise," she demands. "You have to promise."

"I promise."

"I want to believe you," she tells him.

"You can believe me," the father says.

The mother raises her cup. "To second chances."

The father raises his cup. He says, "To second chances," and they drink. The mother grabs for the Jim Beam but knocks it over. "Shit," the father barks as the mother fumbles the bottle, spraying more whiskey over the table and onto the floor. She gets control. Then she pours another cup with a grin on her face. The father stares at the spilled whiskey. It streams over the table. It collects at the edge. He notices the whiskey is about to overflow. He sighs. He can't take it. So he grabs the old newspaper off the table and he lays it open over the spill.

They drink. The mother pours out two fingers of Jim Beam into the cups.

"I want a new car. I like those Subarus," she says.

"How about a TV?" he says. "I want a flat screen."

"We could buy a house," she says. She laughs. "You know?"

They drink the whiskey and the father refills the cups and the mother gazes down at her drink and she smiles. They'll enroll their daughter in school. She'll take classes like children are supposed to do. The mother can take her shopping for new clothes at the South Ridge Mall in Des Moines. It's only a fifty-mile drive. They can have lunch at The Cheesecake Factory. Then she'll call that salon in town. The mother stands. She hurries to the sink and turns on the faucet.

"What are you doing?" the father asks. His face is red.

"I'm cleaning," she says as she soaps the dirty dishes.

"Cleaning?" he asks. He caps the Jim Beam bottle.

"Yes," she says. She scrubs at the skillet.

"Okay." He grabs the dishes off the table. He takes them to the sink.

7.

The old man tucks the girl's long brown hair behind her ears. He buries his face in her hair. He grabs a bundle of it and he clenches his hand into a fist. He squeezes tight. He should break her neck. He should do that right now. But the old man doesn't. He lets go of her hair. The old man cradles the girl on top of his knee. "Do you know who I am?" he asks. He touches her cheek. He says, "It's okay." He touches her cheek again. "It's okay if you tell me," he says. "It's okay."

The girl shrugs. She says, "I don't know." She touches a flower. Her head lowers.

He lifts the girl off his knee and tells her, "Don't move." He tells her, "Be good."

The old man takes a flip phone from his back pocket. He calls the only number listed under "Contacts." The line rings but he wants to hurl the cell phone into the ditch. When he hears Parker's voice, he glances at the girl. He watches her pull up purple milkweed. He looks over at the gold Chevy parked behind a grove of pine trees. He could take the girl. They could go west. They could travel to Utah or to Montana. He could take the girl away from this place.

"I was wrong," the old man tells Parker. He turns his back to the girl. "It's not them."

As he disconnects his call, it happens. The girl clubs the old man over the head with a pine branch.

He collapses. He mumbles. He says, "Val—"

"No," the girl screeches. She drops the branch into the grass.

"Honey," the old man cries. His eyelids twitch. "Honey Honey Honey Honey."

The girl lugs a rock out of the ditch and stands over the old man. She stares down at him with a cold gaze. Then she shuts her eyes and pictures a time when her parents had taken her to Forest Park in St. Louis. They often walked there from their apartment in the Delmar Loop, especially on the weekends that summer. They followed the rock trails past the sculpture gardens to the playground near the sandstone cascades. The mother always sat in the red gazebo, and she always munched on fruit that she'd toted in a picnic basket. The girl sat on a swing and her father pushed her. The girl soared and the wind slid through her hair like fingers. She said, "Higher."

"Higher," the mother called out. "You heard her." She yelled, "Higher."

"Higher," the father said. He laughed. "Higher," he said, and pushed her.

"Higher," the girl said as she kicked her feet into the yellow sun and the blue sky.

The girl opens her eyes. She hefts the rock above her head and a black wave spills over her. She heaves the rock down onto the old man's face. He groans and his legs kick and his feet pedal in the weeds. "Little," the old man babbles. "Little—" The girl brings the rock down again. She hammers his head and she strikes him harder with each blow. The old man's skull finally gives and the girl tosses the rock onto the ground next to his body. There's blood everywhere.

The girl claws dirt over the face. She piles leaves and weeds over the feet and stacks pine branches over the body. She cleans the blood off herself in the ditch water. Then she runs. She runs out of the woods and she climbs the rail fence. She runs across the backyard and past the magnolia tree. The girl runs. She runs to the back door. But she stops. She turns and searches the porch for the Nikes her parents bought her at an outlet mall in Chicago. She finds them. She tugs them on and ties the laces. The girl grabs the doorknob, then lets go. She grabs it again, turns it. She turns the knob real slow and just like that, she opens the door.

ABOUT THE EDITOR

Michael Bracken has edited several previous crime fiction anthologies, including the Anthony Award-nominated *The Eyes of Texas: Private Eyes from the Panhandle to the Piney Woods* and the three-volume *Fedora* series. He co-edits (with Trey R. Barker) the serial novella anthology series *Guns + Tacos*. Stories from his anthologies have been short-listed for Anthony, Derringer, Edgar, Macavity, and Shamus awards, and have been named among the year's best by the editors of *The Best American Mystery Stories* and the editors of *The World's Finest Mystery and Crime Stories*.

Bracken is the author of eleven books and more than 1,300 short stories, including crime fiction in *Alfred Hitchcock's Mystery Magazine*, *Black Cat Mystery Magazine*, *Black Mask*, *Down & Out: The Magazine*, *Ellery Queen's Mystery Magazine*, *Espionage Magazine*, *Mike Shayne Mystery Magazine*, and *The Best American Mystery Stories*. In 2016 he received the Edward D. Hoch Memorial Golden Derringer Award for Lifetime Achievement in short mystery fiction. He lives and writes in Texas.

ABOUT THE CONTRIBUTORS

J.L. Abramo is the author of the Jake Diamond private investigator novels, including Shamus Award-winning *Circling the Runway*, as well as *Chasing Charlie Chan* (a prequel to the series), *Gravesend*, *Brooklyn Justice*, *Coney Island Avenue* (a follow-up to *Gravesend*) and *American History*. Abramo has served as president of the Private Eye Writers of America.

Ann Aptaker's Cantor Gold novels have won the Lambda and Goldie awards. Her short stories have appeared in the *Fedora II* and *III* anthologies, *Switchblade* magazine, and the online zine *Punk Soul Poet*. Her novella *A Taco, a T-Bird, and One Furious Night* is featured in season two of the *Guns + Tacos* crime fiction series. When not writing hardboiled and noir fiction, Ann is a professor of Art History in New York City.

Trey R. Barker is the author of the Barefield Trilogy, the Jace Salome novels, and *The Unknowing,* as well as hundreds of short stories and non-fiction articles. His battle with cancer is detailed in a series of blog posts written during his time undergoing chemotherapy treatment and are collected in *The Cancer Chronicles.* Trey is a Texas native who now lives in Illinois, where he works as a patrol sergeant with a small county sheriff's office.

Barb Goffman has won the Agatha, Macavity, and Silver Falchion awards for her short stories. Her work has appeared in *Ellery Queen's Mystery Magazine* and *Alfred Hitchcock's Mystery Magazine*, among other publications. She edited *Crime Travel,* nominated for the 2020 Anthony Award for best anthology. Her 2013 book *Don't Get Mad, Get Even* won the Silver Falchion for the year's best collection. Learn more at BarbGoffman.com.

David Hagerty has authored four books in the Duncan Cochrane political mystery series, each inspired by a crime during his childhood in Chicago. The latest, *They Tell Me You Are Cunning,* was released in 2019. He has also published more than twenty short stories, including five from a collection about the Navajo reservation.

James A. Hearn is an attorney and author who writes in a variety of genres, including crime fiction, science fiction, fantasy, and horror. His fiction has appeared or is forthcoming in *Alfred Hitchcock's Mystery Magazine*, *Black Cat Mystery Magazine*, *The Eyes of Texas*, *Guns + Tacos*, and *Monsters, Movies & Mayhem*. Visit his website at JamesAHearn.com.

David H. Hendrickson's short fiction has appeared in *Best American Mystery Stories 2018*, *Ellery Queen's Mystery Magazine*, *Fiction River*, and *Pulphouse*. His awards include the 2018 Derringer Award. His novels *Offside* and *Cracking the Ice* have been adopted for high school student required reading. Visit him at HendricksonWriter.com for news about his latest releases.

Jarrett Kaufman is a Ph.D. candidate in English at the University of Louisiana. His fiction has been nominated for a Pushcart Prize and has won numerous awards, including the Mary Mackey Fiction Award, the Tennessee Williams Short Story Award, the Missouri Writers Guild President's Award for Fiction, and the Ernest Hemingway Flash Fiction Prize. His stories have appeared or are forthcoming in *The Saint Ann's Review*, *Fiction Southeast*, *Arkansas Review*, *Another Chicago Magazine*, *The Storyteller Magazine*, and *Short Story America*, and many other publications.

Mark R. Kehl is a technical writer who lives in Pennsylvania. His short stories have appeared in anthologies such as *Darkness Rising* and *The Ghostbreakers: Sinister Sleuths*.

Hugh Lessig is a former newspaperman who works in public communications and lives in Tidewater, Va., where "Last Exit Before Toll" is set. His short fiction has appeared in *Thuglit*, *Needle: A Magazine of Noir*, *Crime Factory*, and *Shotgun Honey*. He is a Derringer Award finalist.

Steve Liskow's stories have appeared in *Alfred Hitchcock's Mystery Magazine, Black Cat Mystery Magazine,* and several anthologies, earning an Edgar nomination and two Black Orchid Novella Awards. He also has published fifteen novels and was a finalist for the Shamus Best Indie Novel Award in 2015. He lives in Connecticut. Learn more at SteveLiskow.com.

Alan Orloff's eighth novel, *Pray for the Innocent,* won the 2019 ITW Thriller Award (Best E-Book Original). His debut mystery, *Diamonds for the Dead,* was an Agatha Award finalist; his story "Dying in Dokesville" won a 2019 Derringer Award; and "Rule Number One" was selected for *The Best American Mystery Stories 2018.* His first P.I. novel, *I Know Where You Sleep,* was released by Down & Out Books in February 2020. Learn more at AlanOrloff.com.

Josh Pachter has published more than 100 short stories in *Ellery Queen's Mystery Magazine, Alfred Hitchcock's Mystery Magazine,* and elsewhere. He is the editor of *The Beat of Black Wings: Crime Fiction Inspired by the Songs of Joni Mitchell, The Misadventures of Nero Wolfe,* and other anthologies; translates Dutch and Belgian writers for EQMM's "Passport to Crime" department; and was the 2020 recipient of the Short Mystery Fiction Society's Golden Derringer Award for Lifetime Achievement.

Steve Rasnic Tem is a past winner of the World Fantasy, Bram Stoker, and British Fantasy Awards. He has published more than 450 short stories. Some of his best stories are collected in *Figures Unseen: Selected Stories,* from Valancourt Books. His latest collection is *The Night Doctor and Other Tales* from Centipede Press.

Mikal Trimm has sold more than 50 short stories and 100 poems to numerous venues, including *Postscripts, Strange Horizons,*

Realms of Fantasy, and *Ellery Queen's Mystery Magazine.*

Bev Vincent is the author of *The Dark Tower Companion,* the co-editor with Stephen King of the anthology *Flight or Fright,* and the author of more than ninety short stories, including appearances in *Ellery Queen's Mystery Magazine, Alfred Hitchcock's Mystery Magazine, The Eyes of Texas,* and two Mystery Writers of America anthologies. His work has been nominated for the Bram Stoker Award, the Edgar, the Ignotus, and the ITW Thriller Awards. Learn more at BevVincent.com.

Joseph S. Walker is a college teacher living in Indiana. In 2019, his stories won both the Al Blanchard Award and the Bill Crider Prize for Short Fiction. He has published more than thirty stories in a variety of magazines and anthologies, and has twice had stories named to the Other Distinguished Stories list in *The Best American Mystery Stories.* Visit his website at jsw47408.wixsite.com/website.

Andrew Welsh-Huggins is the author of the Columbus-based Andy Hayes private eye series, featuring a former Ohio State and Cleveland Browns quarterback turned investigator, and the editor of *Columbus Noir* from Akashic Books. His nonfiction book, *No Winners Here Tonight,* is the definitive history of Ohio's death penalty.

Stacy Woodson made her crime fiction debut in *Ellery Queen Mystery Magazine's* Department of First Stories and won the 2018 Readers Award. Since her debut, she has placed stories in *Mystery Weekly, Woman's World, EQMM,* and other anthologies and publications. Visit her at StacyWoodson.com.

BOOKS

On the following pages are a few
more great titles from the
Down & Out Books publishing family.

For a complete list of books and to
sign up for our newsletter,
go to DownAndOutBooks.com.

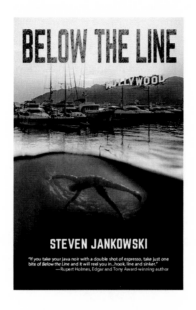

Below the Line
Steven Jankowski

Down & Out Books
November 2020
978-1-64396-154-5

Between gigs as a Hollywood movie Teamster, Mike Millek freelances as an armed chauffeur to the stars.

When Mike arrives one night to pick up his successful but deadbeat rap producer client, whom he finds freshly murdered with a satchel full of cash, Mike decides to take what is owed him, leading him down a path into the sordid underbelly of the Hollywood power elite.

Don't Shoot the Drummer
A Lou Crasher Novel
Jonathan Brown

Down & Out Books
November 2020
978-1-64396-150-7

A security guard is murdered during a home robbery of a house tented for fumigation and Lou Crasher is asked to solve the murder. The rock-drumming amateur P.I. is up for it, because his brother Jake is the one asking. Lou fights to keep his musical day job and catch the killers.

When the bullets fly he hopes all involved respect his golden rule: Don't Shoot The Drummer.

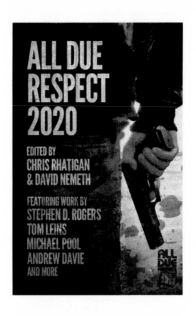

All Due Respect 2020
Chris Rhatigan & David Nemeth, editors

All Due Respect, an imprint of
Down & Out Books
November 2020
978-1-64396-165-1

Twelve short stories from the top writers in crime fiction today.

Featuring the work of Stephen D. Rogers, Tom Leins, Michael Pool, Andrew Davie, Sharon Diane King, Preston Lang, Jay Butkowski, Steven Berry, Craig Francis Coates, Bobby Mathews, Michael Penncavage, and BV Lawson.

Shotgun Honey Presents Volume 4: RECOIL
Ron Earl Phillips, editor

Shotgun Honey, an imprint of
Down & Out Books
May 2020
978-1-64396-138-5

With new and established authors from around the world, Shotgun Honey Presents Volume 4: RECOIL delivers stories that explore a darker side of remorse, revenge, circumstance, and humanity.

Contributors: Rusty Barnes, Susan Benson, Sarah M. Chen, Kristy Claxton, Jen Conley, Brandon Daily, Barbara DeMarco-Barrett, Hector Duarte Jr., Danny Gardner, Tia Ja'nae, Carmen Jaramillo, Nick Kolakowski, JJ Landry, Bethany Maines, Tess Makovesky, Alexander Nachaj, David Nemeth, Cindy O'Quinn, Brandon Sears, Johnny Shaw, Kieran Shea, Gigi Vernon, Patrick Whitehurst.

Made in United States
North Haven, CT
28 June 2023

38351529R00188